White and Red

Dorota Masłowska

White and Red

Translated by **Benjamin Paloff**

Atlantic Books
London

First published in English as *Snow White and Russian Red* in
the United States of America in 2005 by Atlantic Monthly Press,
an imprint of Grove/Atlantic, Inc.

First published in Great Britain in hardback in 2005 by Atlantic Books,
an imprint of Grove Atlantic Ltd

Originally published in Polish in 2003 by Lampa i Iskra Bola as *Wojna
polsko-ruska, pod flag biaBo-czerwona*.

1 2 3 4 5 6 7 8 9

A CIP catalogue record for this book is available from the British Library.

ISBN 1 84354 423 7

Printed in Great Britain by Creative Print & Design (Wales) Ltd

Atlantic Books
An imprint of Grove Atlantic Ltd
Ormond House
26–27 Boswell Street
London WC1N 3JZ

White and Red

FIRST SHE TOLD ME she had good news and bad news. Leaning across the bar. Which do I want first. The good news, I say. So she told me that in town it looks like there's a Polish-Russki war under a white-and-red flag. I say, How do you know, she says she heard. So I say, Then I'll take the bad. So she took out her lipstick and told me that Magda says it's over between me and her. Then she winks at the Bartender like that if something happens, she wants him to come over. And that's how I found out that she'd dumped me. Magda, that is. Even though we'd had it good, we'd had our share of nice times, a lot of nice words had been said, on my part as well as hers. For real. The Bartender says to me, Fuck it. Though it's not so simple. The way I'd found out how it was, or rather, how it wasn't, it wasn't like she'd told me straight to my face, only it was just the other way around, she'd told me through Arleta. I chalk it up to her being a total asshole, to her disrespect. And I'm not going to hide it, even though she was my girlfriend, about whom I can say that a lot of different things had passed between us, good as well as bad. Anyway, she shouldn't have

1

said it through a friend like that, so I'd be the last to hear. Everybody knows from the very start, since she told others as well. She was saying that I'm sort of the more explosive one, and that they had to prepare me for this fact. They're afraid that something might set me off, because that sort of always happens. She said I should step out to get some air. Gave me her shitty cig. Meanwhile, I just feel sadder than ever. All the worse that it wasn't told straight to my four eyes, by her. Not a single word.

Leaning over the bar like some salesgirl over the counter. Like she wanted to sell me some crap, some chocolatey product. Arleta. Rusty water in her beer glass. Easter-egg dye. The candy she'd sell would be empty in the middle. All foil. Which she wouldn't touch with her own fingers, their nails bootleg and false. Since she herself is false, empty inside. Smokes her cigs. Bought from the Russkies. False, bogus. Instead of nicotine there's some garbage in there, some unfamiliar drugs. Some paper, sawdust, stuff the teachers wouldn't dream of. Stuff the police wouldn't dream of. Though they should put Arleta away. The ones no one knows but she's always chatting up, straight to their faces. To her phone, to the ring tone on her phone.

Now I'm sitting and staring at her hair. Arleta in leather, and next to her Magda's hair, long bright hair, like a wall, like branches. I stare at her hair as if it were a wall, since it's not for me. It's for others, for the Bartender, for Kisiel, for the different boys who come and go. For everybody, but all the same not for me. Others will put their hands in her hair.

Kacper arrives, sits, asks what's up. His pants too short. And his shoes are like a black mirror in which I see my reflection, the bar neon, the gambling machines, other things lying around. Here, in a clasp, you can see Magda's hair, an impenetrable wall. Fencing her off from me like brickwork, like concrete. Beyond which there are new loves, her moist kisses. Kacper is clearly hopped up on speed; he's grinding his shoe. Which is why the image blurs. He drove here, is chewing mint gum. He asks whether I have a tissue. I lose Magda in the crowd.

I tell him I don't have one. Though maybe I should have one. Kacper has speed, a whole car full of speed, the whole trunk of his Golf. He looks around everywhere, as though an army of Russkies were lying in wait on all sides. As if they wanted to come in here and stick all their Russki cigs between his clattering jaws. He takes out an LM Red. Asks why I'm sitting with my face to the wall. I say, Maybe I should sit facing forward, maybe that would change something, right? Maybe Magda would be here with me, only I'm facing forward, and she races up and squats down on my knees, her hair in my face, places my hand up between her thighs, her kisses, her love. I say no. Though I'd rather say yes. But I say no. No and no. I refuse. Even if she wanted to come here, I'd say: Don't come closer, don't touch me, you stink. You stink of those guys who touch you while you're not looking, and you think you don't know they're touching you. You stink of those cigs you bum off them, that they treat you to. Of fucking LM Menthols. Bought cheap from the Russkies. Of those drinks, that swill they buy you in a glass swimming with bacteria from their mouths like fish, like sea sluts. And if she wanted me to take her like that now, she'd have another thing coming. I wouldn't say a single word. She'd give me her drink, I'd say: No. First get rid of that gum you stuck under there, since it's just come from the mouth of one of those dirty guys, from their mouths, that gum, though you think I don't know about that. Then wash yourself off, and only then, maybe, you can sit with me, when you're cleansed of those bootleg cigs, of that bootleg speed you drink in your drinks. Only after you take off those rags, that plumage, which isn't for me.

Of course, I'm still a bit resentful then. I turn around, I don't want to chat with her. I say that if she's going to be that way, I'll fuck up the whole bar, all the glasses will go to the floor, she'll walk on glass, she'll snap her heels, she'll bash her elbows, she'll tear her dress and all the laces that went into it. She asks me to come back to her. Says she'll be good like never before, more good, more giving. I say no to that. I say: If I have to explain it to you once, I have to explain it to you twice, that I never want to be with you again, and either you go away or I'll do it myself. She says that she loved me. I say that I loved her, too, that I always liked her, though first she was Lolo's girl before she was mine, and his car was better, everything Lolo had was better, better shoes, better pants, better money. I say that I wanted to kill him because he wasn't good for Magda, just harsher. But that later she was mine, I always stood up for her, I was always behind her. Though things weren't always good, like I was saying, like indeed when she shoplifted some used clothes, tore off the tags in the dressing room. Earrings, handbags, eye shadow. Everything into her purse and into her tote. It wasn't good, because then I had to express it with my eyes, though seriously, she got away with it, and it had a nice effect on her humor. Besides that, she had the disadvantage of being young, which my parents looked down on anyway. Besides that, everything was cool, she often said there was no other boy but me, so her affection was for me and not for them.

Lefty arrives, says that he knows and that Magda is a nastier bit of skank than the ones who hang out at the station. Grubby-faced, dirty. Like the Russkies' girls. I get it, but I can't allow that sort of thing. That somebody of Lefty's ilk would say that, so I stand up. That somebody with a computerized tic might tell me what my life is like, where my affections lie, what I have to do, what not, whether Magda is good or she isn't, because even in the grave no one can prove what the truth is about Magda. That he would judge her conscience though he was the one running Arleta down with his car, with a feeling of vengeance, which no one would do to Arleta, though she is how she is. So I stand up. I look him in his quivering eye, point-blank, so he knows what's what. He looks silently deep into his beer. He says that in town in recent days there's been this Polish-Russki war under a white-and-red flag. He thinks he's changed the subject. The subject is always the same, Lefty. I know that, whether there's this war or there's no war, that you had her before Lolo, I know that you all had her before me and now you're all going to have her again, because from this day forward she's yours, because from this day forward she's drunk and open twenty-four hours, eighty-watt bulbs shine in her eyes, her tongue shines in her mouth, her neon nightlight shines between her legs, go get her, take your turns. You, Lefty, have the first shot, because I know you, I know what you're like, the freshest meat for you, because you must have the very best things in life, the head of the beer, the coffee with cream, the fastest computer, the best keyboard, a golden phone on a golden tray, so whatever you want, Magda's yours, because she's the best, she has a heart of gold. She has a heart of gold when she lays her hand on your head and says what she wants. She has a heart of gold, she manages to get everything, but in such a way that even if you're paying for it, you feel like you're borrowing it. You feel like you've pawned yourself at a pawnshop. She has a heart of gold, she's delicate and romantic; for example, she likes animals and says over and over how she'd like to have different animals, she loves to watch hamsters in an aquarium. Maybe she'd even like to have a kid later on, but only a five-year-old, the kind that would be born five years old and would never grow up. With the right name. Claudia, Max, Alex. A little kid, five years old, and she would always be seventeen, would lead it by the arm around the square, in her skimpy dress, in her heels.

She'd carry it in her handbags with her lipstick in a special compartment. She would dance with this kid at the disco, the newspapers would come and take pictures of her hair, so shiny and sparkling, but the kid's ugly, because it's yours, Lefty, born with a broken nose, born with a computerized tic, ugly from birth, a son of a bitch from birth, because your son would be a son of a bitch from the get-go. Because you wouldn't know how to be good for Magda, how to make her happy. How to give to her from yourself, you wouldn't show her the world, just your computer games, blood, despair, pain. That's not what she's for, she's for making delicate things with.

Because that's Magda. Arleta came up for me to give her a light, she says like I'm causing a circus, allegedly that's what Magda's saying. Thank you very much, and here are the elephants that walked through me and trampled my heart, here are the fleas. Here are the trained dogs, since I was like the trained dogs that don't get anything in return but more whipcracks in the face and no "good boy" or fuck off. Here I am, a dog trained to drive a roofless car. I don't have a light. Because I'm burned to a crisp. And now I want to die. At the last moment, when I'm about to die, I want to see Magda. As she leans over me and says: Don't die. Don't die, it's all my fault, now I'll be with only you, just don't die, it's not about that, after all, it's about having some fun, and that was all fooling around, so that I wasn't really with anyone before you, I wasn't with any others or wasn't even at all, I was just joking to piss you off, you jerk, now everything's going to be fine, we'll have a kid, Claudia, Erica, Nicole, you know that's what you always wanted anyway, we'll push it in a carriage, you'll see how it is, just promise you won't die, but now I have to go to the bathroom, since Arleta's flirting with one of those guys now, he says he's in management and knows everybody, supposedly he even knows you besides, says: Nails, I know that guy, and not a word from me, quiet, I didn't tell him you were my boyfriend, because it was different, but now I'll tell him the truth, so he knows how it is.

So I'll do it later, as a last resort, because Arleta says that Magda's just gone off somewhere. She says she doesn't know where. She says she doesn't know who with. I say to her, Are you my friend, or are you another one of those sluts like Magda? She says, Your friend. I say, So what the fuck's going on? She says, With Eric. That Magda went with Eric to cruise around town, to check out the cars, to stay friends, that's all. And so with Eric. And so the kid will be ugly anyway. More worse than with Lefty. Genetically abnormal. Genetically deviant from birth. Genetically scrambled. A genetic son of a bitch. From the start with a genetically congenital pocket in its gums for hiding things, with congenitally dirty fingernails. Someday I'll be on a train and some kid will ask me for something to grub on, and when I look into its face, I'll see Magda's eyes, Eric's stutter, and my own ears protruding slightly from this other person, since some of me must have remained in her as well, some genes. The scar on its forehead is also from me, from when I once hit some glass, the broken nose is from still someone else, the very face of despair, the world's ugliest kid. Then I'll ask him where his mother is. And he'll say she's gone, that she died, so okay, I'll give him something. And if he says he's with his daddy, it's curtains for him, better not to come across me, since that would be better for him as well.

Magda comes in, but without Eric. She looks like something's happened, like she's been shattered into little pieces, her hair this way, her handbag that way, her dress to the left, her earrings to the right. Her panty hose all muddy on the left. Her face on the right, black tears flowing from her eyes. Like she'd been fighting in the Polish-Russki war, like the whole Polish-Russki army had trampled her, running through the park. All my feelings come back to life within me. The whole situation. Social and economic in the country. It's the whole her, it's all of her. She's drunk, she's ruined. She's hopped up on speed, she's stoned. She's never been so ugly. Black tears are running down her chin, because her heart is as black as coal. Her womb is black and tattered. A tear is running through her whole womb. From that womb she'll give birth to some Negro kid, black. Angela, with a rotten face, a tail. She won't get far with that kind of kid. They won't let her into a taxi, they won't sell her white milk. She'll lie down on the black earth of vacant lots. She'll live in greenhouses. Eaten by grubs, eaten by worms. She'll feed that kid black milk from her black breasts. She'll feed it garden soil. But it'll die sooner or later anyway.

Arleta comes up. I tell her to let Magda know that I hope she eats shit and dies. Arleta blows a bubble with her gum. After which she winds the gum around her finger and eats it. She makes it look like nothing else is going on in her life, she just blows bubbles and winds them around her finger. Like that's her job, for which she makes totally good cash and uses it to buy herself all those rags, all those Russki cigs. She could star in *Funniest Home Videos* with all that portable crap. Arleta says I have shit for brains, that I shouldn't say what I'm saying, because it could come true. She says that's already happened to her a couple times. For example, in school she told the vo-tech teacher to drop dead, and then she allegedly ended up in the maternity ward, confined to her bed. Likewise, she allegedly once said "break a leg" to a friend in her phys-ed class, and that girl broke her pinky finger. She also says that she never smokes LMs, because they're unhealthy and are the most carcinogenic cigarettes. She's also supposedly superstitious and makes sure she doesn't say anything jinx-worthy. If you say something, and it happens to be the witching hour, there's no way out and it'll happen, and you can't take it back, there's no "I'm sorry." It's something maybe connected with religion, with the life of the paranormal, it's a certain quality of paramental life.

*   *   *

But what Arleta has to say on this score, I don't give a shit, with all due respect. Where was Magda with Eric, I'm asking you, I say to Arleta. You fucking godmother. The two of you will have all those bastard kids together, they won't let you into a single goddamn place. Tell me what he did to her, that thief. He stole her clean heart, all her delicateness, all her hair, he ruined her panty hose, made her cry. He hurt her. And I'm going to crush him for it, but later. Now I want to know, Arleta.

But from her jeans pocket, however, the right tone rings out and Arleta receives a text message. It would be great to talk to me if I weren't such an asshole, she says, and goes somewhere fast. Then the Bartender comes up and says to me that there's shit going down. I say, Like, what kind of shit. So he says that Magda was always a bit given to hysterics, that she loses it pretty easily. I say, Like, so what's up. And I'm already pretty fucking pissed, because I don't like when things don't go according to plan.

So he says that there was once some story about Magda going around. Not a story, really, but the Bartender's not a bad fucker, so instead of Magda telling me about it herself, he says it in her place.

Then I go to the john, because Arleta's calling me, she's all smoked out, she's smoking two menthols at once, LMs at that, she's holding both in one corner of her mouth, and with her other hand she's holding Magda up. I'm a bit uneasy, because

I know that Magda hurt me, that she fucked me up. So I ask what happened. She says it's a cramp. I say that maybe it's the speed, that it's too much speed. Arleta says that she'll leave us alone then and closes the door from the outside. So I'm waiting. Magda has a cramp in her calf and is sitting on the toilet. She's holding on to her calf with her left hand, at the same time crying, at the same time being hysterical. Now I don't even know whether she's beautiful or ugly, and actually it's hard for me to say. One thing's for sure: she's pretty in general, but currently in bad shape, if it's a question of her looks, since her black tears are everywhere, and her mascara is gushing like from a rainspout, her panty hose are torn down to the skin, as though they were way too large anyway, and her face is pretty tenderized—it reminds me, not to be unpleasant, of a red fire engine. Thus I'm mulling over whether I still love her when she moans pretty loudly, not even looking me in the eye or saying a single word to me. But then I almost can't stand it anymore.

Did I do something wrong, Magda—I say to her and latch the door. Did I do something wrong, that we wouldn't be able to start all over again? You always looked happy when I loved you, why don't you want me now all of a sudden, is it some whim, did I bore you? Remember that time those cop bitches were writing you up at the stop, and though you were there with Masztal then, and though they wrote you up with him, and though you know that he'd been caught dealing. Who was it who went to check your mailbox so that your parents wouldn't get the police summons while you were at work? Did Saint Joseph check? Did Masztal go check even once?

Tell me yourself, wasn't I good? Lovey-dovey, romantic shitdrops.

Now you don't know what to say. You moan and I'll tell you it's a shame, because now you're nothing, you're like a kid, you're embarrassing yourself so bad. You're staring at these brown tiles that've seen us together more than once, how we were so very close to each other, the way only a girl or a woman can be with a man. We're still repeating on that tile, whatever happened before, I'll tell you that much.

Your name is pretty, Magda, just like your face. Your hands are pretty, your fingers, your nails, can't we stay together? If you want, I'll take you away from here to anyplace you want. Maybe even to the hospital, if that's absolutely necessary. You're asking yourself if I've been drinking, well, so I've been drinking, but it's nobody's fucking business if I've been drinking or not. If we're going, let's get in the car and go, I'll take you everywhere, even if ten thousand Russkies want to give us drug and alcohol tests. You tell me not to bullshit you, to get off it. You say that maybe it's the cramp in your calf, that you took the test and maybe it's possible that you're pregnant, though you're not absolutely sure about that. You say that that's why you chickened out, why you didn't want to be with me anymore, because you knew I'd be mad. Tell me when I've been mad at you for longer than a day? If you have a kid, and maybe it's even my kid, you can always go to the doctor and check it out 100 percent. And in the meantime, we're going. I take Magda in my arms and she screams bloody murder, just lets out a roar, though just a moment ago she was hushed and meek like she was sleeping. Arleta runs up right away with that bubble sticking out of her mouth, she wants to know everything that's going on, what's with that cramp and whether Magda wants some help from her end, some water, some Tylenol. I tell Arleta to fuck off, and the same to the Bartender, who's staring like he doesn't know what's up. Others are looking on stupidly as well, Lefty, Kacper, Kisiel also with some girl I don't even know, she must be new, though not too bad, the music's blaring, what a fucking mess. Arleta's sent me a text message that it could probably be a lack of permanganate or potassium in the blood, considering her bad nutritional habits. I write back to her that she should fuck off, since I would write more but my phone's running out of batteries, and the only thing I can manage is exactly that: *fuck off arl*. I would write more, that she should take her bad prognostication, her bad instigations, since she's probably the one who provoked Magda to get such a very painful cramp with her paranormal fucking cursing, her incantations about that geography teacher.

So then we leave and I put Magda into the first taxi, then I get in myself, she says we're going to the hospital, and he, whether something has happened. I say, Is this an interview for the newspaper or is this a taxi, and is this a confession of

sins and an absolution, are you driving us, because otherwise
I'm getting out and Magda's coming with me, no fare and on
top of that a rock through the windshield, and maybe he
shouldn't show himself in town. He says nothing for a moment, and then puts in that lately we're supposedly fighting
the Russkies under a white-and-red flag. I say, Surely, though
we're not really so very radical on that issue. Magda says that
she's really against the Russkies. Now I get pissed off, I say:
And how do you know you're against them, exactly? The
radio's on, the news is on, various songs. She says that's just
what she thinks. I say that she's on speed and laying down a
big judgment, laying down big opinions, how does she know
she really thinks that way and not some other way? She's a
little afraid. I tell her to leave me alone, not to piss me off.
She moans, because her cramp hasn't gone away.

Then she goes off on her own, tells me not to touch her.
She's crippled. She says that I'm brutal, if I so much as touch
her I'm going to kill our kid and her. Because she'll burst at
the seams and our kid'll die. I'm shaken up enough. In admis-
sions, we're met by the chief or an orthopedist, I don't know
anymore, since I'm afraid they'll draw her blood, because
besides her lack of potassium, they'll also find her dealings
with speed, because now she's sprung like a chicken, they'll
find out about the speed and take away her kid. But the main
thing is her leg, because the cramp is massive and is metasta-
sizing. The orthopedist tells me to go out during the exam,
which pisses the fuck out of me, she's my woman, right? I look
him right in the very center of his eye, right into the whites,

which are pretty overrun with blood, so he'll know how it is and won't try anything, no orthopedic tricks. Magda begs me with her eyes to be calm, so I calm down a bit. Like most probably it's a shortage of potassium in her muscle that's causing her pain. So then I'm waiting and I'm calm, though it makes me want to blow the shit out of the hospital. Because of that orthopederast and the other pervs who work here, because of those starched princes among them with rods in hand, with stethoscopes, since as far as expressing opinions is concerned, I'm pretty much on the left.

I don't really agree with taxes, and I propose a government without taxes, where my parents won't tear their guts out so that all these smock-sporting princes will have their own apartments and telephone numbers at a time when things aren't like that. At any rate, like I've already said, the economic situation in the country is categorically fucked, the government's ostentatiousness and, generally speaking, the chickenshit authorities. But I'm straying from the topic, which is that Magda leaves the doctor's office. Still crippled. But combed. Fuck whoever combed her. I'm not going into this anymore, since this evening is filled to the brim with stress. She tells me to take her to the sea. I say, How is it she wants to go to the sea with that gangrene on her leg. She says it's fucking fine, Polishly speaking. After which, because there's not a naked soul in the hospital corridors, she rips off some crutches. I say that it's not the hour for the sea. She says exactly, that it's the best hour, and that she wants to go there only with me, probably because this feeling in her that she feels is just for me. I say she's fucked in the brain, but generally I warm a lot to the idea that she loves me and admits as much without a shadow of falsehood.

She says she has this premonition, this impulse almost inside her that she'll die soon, that it's already her time. The kid in her is killing her, Magda says so, it has a prematurely developed set of teeth that makes it gnaw her from the inside, eat through her stomach and then her liver. She says it's already curtains for her, and the sign of this, like stigmata, is that cramped leg, which means the kid is already pulling her strings from the inside. It's destroying her internally, mentally as well, it's simply devastating her, destruction, decomposition. It hurts me, since I probably have a share in this kid as well, and it makes me really sorry for this girl that it's turned out this way, that it's developed inside her. I see how much she suffers, even without considering those crutches, which are supposed to help her but which cause her all the more anguish, since she has on pumps with heels that impede her normal movement. Which is to say that, generally speaking, we're going to the sea. Magda is very enterprising on that end, she should make money off it, in one of those companies that goes to the sea, clips tickets, takes care of everything that deters people from going to the proverbial sea. Regardless of the fact that she's crippled, even given that. All things considered, I say it's already late. She says: So what that it's late. Am I a goddamn idiot who thinks that they're going to close the sea on me if I get there late? Won't the sea be enough for me? I say I have nothing more to say to her on that score. Because if she wants to behave like an asshole, regardless of the fact that we were in the hospital together, that we'd lived through a lot of the worst or the best moments together, and if she has to behave in that way, well thank you very much, let her take my ticket and go herself across those kilometers that'd otherwise be mine as well. And it would be best for her to stay there, because it's the only place for her. Magda says that now I should get off her back, since she's dreaming about something else, and am I going with her or in front of her, she being disabled so she can't walk so fast.

I ask her where she got that speed from, since on her face and in her look in general she's really flushed, unhealthy, to tell the truth, she looks like she just gave birth to the kid, only she lost it somewhere and is currently looking for it around the station. She tells me I'd rather not know, because it's from Vargas. I tell her it's bad shit, impure, cut. She says it's fucking great. I tell her not to get on my nerves, not because it's bad, but that it's shit, and not speed. She says I'm fucking her shit up. I say that it's good how she wants to get fucked up off of Vargas, it's a free country, that bathroom cleaning powder is now hers forever, but if that kid is born a monster, one leg longer, the other shorter, and congenitally hairless, I wouldn't have any hand in that. To that she answers, Good, have it your way, we'll see. And as soon as the train pulls up, as soon as we get on, indeed she takes a circular from the Hit Market and cuts me a line.

* * *

And when I wake up by the sea, I remember just enough from the time when I still associated various facts that I'm doing a line through a pen on which it says Zdzisław Sztorm, Sandworks, something-12th of March Street. How I imagine that sand, which is made by modern technology, modernly processed, modernly packed in bags, modernly passed on to manual and active distribution. I remember my thought of a truly economic character that could save the country from the very annihilation I mentioned earlier, an annihilation prepared for the country by the fucking aristocrats, dressed in overcoats, in aprons, who, if only the conditions were right, would sell us, the citizens, to whorehouses in the West, to the German army, for organs, for slave labor. Who finally want to sell our country out, like some old secondhand crap, a bunch of rags and ancient coats labeled Mińsk Mazowiecki, sweaty old belts, if you'll pardon my saying, because the way I look at it, the only way is to drive them out of their homes, to drive them out of the apartment blocks, and to turn our fatherland into a typically agricultural fatherland that produces, even if only for export, normal Polish sand that would have a chance on the global markets in all of Europe. Because these are my quite leftist views, which makes me figure that one would have to expand the garbage system in the apartment blocks in order for the farmers—because in my estimation it is on the farmers that the country should depend—to be able to toss out more crops, living in the apartment blocks, that's what it's all about, that in this way their lives would become more mechanized, simply put, more good.

And now when I wake up, I remember this well, because I could say every word I was thinking, but when I wake up, Magda's no longer here, though maybe she's not here yet or she's not here at all. I get up from the ground, which at this time of night is cold, and I shake off my jeans, I shake off my layers. Magda's not here and I notice it right away, right away I get pissed off, though upon further consideration it turns out that I have both my wallet, which is crucial, as well as my documents. I also don't really know what was going on when my vision of economic nature had already vanished for a time, when I was doing something, before I woke up here. It's worse, more than—forgive the phrase—blacking out. I see all the sand, which I take for economic squander, which, I must confirm with regret, totally pisses me off. Just gives me a raging case of fuck-off-itis. So when I'm walking and I find a plastic bag, without a moment's hesitation I fill it with sand. After which I twist it shut and keep it, since in case I'm out of cash, in case the bottom falls out of the market, it could turn out to be a valuable thing, or rather an asset. Then I find two shopping bags from the Hit Market, which also makes my heart ache, this lack of any kind of economy in a country where perfectly good shopping bags are tossed to the ground and left to waste. And first of all to the mercy of the lumpenproletariat. So that after a solemn promise that Magda will certainly come, since hypothetically she just went to take a leak, I go to get sand. I figure it's necessary to collect it all as quickly as possible. Because if it doesn't end up in our hands, that's it. It will all be snatched up by the traitors.

So then I meditate in a similar manner. What's rare, I even start to scratch these different thoughts, these calculations, on the ground. Unfortunately, I write fast. Which has an impact on whether those are letters, or whether they're basically indistinct numbers. But fuck that, because somewhere nearby, since it's totally dark, I hear Magda, who is most distinctly laughing at something. I puzzle over what's so funny about that. Not about that, but rather in general, what's so funny. So then I see her, though she's distinctly not alone, but is with somebody. Or rather with men, two at that. Which compels me toward inter-action. Toward reaction. Because despite all the bad that's gone down between us, her love, as I recall, is mine, and her body is likewise mine. Therefore, there's something here that I don't get, when she goes off so playfully. Shakes her little ass. Sweetness itself. Her leg no longer lame. A model-actress-singer all at the same time, all in one. Fucked through and through. Her holey panty hose advertise, Buy holey panty hose, right now they're the in thing, they're all the rage. And of course crutches under your armpits, ripped off of course from the fucking hospital.

What the fuck?—I say to her, because this suddenly apparent situation has knocked me completely out of my contemplations. And she says to these guys: This guy here's my psycho-physiologically handicapped brother. So how are you getting along?—she says to me. You're writing for yourself in the sand, that's good for you. Because I still have some matters to attend to with these gentlemen here, I'll leave your crutches for you here, in case you want to go back home or maybe go off somewhere, just press the crutch into the ground, that will be easier for you.

I stand that way with the stick for a moment, and one of these guys, who looks like a total letch and latent pervert, black skin, a striped sweater, says: You know what, Magda, you don't look much like him, even though you're siblings with him. To which she says: So. That's life. We still have the same last name. Then she says to me: Nails, listen, what's your name?

Andrzej Robakoski—I answer in accordance with my beliefs. And that slut says back cleverly: Exactly! And that's my name, too. Robakoski.

Then I keep quiet. The second guy comes up closer, he's one of those more sportily dressed types, and says: Look, he wrote something here. Then they all stand above my writing, like some Ministry of Sports and Education, and they try to decipher it. As I already mentioned a little earlier, the letters are unclear, those signs are a little more abstract, not to say nonexistent.

Because he's not entirely normal—Magda says. That's why he has handwriting like that. That's how the mentals with Down's write.

They already want to leave. Magda's already almost close to having a quickie and passing into the chasm, passing into the pussy with these two bums. A three-person commission of

sports and educational affairs, this faggoty fag from education and penmanship affairs, and Magda does sports with this
one in the tracksuit, does it wonderfully, I can just see it.

So I say: Come over here, skank, for just a minute. Come here,
don't be afraid, I'm not going to fuck you up. Since from the
shock, from the shock this has done to my outlook, to my
feelings, I'm at a total loss. Totally powerless. I'm not so delicate by nature, because I'll even say openly that in my past,
which wasn't even that long ago, I was pretty impulsive, which
put its own stigmata on my relationship with Magda besides.
Willing to go solo right off the bat, ready right away. But this
festering trouble, foisted upon me through very little fault of
my own, it's suddenly made me delicate, gentle. Because it's yet
another wrong that's been foisted upon me all over again, like
on some victim.

So I say: Come here. I want to talk to you for a minute. I see
how unsure she is. She wavers, I'd say that she's afraid. She
knows what she's done, that everything will be different between
us, so she shakes off her butt, smoothes down her dress, looks
first to the right, then to the left, then straight ahead. She looks
in various directions, mostly here and there. Is she completely
stupid, that's what I ask her, because things are already worse
and worse with me, because my feelings are in shambles, I've
been destroyed by her, my nerves and psyche are shot.

These two dudes are looking at me. They're sympathetic
enough, but they want to leave already. Magda glances first

at the one with the tracksuit, then at that fag, who—I later learned—is nicknamed Swallow.

His ass's come back to life, he says, pointing at me, then he says quickly: So then let's go over to them.

Now I'm fucking pissed, no joke. Now there's no possibility of forgiveness, none, that Nails, a good soul, an altar boy who served at church during Mass, the very picture of gentleness, of a good heart. Dear beloved Nails, who does good deeds for others like it's no big deal. Nails, staring down store managers for some stolen rage, even the tasteless kind, without any sense of taste. Because Nails is the sort of deal who, if you want to call it quits, then you have a cramp in the calf, it's quick, a phone call, Nails is there licking the floor under your legs so you'll have a clean place to walk. Nails will perish for you in the Polish-Russki war, shielding you from a blow with the standard, the white-and-red flag. Though all your friends will gladly want to use it to fuck you over for all your rather simply not-so-moral excesses. But Nails stands and protects you. There's no forgiveness, babe, now when I look at you, I know that my love for you was basically unfounded. And that for this vulgar disrespect I've now endured from you, you will have to pay dearly.

It's right now that I decide I will no longer feel this feeling that you stirred in me when I spotted you for the first time in Lolo's car. Right now I drop the stick, though a moment ago I used it to jot our plans for the future in the ground, the number of children, the costs for the apartment, our laundry, the costs for our wedding and burials, everything for a common future. Now, with one gesture, I manage to cross that out, to erase it. Now I come right up next to you, in one hand I take your hair, which I once loved so much, which now I don't feel anything toward. I wrap it around my fist. Now I'm cool with the cool of someone who works in a slaughterhouse, that's how I'd put it, of someone whose job is beheading chickens.

This is what I say, though my whole body's trembling, though not from fear, but from grief: Gentlemen, here's the deal. This is my woman. She's so wrecked on speed that there's nothing left of her for you. I'm not retarded or abnormal. Now I'm taking her back. And for you, boys—respect from Nails, kind of you to bring her here, this slut who, for all her bullshit, is soon to get what's coming to her.

I'm smiling on the inside. Because that really humiliated them, took them aback. This is my domain, this is my sadness under control. It completely took them aback, rather surprised them. The Special-Ed faggot was still muttering something, the same with the one in the tracksuit. And I pulled her back by her hair, all cultured, cool, no fooling around, no shit. They were frozen where they stood, Magda keeps her trap shut, quiet as a mouse, I walk coolly, coldly, dragging her after me. Then these two are still muttering something, they're like murmuring something, whispering something. That also fucking pisses me off. I turn and say forcefully: What the fuck, a riot in the state lockup?

Then they both abruptly fall silent and say: Respect.

I moved a little, softened. Since, however, in the face of pure rudeness, of pure hatred for another person, of trickery, of evil, but they manage to talk man-to-man in solidarity, to fight these things in solidarity. Those are my views, anyway, but I'm trying not to say them aloud. But that's exactly how I see things on this matter: respect for a person, high regard standing shoulder to shoulder, since it's not his fault he was born that way, in that form. That's how it is, though in the olden times I had strong feelings of a religious, sacral nature. And it's remained in me, it's stuck in me to this very day, that feeling I've fostered for the Fatima Mother of God, and for that matter for God as well.

Boys!—I call out like that, because after all, Magda and I are getting farther and farther away. When you're in our town, ask for Nails. There's a Polish-Russki war in town. You want someone, something, some smoke, ask for me, boys.

They're still looking toward us pretty much in shock, but at the same time they say again for the last time: Respect, Nails, because despite the fact that I'm far away, I can read it off the movement of their lips.

So I've talked things out with them to pretty peaceful terms, to a settlement. And now it's time to strike up the polonaise with Magda. I sit her down on the bulkhead by the beach. She has pain inscribed on her face, on her mouth, since I'm holding her by that dyed shag exceedingly hard.

It's hard for me to say at that given moment just whether she's pretty or enticing. One eye is completely smudged. The string of her dress is torn, held together by a safety pin. She's in a rather bad state, her teeth are chattering from that amphetamine she overdid. Like if someone were to propose to legalize amphetamine farming at her place, go right ahead, with a kiss. On the hand, on the mouth, and on the cheeks. Even if it had to be at her expense, at the expense of her folks, her neighbors, and her pals.

The first issue—I say to her, because she's grimacing from the pain, maybe, and maybe also from shame, from a sense of guilt—where's that gangrene on your leg?

She's silent. She grumbles something. She says: What do you think? That I'm going to walk around crippled, paralyzed for the rest of my life? You'd love that, I know. But that's not how it's going to be.

So I say, since my nerves are getting frayed all over again, In my eyes, what you are, Magda, is mental. Paralyzed, but mentally. Emotionally.

What's more—I say to her further: Either you have that crippled leg, or you don't. There's no such possibility, in an honest, apolitical life, that for me that leg is crippled and requires an operation to be performed by the chief of staff, but next, for those gentlemen, it's healthy and walking. *Nyet* on that possibility. It's one way or the other, and this is one thing I'll tell you, Magda, straight to your honest face, if that's the way it is, you can go and register yourself with the House and the Senate and spin the threads of your lies, of your slander, there, because that's the only place they'll fit right in.

I'm cool, I'm like stone. She starts to cry, which looks rather unspectacular, a little TV. I light up a cigarette, since I have to stress that in recent years I've fallen into this unpleasant addiction. But it's my way of expressing my opposition, my way of expressing my defiance to the West, against American dieticians, American plastic surgeries, American crooks, who are suave but betray our country on the sly. I was saying this to Magda once already, in this conversation of a friendly nature, that when I go to America, I'm going to smoke cigs right on the street, despite the fact that they mostly look down on that there, since the entire West is cutting back on smoking.

At this very moment she says, in a pretty dreamy voice that surprises me: Oh, Nails, I'd like to get away from here. To chat up managers, executives, to chat up all those filthy-rich orthopedists, to squirrel away some wad of cash. To get away. With someone I love. Anyway, maybe even with you as well. Maybe even with you first of all, Nails, since I'm so safe with you. Because there's no future in this country, our love has no chance to grow here, wherever you look there's violence, even this Polish-Russki war now taking place in town, which you can't enter without running up against Russki pervs.

Everywhere there are staffs, everywhere white-and-red flags. When all I want is your affection, and at every step I can be beaten or even killed. By anybody. Man is a wolf to man. A friend betrays you.

It's very late at night, deep, the sea and the beach. Not a living soul, because those two, their leather tails between their legs, have long since vanished into thin air, as if they never existed. Even so, given the insult that's been perpetrated against me, I simply can't pass over it lightly. I simply can't take it. Because think what you want, but that had been rudeness on her part, though now she's tender and sensitive, all dreamy.

Don't talk like that, Magda, because I'm not listening to you anyway. I don't want you anymore. Not to listen to you, not for anything. Since there's a lie in those very words, the very poison of falsehood. Which I won't take anymore. Even today you tossed me aside, without looking at the marks of time. Because according to the rules of the watch, it was like still yesterday. But at any rate, you tossed my feelings aside. But then you say no, that you have a cramp in your calf, that you have a kid. You claim it's killing you, you accuse me of being the father. Then you leave me for dead on the beach, you go off with some dickheads. All of a sudden the cramp in your calf's gone. The kid as well. A complete mobilization, like a fish when it smells blood. About me, you claim aloud, like Judas, that I'm mental. Yes, don't deny it, those are the acts that you've committed. Though now you stress your love for me all over again, I, Nails, am telling you that it's over between us.

So I say it. Without getting all dark, without special Lenten hymns, without fucking around with any old tears, with any old feelings. Since given the fact of what Magda's like, there isn't a ghost of a chance of being understood. Her empathy horrifies me, it devastates me. Magda's crying grows still worse, simply put, more advanced. She says that no one has ever wronged her more in her life than I have with my brutality, with my coldness, with my mental, emotional shell. Or rather, a husk that covers me. She says that those two wanted to kill her the way you'd kill a dog, and to kill me as well. Because if she hadn't told them that I was mentally abnormal, they would have fucked me as well. They had guns, championship air rifles, hunter's knives, various weapons. Everything under their jackets, because they showed her. She had to pretend that I'm her brother who has shit in his skull, seeing as she wanted to keep me from certain death.

Since I'm at the limit of what I can take, of shock and of something else I can't name. Because what I'm hearing is over the top, a stretch, pure ethical flimflam that, in the longer run, is not to be tolerated. Magda takes advantage of the moment of silence between us. She rolls out a monologue on the subject of her goodness, of her devotion, and suddenly she became mad talkative, like a mental whore, like a mental escort. So I say: Listen, Magda. She's further afield. To which I say, in the following manner: You have a cramp in your calf, or not?

To which she says, in the following manner, though she speaks with a distinct heaviness, because the amphetamine locks up the jawbone, which is trembling involuntarily in her face: Do I have it, don't I have it, that's already your deal, because I'm jetting, I'm leaving here, I'm taking my purse by the strap and fucking off, because those assholes, assholes without a speck of culture, never mattered to me, I never had any feelings for them, I'm interested in culture and art, a certain delicacy of manners, true love for all time, the true sensitivity that can transpire between people of the opposite sex. I don't give a shit about your lesbian interests, though you always mention how lesbians turn you on, so I'll tell you something, you're a common perv like all the others, and it's the only thing that interests you, and in a typically perverted manner, which you know doesn't interest me, it grosses me out, something like that. And maybe you're even of the gay persuasion, which I can't prove to you, because that's always a tough thing to prove, but I can say it to your face, because with regard to you, that's exactly what I think. So now I'll tell you: I hate you, because you're simple, shallow. You're not interested in pictures, magazines, film, which I have always loved, much as I haven't had occasion to show it, what's more, I'll even tell you, is I've been afraid to reveal it, because you could respond in the negative, no. I'll tell you that I'm not interested in the kind of love you want to make, that's why the topic of our conversations was always brittle, it broke. Since my worldview depends, to a high degree, on liberating women from the yoke, on putting an end to feudalism on this score, on this issue. I'll tell you it's enough, and that I'm raising my fist against those very people, like yourself, who are all about one thing, the Prussian fealty at their feet. If it were to go on any longer, I'd lose my individuality to no end, my personal, individualistic dimension, my way of behaving, my views, which I'd lay out for you as abject tribute. I'll tell you this one thing, no matter how much my life turns into a nightmare on your end, that the feeling had already burned out in me yesterday, and I'll tell you that back then I was looking at Lefty, that he's definitely better than you, more sensitive, that when I was with him, the whole world seemed to me overfilled with depth, suffering, but through just that sort of existential strain in his behavior I felt that that's what life's about, it's about wisdom, readership, computer maintenance. That spread before me is a future that's mechanized, computerized, learning the basics of photocopying, learning the basics of English, trips abroad. Then your appearance in my life through Lolo, though even with him I was happier, though he was a dry person, stern, not free with his voice, with his opinions. Your presence destroyed everything in me, every wish that rose up within me. On the whole, I don't know why I was with you, because it was actually bad between us from the beginning, various tensions, paranoia, and though I'll never say what Lefty revealed to me then, he revealed to me that you're a common, uneducated jerk who has no idea about a girl, that I'd probably even be your first initiation right after Arleta, who's my friend, though you won't admit it, since hypocrisy is your main principal trait. He revealed to me that he'd never let me be with you, because never in your life have you ever used the three magic phrases, please, thank you, excuse me, or opened a door for a girl. Or just offered a symbolic proverbial perspective.

* * *

You say something?—I say, because from my guts there suddenly arose a squeaky voice, I'd almost say: feminine. That's an effect of feeling the anger that all at once engulfed me like an ocean and cut me off from all rational impulses, from all rational messages. And I caught on that I don't want her to answer that question. I want to kill her, now that I see that this sensation is my impression pertaining to the entire evening.

Magda, though I hate that name to no end, I want to X out each of its letters in a row, she's horrified by what she said a moment ago. She's wiggling her butt at having hurt me. She looks like someone who's about to get her ass whupped. Shrunken, diminished, her head concave, her leg drawn in.

I didn't say that—she says quickly, shielding her empty-to-the-last-drop head with her hands—Lefty said it.

What Lefty, what the fuck Lefty, you just said it, you slut, here and now, and I am the key witness that you just said it right out of your mouth?—I say, and in light of the big line of crank I enjoyed earlier, it's hard for me to talk, referring to my trembling jaw.

Well, Lefty said it, and not me. But you also can't take Lefty as a serious person. You know how he is. Abnormal, which is why the good times ended between us anyway. Particularly because of that tic he has with his eye. I saw that he has a tic. Teeth totally out of whack, not set in a row like with every normal person, only otherwise, just as you please. That disgusted me while I was kissing him as well. But really especially it was his tic, she says.

Regarding Lefty, we'll deal with him later, I think to myself. As soon as we get back to town, we'll go ahead. That's what I think to myself in my soul. The Polish-Russki war has no chance here. Standards, flags won't help at all, asking, begging, forgive me, Nails. No good will come to him in this crusade that'll transpire between him and me. On one side me, on the other Lefty. On one side Nails, against the fucked-up Captain Eye, with his duplicitous view of the world.

And now enough with this shooting the shit, enough with the pity, with the scruples that have beguiled me thus far. Now there'll be a slaughter in actual fact, now it's after ten o'clock, now close your eyes, please, children, and those with weak nerves.

Shake a leg—I say to Magda, because I've had it up to here with her liberated fucking around like out of the newspaper, like read from a handbook in the dark. A head-fucked handbook on left feminism. Enough. Enough with goodness, with gentleness. To which she says: Leave me alone, you stupid nut, what are you trying to do? Give me your leg, no funny stuff—I say in a low voice, all cruel like I never happened to be at my very worst when I was single, against the worst enemies straight up on steroids, on coke. Not that one, the one with the cramp, the one that had such a fatal deficiency of potassium and polychrome. At that she starts to howl and squirm and moan, saying: Whatever you want, just let me go, I'll tell you everything. About the truth about that leg. Just let me go. Your loneliness has gone to your head. The amphetamine's gone to your head. You've turned into a bum, amped up on speed. Jakub Szela. The fucking vampire from Zagłębie.

Enough of you, Magda. It doesn't mean anything to me anymore. What you say. It's simply senseless, 100 percent sensefree, because you're totally without sense from the inside out, your literature and education, your pro-feminist pretensions, your ploys with fine art, all of it, I've had enough of it. No more of your sway with me, no more of you making me crazy, for I know the truth about you, about your whole quasi-liberationist fooling around, about the whole paramental mudpit that, forgive my saying, you play up with that devil Arleta. Shake a leg, because I can't get a handle on my anger. Which is great and will only get greater. Shake a leg. You ask me that if you give me your leg, will I tell you what I want to do. And so I'll tell you, so get ready. Better yet, close your eyes, cover your ears, because here come some dirty words. And give me that leg, no funny stuff, no fooling around, and straighten out your panties, so it won't be unpleasant for you, and get ready for a quick death. And right before dying, in the last moments of your shitty life, look for yourself at how beautiful the sea is tonight, how nicely it rushes about, to the left, to the right, then forward, then back. Because you're no longer going to see it later on, except maybe in hell. If of course your lovely little Arleta wants to send you a card from Jastarnia to the cauldron you're in, with best wishes for a worthwhile stay, since she's having a great time and has met a sweet forty-year-old businessman without kids. You ask what I want to do to you with that leg, you say only don't let it be too painful. And I'll tell you one thing, you'd better shut up, you'd better snort whatever shit you still have left, and if not, then I don't know what you should do, snort up some of that fine Polish sand, since it's really going to hurt, what I'm going to do to you. Because I'm going to kill you, I don't know if you know that. That is, it's more that I'm going to saw off your most fashionable leg in its panty hose, which in your case amounts to death. That's what I think. That even if you don't die during your puerperium, in a so-called hemorrhage, all the same it's curtains for you. You won't be able to put out, your ass'll shrivel up because of it, which for you will also amount to death. Oh, certainly, I'll set out your crutches. Three meters from here and that's how I'll leave you, watching you crawling, creeping toward your shitty death like some marine vegetation.

That's what I say to her, to that idiot Magda. To which she bursts out laughing. She squeals with laughter, tells me to leave her be, because she has the giggles, and on top of that premenstrual cramps, so she's more neurotic still, primed to be irritated. Then suddenly she sobers up and says: Nails, you're not serious, are you? What are you doing with that blade, with that little knife there, huh? Have you gone flat-out stupid? That you're so impulsive, that always impressed me about you. But that potato knife, keep it to yourself and get it away from me, because I'm squeamish with regard to blood, even if it's mine. Did you rip that piece of shit off from your mom's drawer? You want to cut me up? Are you a perv? You want to set up a live-person-butchering contest for me here? In general, are you fair or not, are you my friend or some homo after all? If you want to screw around like this because it turns you on, then do it to yourself, or go to the Polish-Russki war and jab at the Russkies with it, because I know you're an enemy of the Russkies, though you won't 'fess up to it. What basically comes clear is that you're false, that you're bogus toward your true feelings, because you'll never 'fess up to them, you won't come out with your own views, which I know about, that they're quite extremely leftist, right?

Then, though I'm insulted, I look at her, and she seems pretty to me, which I can't deny. And which compels me toward various gestures. Generally speaking, she's so pretty, so fragile, that when I look in her direction she makes me sorry for all the words, all the expressions that'd been uttered. She makes me feel sorry for her, since maybe she had a tough childhood, worse than tough. Maybe she hasn't had it the best in life, cast aside from the start, all the time led astray by the government, by the state, no chance for prospects. When I look at her like that, it occurs to me that maybe her drama comes from having been born out of place, out of time. I imagine to myself that in another town, in another state, she could even become the queen of the royal court. And no one would guess that she's just a regular girl, including the king, including the marshal. And if things weren't so bad between us, various clashes, if she hadn't put up all that paranoia, those pretensions about everything and nothing, that grudge one has for another, it would be different. I'd take her and set her down on that little wall. I'd pull down her tights and put them back on again, so that they wouldn't be all twisted around like that, destroyed, I'd tuck up her dress and stretch it out, so that it wouldn't be so out of sorts. And if I had some tissues, which Lefty reminded me about, because those tissues are one thing that everyone, even a badass, should have with him for personal use, and they always come in handy. I'd cleanse her face of that grease that's spreading like a landscape around her eyes. Of that lipstick that's colored like some half-uneaten dessert in the neighborhood of her mouth.

That's what I'd do. But at the same time she's sulky like she was at least the mistress of the manor of that little wall, and I were a hobo, an illegal immigrant here without a passport, without a visa to her, without anything.

It's a pretty day, I start to speak in a more soothing tone.

To which she says: So maybe I'm already coming down from the blow, I feel like puking, and in a moment I'll puke on your pants just like that if you don't tap out even a little line for me. I have the distinct impression that maybe I'm even already dead, that I'm already almost not alive. Just a gust of wind will be enough, one gesture on its part. Forgive me, but now I'm really going to get serially emotional. Because when they cut off the chicken's head on the farm, it still runs like that, headless, for fifteen meters through the whole yard. That's exactly how I feel, like a hen with its head cut off, running through the yard on what's left of its strength. But I know that in a moment, without a doubt, I'll die. If you, Nails, knew how to help me even once, then understand me.

What there was, the remains that I find in her purse—because Magda's pretty clearly coming down already—I tap out onto the Hit Market circular. Which I found near at hand. It's already dawn. I tell her not to die, that that feeling, no matter what would pick at it, destroy it, it exists between us. While she has her head thrown back from her body and nods in agreement. Her face is rather pallid, anemic. More like underneath, inside, Magda had garden soil instead of meat. Which shocks me. We walk to the station, though we could have taken a taxi. But that's rather impossible, since there's the possibility of throwing up on Magda's end, maybe of spewing garden soil, because that's how she looks at that moment. Besides, I think that taking a stroll in the morning is good for your health. Which, in this situation, can be categorically helpful in relieving the symptoms, in changing the whole situation in our favor. On the road we stop in at a gas station, since I buy Magda *Filipinka* so that she can read herself some magazine, a newspaper. Though I'm rather opposed in a declarative way. Magda says that that's a good sign, that I'm tender, romantic, sensitive to her, like no one before me. Enclosed with the magazine there's clearly one of those denim handbags. Which Magda notices right off the bat. Which in her condition is significant, because it looks like suddenly she has to be joyful, happy, though in general she looks awful. Because with zeal, with rapture, she pours everything else from her handbag out onto the sidewalk. It's mostly chewing gum, various feminine doodads like deodorant, lipsticks, cigarette filters, various beauty products. That pretty much pisses me off, because notwithstanding the fact that it's morning-time, that's just fucked up, treating perfectly good stuff like that, so I tell her not to make a mess in the middle of town. She says she doesn't give a shit, since no one sees her doing that here and now anyway, so that she could even take a piss right here, if only she felt like it. So she chucks that handbag away and makes use of this new one, tossing into it everything she has, leaving on the sidewalk just the empty dope baggie, gum wrappers. As well as the pen with the inscription *Zdzisław Sztorm,* the herbal sedative tablets that I'd recognize anywhere. Because they stink like chicken shit.

Eh, keep that pen, maybe it'll still be useful later on—I say. To which she says that she's been on a diet lately and has lost ten kilos from her upper arms, and she's categorically chucking the pen, since it brings her bad memories of Vargas, who she got it from.

I think over where her declarativeness is coming from, this gift for decision. It's obvious, tickets or no tickets, a line, we take a leak before the station, LM cigarettes, menthols, because they're the only kind left. I tell her that women are exceptionally wronged having to piss in this way and that it looks like a flying machine taking off. Magda says I should fuck off, that I should take better care about pissing on myself. She reads *Filipinka* with low energy, says, I'm leaving, I'm leaving this place to go somewhere else, to better states. I say, Like where. To which she says, To like warm countries. In the meantime she cuts into the line, like there's almost no passengers besides us, because it goes without saying anyway, her nausea is overwhelming, to say nothing of the details. Then she keeps reading quietly. She says she'll go to those countries where they have these outfits, these cosmetics, creams made from cucumbers, from everything, because that's the only place she wants to live, if I want to be with her, gels under the eyes, various creams, bath salts. I say that yes I want to, though on this point my understanding is otherwise, I'd say more leftist-patriotic. So then I tell Magda how things really are in our country. I tell her about the general oppression by a race ruling over the working race, of the race of the haves over the race of the have-nots. That they're the same relations like in slavery. That the West stinks, has a polluted environment that litters everything with various unnatural compounds, PVC, CHVDP. That the ones in charge there are Jew-killers, prole-killers, murderers who maintain themselves and their illegitimate children by oppression, by selling people corporate shit in the corporate wrapping sold by the McDonald's corporation.

You're shitting me—says Magda, with no blood in her face, with an excited expression. Like a kid who's just been exposed to the fact that Santa Claus is a fake, another stinking custom devised by a handful of folks from the West. It isn't shit, because I ate it up.

Sure, I ate it up, too, but not wanting to upset you, it really is shit, shit from people, and even of cows, of dogs, of domestic and circus animals. That's how I explain it to her, visually, so that she'll get it. It's prepared shit, chemically altered, changed from its own composition to another composition and flavor. It's already a matter for specialists, technologies, production procedures, precedents. One shit is more for these rolls, from another they make meat, from a third onions, from a fourth, the worst kind of shit, ketchup and mustard.

Magda doesn't want to believe me, she says: How do you know, you're a novelist and a poet in one, huh?

To which, since I don't have material proof, and I don't want to let her down, I say to her, From guides, various textbooks on leftist issues, on anarchist, liberation issues.

To which she stares at me and says: Shit or no shit, it's good enough, that is, tasty.

To which I say: And that's exactly right, and we both look out the window, dreaming about food products, groceries, because for a long time we've eaten neither lunch nor dinner, not counting those drinks, that speed. Then, already silent, we go back to my place, which is just about free, empty. In a minute it's all over, after our like love, because we're pretty tired, exhausted by that whole night full of feelings and many events. And Magda goes to the mirror, straightens her panties, stretches the skin on her face, and says to me right off, with great resentment: Why the hell didn't you tell me?! Why the hell didn't you say anything to me?

About what, exactly?—I answer with a question from the pullout, because I'm pretty tired of this whole situation. She says: That I look like this! Dirty! Bloated, even! It's come off my hands onto my face, all the mascara, all the flesh, it's come off my hands! Motherfucker! Ass-fucker! I look like a hog, a boar! My eye and mouth doubled! Repeated twice onto my face!

Unfortunately, I don't know more, because notwithstanding her unnatural yells and her rooting around at the sink with various cosmetic things, I fall asleep, and when I wake up, it's already a different time. And what I dreamed about, forgive my saying, that's already none of her business.

⋮

On my cell phone I get a text message from Angela. *Hey, Nails, we met in such-and-such a place, and are we still going to get together sometime.* That kind of message. That kind of SMS. At that moment I wake up from my dream, in bed, on my parents' pullout, a dream that was maybe long but might have been short. Because whatever time it is is in doubt.

Maybe it's no time at all, since it's the end of the world with the apocalypse, which reveals itself and puts syndromes into my psycho- and physiology. Because things aren't well with me, in particular physically, physiologically. Then I notice one fact that I can't bear to assimilate or understand logically. Magda is clearly lying right here next to me, sleeping, which shoots me a pretty good movie along these lines. A classic trip. Because she's clearly next to me, but whether she's alive or she's dead, that's in doubt. I'm afraid, I get a not-bad scare on this point, since she looks pretty bad, pretty much not alive, I'd rather say literally dead. She breathes once, then she skips a breath for a change, surely to make my movie all the worse. In the meantime, not moving an inch from the position she's settled in. I try to call to mind some event, some fact from last evening, during which Magda suffered certain death. And I have no recollection.

Just then, though my each and every movement is almost fatal, and pain and suffering are my inseparable lover, I reach for her purse. Much as that costs me in pain in my skull and in all my human organs, since that's how things are in my body. Although I have to chuck all that shit from the purse she carries around with her and that isn't worth shit to me, forgive my saying so. Everything, if only to extract one broken Tylenol in tablet form.

Because maybe I'm even betraying my antiglobalistic worldview, my beliefs. But Tylenol, though it's made from toxic animals, toxic plants, and human waste from the West, from Western minerals, from the acetaminophen that poisons watering holes the world over and is measured out on sterile scales against a sterile weight.

But despite all that, it's good, when we focus on its medicinal qualities. Not important. Whether it's the venom of bees, of wasps, whether it's the venom of death. It has the form of a common, the most common, tablet, suited for and comfortable to swallow. It works against the general pain of coming down, which for example I have now, as well as against illness, fever. Who knows, maybe against cough, the runs? In a word, maybe it can cure everything.

Then I find the Zdzisław Sztorm pen. It's sort of a shock to me. At that moment some like fata morgana stands before me, all the events and all the incidents that took place yesterday. Though looking at it chronologically, maybe it was even today.

It's like at the moment of death: smoke rises, in front of you there's your whole life enclosed in a photographic frame, like on a slide. So I remember it had to do with many events, many words precisely of death, dying, suffering. I look at Magda, who not only has her eyes closed but doesn't even move a muscle. I think about that child she was bragging about, that she has, I think, or maybe, just when I wasn't looking, she gave birth to it and died in childbirth, addicted to amphetamines. But I throw this version out, since I remember as well that I had her later on, on this pullout, which is mutually exclusive, eliminates, since with a child, with that whole biophysiological mess that supposedly took place later on, that's unlikely.

Then I recall the emotion that inclined me toward uncontrollable aggression with the use of a sharp object. I recall that I wanted to sever her leg around the thigh. That horrifies me, because the thought occurs to me that I did just that. And this, that is, this momentary amnesia, had been brought about by the shock of my crime, by that rush of ruthlessness. And Andrzej Robakoski agrees. But were I to have cut off her leg, it's already evicted from her memory, maybe even forever. I slide my hands timidly under the quilt and look for that cramped leg, which, as I remember, is closer to the wall. The leg is there and is in good shape, and it still purrs, as if it were a dog that's satisfied with its own feces. Magda is clearly greenish as well, because she's greenish, strewn across the entire bed, like some murder victim, but clearly she hasn't been killed, nor did she perish in the battle for the Polish red flag, she didn't fall in the war for the flagpole. She even has fresh makeup that she put on for bed, these smeared specks yet newly applied, sort of askew and sort of backward, as if from the amphetamine, from that like unfaulted coming down, her mitts had the shakes and she made herself various lines and dots, as if the entire Morse code had marched across her face. Looking at her, maybe I shouldn't resort to such allusions, but I'll say only that as a not so big boy, until my most recent life, I have never seen the likes of those eyebrows, the likes of those lashes. Indeed, I've seen eyes, but eyebrows and lashes were for me a kind of black magic. The same with a dress and skirt. There's little to add. A Chinese sermon in the Polish National Church. This brought about a literal avalanche of personal, intimate situations in which I behaved wrongly and unfairly. But I somehow always got out of them.

And by the time I know that nothing's wrong with her, I'm sweeping all that inorganic, foreign crap from her purse off my belly. From the purse with the flyer joyfully advertising *Filipinka*. I tear off the quilt and, thinking in precisely you know what way, withdraw stealthily to the kitchen.

Where I glance down at my telephone, on which there appears a text message from Angela. So I call her right away. One-two-three. She's all cheery. Perhaps still drunk from the day before yesterday, which is when I met her. I tell her that she's very beautiful and very pretty, that she delighted me as a girl and as a woman. Various similar male shitbricks, sweet talk, phone numbers, beautiful and pretty, and lovely, and at the same time pretty. I tell her that she has a great personality and that that's what I like about her. She asks me what kind of music I listen to. I say, A little bit of everything, all kinds in general. She says, Me, too. Summing up, we had a nice chat, the discussion's on a high, cultural level. There's some talk about culture and art, she: what kind of movies do I like, I, that she's really hot, but that prettiest of all is her face, I like different movies, and most of all different actors and actresses. That she herself could make a pretty good actress, a model. She says I'm fucking around with her, I say that if she doesn't believe me, that's her business, though I can swear by Saint Jakub Szela and all the saints. To that she answers that she has to get off the phone. To which I ask her if she's seen *The Fast and the Furious*. She, that maybe she has, maybe she hasn't. I propose that we get together to watch the video. She asks whether I'm seeing somebody. I say, Not just now, because I'm having trouble shaking off my last relationship, which was full of a faultless but tragic love doomed to collapse. To which she says that she loves boys who are romantic, sensitive, but at the same time hard and dark. With a sense of humor, who like love, adventure, taking walks as a couple, dinner together, long walks together along the beach, long conversations together about everything, romantic strolls, writing long letters, open and with a cheerful sense of humor, who will be her true friends, buddies, honest, sensitive, in their gestures, in culture, in art, in their honest conversations about the passage of time. I answer that I also like those kinds of girls, pretty, beautiful, with a sense of humor, who like fast action films and listening to good music, who like to have a good time, to dance, who are hot, good-looking. She asks me if I'm fucking around with her. I bridle. Because if I already say something, it's the truth, by the very fact of the words coming out. And even if it isn't, it still may be. Then she asks whether I know that in our land there's a Polish-Russki war with a white-and-red flag, which waves between the native Poles and the Russki thieves, who rob them of customs duties, of nicotine. I tell her I don't know anything about that. To that she says it's exactly how things are, it's what she hears, that the Russkies want to cheat the Poles out of this place and establish a Russki government here, maybe even a Belorusski one, that they want to shut down the schools, the government offices, to kill the Polish newborns in the hospitals in order to eliminate them from society, to impose protection fees and tribute for industrial and grocery products. I say that they're common swine, common informants.

Then she says that she has to get off the phone. She asks why I'm speaking in such a quiet voice, like in a lowered voice. I say that my mother is here sleeping in the next room, because she's coming down. She asks me in what way my mother's coming down. I say that my mother is the sort of mother who sometimes likes to get high, to put a line in her nose for work or for the evening. Angela laughs, says that I have a cheerful sense of humor, which earns me a hundred points with her. I say thanks, that we'll keep talking about that, because she has a great personality and disposition, which is particularly easy for me to see.

I return to the room, where it's utter Sodom and Gomorrah, syph, malaria, the plague. The pullout is folded onto itself, all crazy. Pain in my skull. The Zdzisław Sztorm pen is running through the whole room, like it's going downhill. All over the place. Gumballs, colorful, red, blue, pouring from Magda's purse like hail and snow, atmospheric precipitation onto the linoleum. Lollipops, rags, tights. Everything like a storm's passed through. Rags with no real worth. And a hurricane blows in, flying through the window. The chandelier swaying to and fro. Dirt, dust on the furniture. In a word, chaos, panic. Magda on the pullout in an ambiguous position like some lady on a garbage dump, in my own mother's nightshirt, which completely sets me off. She's playing a dexterity game on her telephone. She sticks her tongue into the baggie of speed that she found in my jacket pocket. She's desperate. She's lazy, good for nothing. Seeing me, her boyfriend, doesn't afford her a shadow of joy. Rather an abrupt disenchantment, a disappointment.

Who the hell were you talking to?—she asks me, and before that she takes the baggie from her tongue.

What, like I was talking to somebody?—that's how I answer, rather unpleasant, but that's exactly the state of grumpiness, of harshness, to which this vision is leading me.

So you were talking, what: you weren't talking, but you were talking? I heard it as well, so there are witnesses. But in a different way, since I was sleeping. That's how fish must hear our, people's, conversations underwater. Mum mum mum, yada yada. I literally heard those things, half-asleep, half getting it. And when it comes down to what I should have understood, it's that over and over you repeated "mother."

So I say to her, because I'm already pretty pissed off, since I have to look at her: Because it was my mother who called me on my cell phone, in case you didn't know. She said that right now she's on her way to our place and that you have to get the fuck out of here with all haste. Because if she sees you, she'll kill you like a dog. Because you, Magda, are not a suitable companion for me. Because she has principles, she believes that a girl's treasure is in her modesty, and you don't possess any, even less than you do culture. That there are rumors about you in the housing development, that you take amphetamines, acid, that you hang around with types you shouldn't. That in general you're done for, that you're draining me morally and mentally. That if you keep coming here all done up in her nightshirt, in her rags, that will be your slow death. So get yourself together quickly, since you don't want to cause problems for the both of us, get us committed. I had to tell her: Mom, don't have a fit. Magda's just sleeping by herself in the den, in the basement, she brought her own screen and made herself a smallish corner down there, where she has a space heater. She's asleep there, she's not touching our things, our banknotes.

Magda's silent, but suddenly she explodes. In an unhealthy manner. Entirely incoherent. In an intermediate manner between cough and fury. She starts to gather her shit, belts, hose, like it's a lightning-quick sorting of garbage. She's clearly full of venom. She says: Your old lady's just as full of shit as you are, just as mental. They talk about her in the housing development, that she put panels from the Russkies on your house and that these panels, this siding, is going to peel off on you soon, in the very near future.

Then she pulls on her tights, which she had mislaid somewhere. She smoothes the runs with her fingers, as if by doing so she could cauterize them so that they wouldn't be visible. She glances at me, sympathetically like, and says: Because it's Russki siding. And that siding's going to peel the fuck off from a great height. Killing your whole family. Take it to heart. And tear that paneling off before it's too late. I'm warning you, Nails. Next there's going to be a cookout in the garden, it's all cool, spare ribs from the Hit Market, your old mom leans over the grill with a poker, your bro with a handy set of seasonings. And Nails, suddenly you're all leaning over the grill, looking at it like it's a revelation, like at a solar eclipse. And then fuck, fuck, fuck, the panels are flying into your genetically shithoused skulls like some fucking meteorites, moons or planets from the sky. One on your brother. For dealing, for his egoism, his depravedness, for screwing Arleta and then dumping her, deserting her at the first stop. For holding on to fivers for the Russkies. Fuck him in the head. And to the hospital's isolation ward with him. Or better, lock him up right away. Fuck him! And your mother next! For her rumors, for the whole Zepter thing, where she does business and makes pretty good bank. For the criminal prices in the horrendous solarium. For all her evil, for destroying our love, Nails. Fuck her. And to the ward with her.

Then Magda, since she sees that my silence notwithstanding I'm already set to react, smiles apologetically, but at the same time venomously. As if she wanted to say to me: Sorry, Nails, that your family is that way, which fucks things up for you all over town. I can't help you with that. At most you can hide it, not show it. Because you don't have a chance among normal people. So generally, she drags herself around the apartment. She stomps across the linoleum. Desperate. In her tights.

And the next panel onto your dog. Fuck him! Right onto her skull. Because she's an abnormal, pathological dog, she only has a stomach. Zero legs, zero arms, a vestigial head. Like your whole family.

Saying this, Magda brings my mother's toothbrush in from the bathroom, squirts some toothpaste onto it, and, reaching the peak of her gall, scrubs her not so perfect teeth. But that's not the end of her speech, because despite the resistance posed by the act of cleaning her teeth, she continues to yap. Now she's talking, and this is the culminating bullet point in her program. And the last panel is going to fuck *you* up, Nails. You should know how I spit on you, how I don't love you. You should know the truth about yourself. That you're nobody, dirt under my fingernail. Which I have somewhere, with all due respect. Because it's not just that you were such a wimp that you drove me into that story about the kid. Which is already the least bad thing, since maybe Claudia or Donna, Nicole or Marcus wouldn't even be your kid, only mine, and you'll die. It's not important if it's a boy or a girl. What's more important is that you attempted to kill me, that you came at me with a knife. That you showed no understanding for the fact that I was coming down. Because your leftist soul is totally fucked all over.

*   *   *

Having uttered these words, Magda spits her foamy tooth-paste out onto the carpet.

Watching this, I ask: Which toothpaste did you use? Because right away I become aware of this whole drama, this whole desperation, and I completely lose my cool. Tell me, you fucking trash. The one on the right or the one on the left? She answers that she doesn't quite remember anymore, since she's coming down hard and I shouldn't go all apeshit on her today. Because she's in pieces.

Because that toothpaste on the left was an Easter gift. I say to her: If you used it, I'll kill you like a dog. For the insult to my principles, the constitution of my apartment. And for insulting my mother. Regardless of what she is, good or bad, representing Zepter or PSS Społem. Because a mother's a mother, and I love her because she's mine. And it has nothing to do with you. Here's all your shit, your purse and your mutty rags, here's your portable world. Here it is, I'm throwing it to the stairs like a bone to a dog, you should know your place in life. Whine. Whine like a dog. You won't bother me anymore. I have important business to attend to.

And after saying that, I shove her pretty cruelly, pretty brutally, through our Gerd automatic doors. In her quasi-tights. That's bad on my part, disloyal, I admit it. But depriving me of my balance equals a spasmodic death. And that's what she'll endure. All the consequences for it. One way or another. Left or right.

⁘

Arleta, leaning over the bar, is, honestly, pretty drunk. Like
some exotic puffy-faced animal. She's blowing a bubble with
her gum that pops, covering her up, her face, with its entire
pink expanse. After which she pulls it off and puts it back in
her mouth. It's like some symbol of consumerism. She would
eat everything, she'd eat the whole world down to the last
crumb and leave some like plastic wrap. She'd smoke all the
cigarettes from the pack flat-out at once, if only she could
wedge them in somewhere and light them. She'd lick the remnants of her drink off the counter.

She's got a smoke stuck to her hand called Viva that she
puts to her lips with a pretty drab expression on her face. She
says to me: Listen, Nails, I have a question for you, on the
DL. I say: So keep going. To which she says: Will you tell me
what really happened between you and Magda? I say it has
shit to do with her. To which she says that she's very well
aware of that, so I don't have to tell her anything at all, because she already knows. To which I say: So what, what happened between us according to you? She says: You could still
change everything, put everything right, when you were at the
sea and Magda wanted to be with you. She confided everything to me. But you were jealous, and in the morning, waking up in that apartment where you'd tricked her into going,
she told herself deep down that she can't be with you. So she
walked. And it's what you've accomplished, that's what I
wanted to hear from you, Nails.

I put my hand over my face. Because it was well and good that she wasn't here today, her raggedy hair, her little bird's voice, her laugh like that of a woman breaking down at menopause. Because today she wouldn't have made it out with her life, not a chance. I look for her like, like what, I'm going to kill her, destroy her. Music, lights, neon. She's nowhere for now, so, having looked around, I say to Arleta: Where's Magda? She says, because she sees how I'm unusually, extremely fucking pissed: She went to the lot with Lolo.

To what lot she won't tell me. She's trembling at the idea that I might go there and kill them both at the same time with one blow. Squash and trample their faces with my own foot. Drive an aspen peg into the earth under a garden shack, and having soaked the soil in that place with solvent, with rubbing alcohol, so that they'd never manage to get out. So that they could make underground, nonpublic love in the dark and cozy recesses of the garden soil. Arleta will not, will not allow such a cunning crime, because she's quaking right down to her ass about whether in the course of the investigation there won't emerge the issue of her excesses against the law with Russki cigarettes.

The Bartender says that I should fuck it. And indeed, that's exactly what I do. But not because Magda doesn't mean anything to me, but because today I have bigger fish to fry, some business. But that's yet to come.

And I sit there. Cool clothes, because I dressed up, because when I got up this morning, I was wearing just my drawers.

Clean pants, too. Then Angela comes in and walks like she belongs to the whole bar, to the contests and the billiards and the pinball machines. Apropos of that, it occurs to me that all in all, I didn't remember so well what she looks like, this Angela. Someone, something rings a bell, but who knows what church, parish or provincial, she comes from. Now I recognize her for sure and stand up at her greeting.

Angela is a girl of a different stripe from Magda. Different to the touch, different in general. Her style is more of that gloomy dark sort. Some kind of black velvety skirt, as well as laced-up boots, abnormal stockings, but quite provocatively netty. Chain mail, brass knuckles on her hands and ears. She's all nail polish, of the black variety. All smeared black, but evenly and carefully. Around her lips, as well as her eyes. From which there extend eyelashes glued on for all eternity.

You have a cool, interesting style—that way I cut her off right off the bat, straight off, with a compliment.

In a moment I see that it delights her, talking about it. To which she answers: What style do you mean? I say right away: Well, you know. Clothes, behavior, way of carrying yourself.

She says that that's just the way she is already, that it's not her copycatting someone else, just something she chose. That she carried herself that way her whole life, like me and you, like all of us, but one day she said to herself that she wants to be herself and have her very own inimitable style. Like herself on the inside, gloomy and dark.

I say that that's really interesting and engaging on her part. That it's the most important thing in life, to be yourself, not someone else. She says that she's found that to be the case, too.

Then the conversation breaks off for a while. Angela, sipping at her drink, looks around the room.

Are you having fun?—I say to her, to get the conversation going.

Sure—she says—fun. Though I mostly hate people like you. I'll tell you that right off.

That completely takes me aback, to hear that kind of shit-talking from an apparently nice girl who still seemed so likable over the phone. I look straight at her. To which she says as follows: Because, you know. I don't mean you in particular, because you're pleasant, neat, simply intelligent. I have more in mind these disco-assholes, these disco-whores, who I simply hate. Look at your friends. Sluts, assholes, yearning for each other. Everybody thinks about finding a husband. It's a total embarrassment, rooting after breeding rights. A lack of contraception. But you're different, which I noticed here right away. Romantic, because I recognized it straightaway in your true nature. Romanticism, sensitivity, going together on walks, motorcycles, water bikes. That's what I love.

Then she asks whether I have some girl. To which I answer not yet, because I can't get over the girl I had to get away from because several times each day she wrecked my spirit. To which she says: Right, it's good that you broke it off with her. I, for example, am not like that. That is, shallow, dumb. Consider, for example, that I don't eat meat. Meat is the product of a crime. Sugar is made from the bones of animals, so I don't eat sugar, either.

I look at her like a deer in the headlights. It occurs to me that perhaps she's some kind of lunatic that slipped out of the hospital and is looking at me as her next victim. And now I should get the hell out of here, pay my tab, tell the Bartender that there's a damn fine piece of ass that wants to get to know him, and get the fuck out of here with all speed. But I don't do that. I don't have the animal instinct that saves us from the eradication of our kind. I sit and look at her, her dress, her legs. What will be will be.

She sees that, finishes her drink. Do you know that I don't eat eggs, either?

This I can no longer bear, because to grasp such preposterous views, I can't do it. I say to her: What's with you, are you retarded? Did eggs do something bad to you?

She looks at me, pretty outraged, as if I didn't know about basic moral fundamentals. So she says to me: And how would you feel if you were to be killed without your consent? If you weren't even aware of it, if you were defenseless? You'll come around to this anyway. Because the world is already on the brink. When I look over the balcony in the morning, all I know is that the world is perishing, dying. The natural environment.

Humanity completely degraded. Widespread heaviness, obesity. Sadness. Americanization of the economy. Do you understand all this? CV contamination. Asbestos. VTC. As people, we're finished. The end.

This is what the discussion hinges on. So I say, since this has knocked me out of my balanced equilibrium: And do you know that that's sometimes just the way it is, and it happens that hens, roosters, peck through their own eggs and eat them?

Which irritates her all the more: Because they're rebelling! They're speaking out against the evil people who unlawfully deprive them of their only progeny. They prefer to destroy them than to nourish the dismal human race.

Though I myself postulate for nature unpolluted by American enterprise, her speech sort of shocked me. They're like my thoughts, of an antiglobalistic character, but not quite entirely. More hysterical, without sobriety, without balance.

I think that your views are too radically pessimistic, I say, putting my hand on her thigh. She says that she's just realistic. Last month she got dumped by her boyfriend, amen, that's the story. Since then she has no illusions, she's no longer so naive as to get tied up. The world horrifies her, overwhelms her. But if only she could meet someone who loved riding bikes, playing sports, badminton, beach ball. Who shared her hobbies. Who would help her discover the beauty of the world. Friendship, love, romantic strolls. She'd manage to be devoted, giving. She'd answer the call.

Don't think, since it won't be that way, that then your problems will vanish all of a sudden—I say to her, surprised at my own inner depth, my spirituality, which is getting the upper hand on me. So I say: There won't be those problems, those troubles, but other ones. Life isn't so simple.

To which she makes the following confession: I don't know if you know, but I don't believe in God. There is no God, because He sentenced His children to suffering and death. So there isn't a God anymore. Not in church, not anywhere. I categorically don't believe in it, even if you try to convince me. There's only Satan. No argument will work against my views, even if I would give them up. That's all I'll say to you on the subject. The Black Bible, you have to read it, analyze it, because it's the best reading I've done in my entire economics high school, my best schooling in ideas. Especially the chapter where they talk about the so-called energy-vampires, which suck up your energy, leaving nothing, these people. That's exactly what my boyfriend Robert Sztorm was like, who took everything from me.

*   *   *

Right away I latch on to this Robert, because I don't have the slightest, not the slightest riposte for her judgments about religion, about the sphere of sacrum and profanum. But if I do, then I don't want to utter them aloud. That's the deal, everyone has his own ideas, and there's no reason anyone else need know about them.

Robert Sztorm, where do I know that dude from—I say to her. To which she says that maybe from school, from the disco, or from a club, the market. I say, Wait a second, wait a second, is his father named Zdzisław? To which she says of course, and do I know him? I say, Yeah, sure, for certain, they're the owners of a sandworks with whom I do good business, make bank. To which she's already a lot cheerier, now that things aren't turning out so bad. I say, Me too. She, that she never expected it. To which I say, Neither did I. That I have a transport company, a tourist company. But that first of all I have an amusement-park factory as well that takes up a lot of that very sand. The fact of the matter is that these amusement parks have to be built on something, and the experts have shown that the best thing is to build on a sandy bottom.

I also add: ferrous, and some less comprehensible Western name, so that she'd know that in our line of business we know our stuff.

Regarding this amusement-park factory, she says that I don't look it. I say that regardless, that's the way it is. Then she, that if it's so, then I should give her my business card. I say that they're being prepared by my secretary, Miss Magda. Instead I can show her the Sandworks company writing instrument, which I supposedly got from Sztorm personally. I show her, she's delighted. I tell her that if she'd like, we can do some dust, since after a whole day of doing estimates, of business lunches, which are usually bountiful, consisting of unhealthy, most often American grease, burned. Dutch salad in dog manure. That after all these daily banquets, buffets, after my daily read of the newspapers, magazines, I'm tired, I suffer from chronic fatigue. To which she says that Robert would never let her. Then I'm already pretty peeved and tell her right to her face: Did you come here with me or with this virtuous saint Robert-son-of-Zdzisław of yours? We're going to snort some crank or we're not. Eeny, meeny, miny, mo, and you are it. To which she ultimately delays, hums to herself, throws on her leather. The Bartender gives me the eye. But if Lefty were to give me the eye, I'd kill him and his whole family, cousins included.

It's okay, we go across from the bar. Wanting to be all protective, I suggest to her that if there are some troubles with Robert Sztorm, just let me know. It's no problem getting into his place. The boys will rip him off for free and will even have a good time doing it. And then he can calmly buy back his stuff with interest or pay installments, so no harm will come to him. Particularly if he's really a rich right-wing exploiter of the workers in his company. A Focus-On-the-Family type. A crazy informant, a Russki LM. She says how come. I explain it to her vividly. Ten guys show up at his apartment, the fridge, the stereo system, audio-video, all the hi-fi goes up to heaven and waits for him in heaven. If, of course, he makes it there. Though most often they don't kill him. They'll just apply various caresses to his shins with a monkey wrench. A curling iron if it's one of the better ones, the toner for his printer, his hair dryer, his Rollerblades, the camera, the computer including keyboard, the mouse, the wife, the crystal, the toaster if he's got one. That is to say, the entire Housewares Department and Polish TV.

To which she keeps quiet, she doesn't really know what to say, and I'm pleased that I've made such an electrifying impression on her. I cut us a line and ask her if she has a pipette or maybe some kind of pen. She says she does. So I tell her to give it over. Then she gives it to me. *Zdzisław Sztorm. Sandworks.* Then I say: Mooootherfuuucker. To which she says: What, is it Russki, bogus? To which I say: No, not that. Just your basic-pen pen. But you women are all the same jerk, the same silly fuck. And I'll tell you something else. I don't want a woman anymore, even if she were to stick to me like flypaper. Because they're all common whores. Once a month they break down and don't want to work. They each have at least one Zdzisław Sztorm pen. Enough already. Even if a woman were to ask on her knees that I take her. Then I'd say to such a woman: No. Get the fuck away from me. Out of my sight and out of my heart. That doesn't at all apply to you. That's for some other bitch that'd dog me. I won't lift a digit, neither in my shoe nor on my hand. At which she looks at me like she wants to be fucked on the spot, here, across from the bar, against this wall. And so she answers me: Nails, you're right. I don't want to be with a woman, either, nor with a man. Because there isn't really any difference, this way or that it's the same dick, one big problem. There is no gender, no separation between men and women. There's no gender, into opposites, or any other kind. There's only sons of bitches and bloodsuckers. All people, regardless of the gender they've gotten at birth, are the same rank. You know which one? The rank and race of the bitch-born, of common potential sons of bitches. That's as much as you'll hear from me. One race, the human race.

So I say to her: Don't talk so much shit, just snort. She snorts it into her nose, one here, one there, colorless tears flow from her eye. Then I snort mine. We stand like that for a moment. I ask her if she's done that sometime before. To which she says not exactly, not really. So I think to myself, only now that the trip's starting, Angela strikes me as a thirty-kilo mountain of living mass. Her hands are more or less like they were the hammer and anvil in my ear. Suddenly she laughs, like she's more than a bit psycho. She says that now she's good, that she feels nourished, that her views seem more definite to her.

Damn if she doesn't projectile-puke all of a sudden! It's an amphetamine puke, with recoil, flying way out in front of her. I get a pretty good laugh out of this, as does everybody standing around. I've never seen such alpine acrobatics with my own eyes, not after vodka, not after smoking. Seriously, I literally shit myself with laughter. What, would you believe it, it seems funny to this puking girl as well. Though I'm surprised at her, in her place I wouldn't be so thrilled. But she's roaring with laughter. Between one puke and the next, she calls in my direction: Saaaatan! After which she pukes more. She looks like in a second she could blow up inside her suede dress and enclose the whole world in puke, it'd echo. That would be her kingdom, a Kingdom of Satan, across which, across its entire width, she'd stretch clotheslines and use them to dry her black dresses, stockings, black panties, and—the main thing, or rather the thing that stands out about her character—her black bra. I've never met such an abnormal in all my life. Though I've come across pukers, even Magda, who took her turn slyly, like off to the side. Smart like that, if we're talking about Angela. I look up at her. How that little fucker, that scrawny disaster, can throw up. Terrible. All the mountains, all the sea, all the landscapes, everything held in the tone of her drink, bluish, exotic Bols Curaçao. Plus some not-called-for food, vegetarian murder on an unknown plant. But that's merely a small percentage, and all the rest is some rough ocean of blue vodka plagued by a storm. Whereas if you ask me, I wouldn't be surprised if what takes leave from her mouth is her black nail polish, black mascara, a black chewed-up marker. And a black crayon, black hair dye with the applicator included.

Okay. We go back to the place. Angela goes to wash off her tatters, her remnants. I look toward her. She's in one piece. Though dirty. Abnormal. But cheerful, playful, given to laughter, intelligent. In a word, cool, despite everything that's gone down. Hey, Nails, says the Bartender, winking at me. Fuck it, she'll puke up your apartment. Which at that moment bugs me, irritates me. Because that's shitty, what he's saying, harsh, besides the fact that he saw the whole incident through the windowpane and doesn't know the facts.

I don't want to be an asshole like he is, but around Angela I can't allow him to be so disloyal. When she's so thin that my lightest breath, the movement of my finger, is enough to knock her off her stool and blow up her skirt. Angela comes back. I say to her: We're leaving. To which she says: What for? I, that I've had it up to here with this place, where there's zero culture or art. She looks at me, because maybe she's rather fallen in love with me, fell in love from the first impression I made on her. She says to me: Exactly. While her eyebrows are done up black, like with coal, which I notice right away. But I decide not to look there, because with her, the soul is more important than the body. Though the body is important, too. Though it's so frail, scrawny. She says she loves to take walks, even at night. That tomorrow it's No Russkies Day in town, that sort of fest, and do I want to go with her. I think to myself, Lovely: No Russkies Day, for sure Magda will not fail to come, if only to seek out trinkets for half off among the various chumps from this here entire district. But still I say that I know I'll run into Magda, that that blackens my soul and my thoughts, I say to Angela: We'll see. She says, Like what. I say, Like shit, that there are various conditions, weather, oxygen pressure, if for instance there will be circumstances to get high, that various things could turn up. And I ask her if she wants to come back with me to my apartment.

She says that maybe yes, maybe no. On her dress I notice a web of bright spots that got there when she was puking and when there were splatters, they completely spotted over the front of her dress. I say that she has a bug on her cleavage, so she glances real fast in that direction, hopped up to the limit despite her vomiting, and she tells me to kiss her on the lips, because she always wanted to do that on a bridge, always among trees. She says: Kiss me right on the lips, that's just what I want, I always wanted to do that in the middle of a bridge, amidst trees and bushes. I always wanted to do that. Now I feel it. I don't know what's making me. You're making me. Some minor, onetime madness, some spontaneity that comes out when it's least expected. For instance in an elevator, on the sea, somewhere where no one would expect it. Because life is so short, Nails, and death so close, ever closer, it pants right into our faces, the Reaper with the yellow pelvis, with the dug-out eyes. And don't say it's not so, since that's exactly how it is, total degeneration, a total general collapse of everything. Despotism, depravity. Nails, any day now we're going to be dead, any day both you and I will perish. And it doesn't matter if it'll be poisoned meat, poisoned water, PVC, or the right, or the left, or the Russkies, or our guys. They'll kill us, and then they'll kill each other and eat each other from the same plate for dessert. For dessert. Because there'll be something else for the first course. Beautiful wild animals of endangered species, deer-herd fricassee, tiger-extermination marinade, and giraffes eaten with disposable utensils made from their bones. It'll all perish, die. We're just you, just me. In general I write poetry. Various poems. Sometimes I can sit endlessly. All wrapped up in jotting things down and rejotting. Writing over and over. Straight into the drawer. Later for a wider readership made up of the whole world, who knows, maybe of the American Polish community. No fooling, I have family there. An aunt and an uncle, simply wonderful Canadians. Cheerful. Resourceful. They run a little store for the Polish community there. Not a big business, but lucrative. They got an inheritance. Got it going. My aunt made deals, though she didn't get through it without aggression on the part of the German autochthons. My uncle imported. You know, Russki figurines, various native national icons that sold there like hotcakes. CDs and publications from the band Mazowsze. Vader sold as well. Which I love. But the dolls are better, matroshki, little rugs, kukla figures, marzanna dolls. Besides that, I love animals. For a long time I've subscribed to *My Dog*. Do you know that magazine? No? That's weird.

That's what it is, a magazine about animals. You know. Different kinds, domestic, pack. It's amusing. How much water can a camel carry in its hump, its reserve stores? Do you know how much, for instance? No? Well, a lot. A whole lot. Or a dog, what are the symptoms of its parasitic illnesses?

It rubs its ass on the carpet—I put in gloomily, from experience. I have a dog, too.

To which she says indignantly: Not just that! There are a lot of symptoms. Anal pain, mange, vomiting, a dry nose. I hate animal-murderers. When I watch programs about the treatment of animals in Poland and the world, I want to die. I've already wanted to die once. Then I destroyed all my letters that I'd kept from Robert. Everything. It was a suicide attempt. Unsuccessful, anyhow. I'm talking a lot. I want to say everything, now I know that. Because life is short, Nails. And if I hadn't puked up all the Tylenol in the world, when I could have died at any moment, it would have been even shorter than it is. By half a year. Since a period of half a year has passed since those events. Degeneration. Decay. That's what I write about in my writings. The world is evil to the core, and I want to die. But not just yet. I want to die jumping off the roof and screaming: Fucking awesome. I want to die beneath the wheels of a speeding train. It's speeding, and I'm across the tracks, it whistles, I do nothing, it hits me, I do nothing, zero reaction. Only then there's a picture in the papers, everyone asks forgiveness, everyone blames himself. Robert is the guiltiest of all, since he's the one who drove me to such an extreme, degraded me, ruined me as a person and as a woman. Obituaries, an epitaph, readings. Nails, and now the question of the evening, do you have the courage to die with me? Amid the smoldering wreckage, amid the ashes and conflagration? Which will engulf us like a study in destruction. Satan will crawl over everything he encounters. He'll touch us as well, and then this movie's over. The land will open up into the face of nothingness. The end. Complete decadence, complete modernism. Snakes, the open wombs of women. Don't say anything, I don't want to know your answer. I prefer to go on in the illusion that it'll happen sometime. But I don't know when. Now or later. When I look at you, I think that you're not listening to me. When we're walking like this. You're not saying anything. You're quiet.

Angela was a virgin. That came out later. When she'd already soiled my parents' pullout. I'd never give Magda my consent for such antifamilial desecration. It's another matter that I never had those sorts of problems with her before or after. But that happened later. There were still a lot of different things that took place before that happened. Still, I'll just mention that Angela definitely didn't give me to understand that she was a virgin, intact. In no way. She underscored that after Robert, everything she had was gone, so that even though she's still very young, I figured that the whole physiological kit and caboodle had gone with him as well. It turned out that that Robert Sztorm left me a bloodbath, for which I will curse his name for the rest of my life. But about that later.

* * *

First it was like this. We're going to my place. She prattles on without end. Like a music box, only a lot worse. That if I could, if it were in my power, I'd drag that speed back out her nose. Then put it in a bag. Then seal it up tight and hide it away so that she'd never see it again with her own eyes. Since even the sight of it could usher her toward that endless avalanche of verbiage that she's indulging without pause, without limits. I don't say anything. Not even half of a broken word. I don't want to spoil anything. I listen to everything like at confession. First it was the fucking politicians, who she doesn't care about, baby-killers, bloodsuckers. But next she started again with the gender, like that there is no gender, there are no organs, no women, no men, there are fucking politicians. Killers of babies and newborns, bloodsuckers of the whole nation. Defilers of the natural environment, murderers of totally innocent animals, to whom she says no. Then all over again with Satan and his retinue, a world enveloped in evildoing and its swift end, an apocalyptic rider on a flesh-eating horse. The beauty of environmental nature. Scenic parks, bike trips, mountain walks and strolls along the seashore, a golden tourist badge, letters and postcards from friends from all over Poland.

I ask if she wants gum or some candy, since we're just about to come to a Shell station, so then I buy gummy bears and gumballs without any clear okay from her. It's an awful trick on my part, but my nerves are frayed, defiled, and it won't take much to piss me off.

So then we're already coming to the housing development. It's nighttime, dark. Leaves flutter in the wind. She's chewing, munching. Just a little, though I wanted to give her more, I wanted to stuff it all into her at once. But then her small sickly body would burst from so great a quantity, and then failure. I'd have to go to my place alone and leave her here in pieces, or even call the police on my cell phone, that I actually killed a young lady by giving her too many gummy bears. They'd think I was making crank calls, and in the meantime she'd croak right here at my feet. She didn't foresee that sort of death in her daydreams, huh. I'd tell her what's up, but I don't want to spoil anything.

I open the door with the key, she says: Nice house, modern. My aunt in Canada has a similar one, only better, Canadian, it's vertically open. Is this Russki siding? Russki or not, in general it's good siding, though sometimes it manages to fall off when no one expects it. It depends on who did it, in this the Russkies don't really lead the way on the world markets.

Is that what you think?—I put in, politely donning my house slippers, which I also give to her, only smaller, my old lady's.

I don't know. I don't know what I think, what I believe anymore when it comes to that. Though my views were well established just yesterday, tonight I'm all out of sorts. It's the effect of the new moon, it's your influence as well. Everything's happening totally faster, like some amusement park is spinning around me.

*　*　*

The thought occurs to me that that's a shady subject, amusement parks. Shady as a corpse. She's staring at me expectantly, frozen in half-gesture, like in a moment, here, I'd have to whip out cardboard boxes full of scrap iron for her, and then before her four eyes build her a house of horrors, little Toyotas, little planes with a target range, and then the best part, that I'd start going, the best part being together with her, on all of them in a row. And at least show her the office built into the wall, the invoices, important papers, my Sunday-best uniform for corporate plans, business meetings. Not to mention, of course, the 2001 Business Cup for the Largest Consumption of Sand in Pomorze Province, endowed by Zdzisław Sztorm. Best of all, I'd sit her down on one side of the desk, then I'd sit myself down at the other side. And I'd start talking her into purchasing a super-quality amusement park on very favorable conditions, prices. On sale, at a discount, between friends. But none of that, Angela, fat chance, there was no talk of that. So I offer coffee, tea.

None for her. Doesn't want anything. In general she's on a diet. Doesn't eat anything, because she heard that that's the best way. A single grain of rice washed down with six glasses of boiling water. In the morning. The same in the evening. The next day, two grains. Then, on the next, three, four, five, six, seven, eight, just each morning and evening one more.

It's easy to keep count. Meanwhile, the number of glasses remains the same. That's how it's done. In order to avoid the murder of animals that pay harshly for our fucked-up consumerism, the destruction of plants, the consumption of paper, the consumption of money. This is her voice of protest against the world.

Then she asks me if I want to die with her. Cuddled up. Me on my back, she on her stomach, or the other way around. Face-to-face. But before that, so as not to feel pain, you have to be drugged, to be all the more beguiled. She asks if I have any more crank. I think: Holy Wajdelota, come and take her from me. Take her from here, even at the cost of the fact that I'll spend tonight by myself, before that I'll make sandwiches. Though she's pretty enough. Hot, depending on your taste. If you like that kind of anatomic mood where you can see each shinbone, then sure, she's hot. But only for some. You have to be a Jew-lover to stand every movement of her skeleton under her skin. But sure. Nothing to add or subtract from her face. Mouth, nose, everything like it should be. Attractive. And on that note I try to get her a bit on track.

You're very pretty—I say. You could be an actress, even a model. To which she says that I should stop fooling, and do I really think so. To which I say, You bet. Then she lies down on the pullout, tosses back her hair, smoothes out her, like, animal-spotted dress. Kicks off my mother's slippers onto the floor and, in such a sleepy and longing voice, says:

Don't you have any contacts, Nails? Some contacts, you know, with some nonshady CEO, with some journalists? Who organize parties, judge art? You know what I'm talking about. Poetry readings, vernissages that could give a real kick to my career as a budding artist. It's not a matter of the costs, which, after all, we could foot together. Nor is it a matter of the underground, since that totally doesn't interest me. It's a matter of making art, culture, poetry readings, vernissages, talks. It's a matter of ideology.

No—I say gloomily. Though looking at her, how she rubs one thigh against the other.

Then she becomes more contemptuous, colder. And she says: What, no? Just like that: no? That's all you have to say to me after I've come here with you? Mr. Big Corporate CEO. Big Master of Mechanical Engineering. Producer of Russki amusement parks. Of electric trains, Donald Ducks with thousand-watt engines. A company, papers, invoices, suits. Capitalist bullshit. A phantom corporation. Zero connections, zero roots in business. Zero ties with culture and art, zero sponsorship.

After which the tinge of her voice changes to conciliatory, soothing. A single journalist would be enough. Even a sportswriter, but with connections. One interview with me for the paper. Let's say, for the paper and a magazine. Not necessarily a local. Maybe put something under wraps, keep something in the dark. Reveal a suicide attempt, since that always comes in handy, it'll wipe away the so-called screen between author and audience. A photo, in which I'll be pictured just like this. You take up a similar position, only sharper makeup, demonic, proper lighting, the right photographer. It'll gush out how, in my art, I express motifs of modernism, of demonism. Of Przybyszewski's Satanism. That always sells, it's in fashion. It'll gush out that I'm totally young and yet already so talented.

At that point in the conversation, which had been sort of one-sided, it's possible that I dozed off. Because the subsequent facts don't add up for me. That is, I wake up at another point in Angela's conversation. When what she's saying to me doesn't really make any sense: So, what's it going to be between us, Nails, huh? Are you going to chat with Widłowy, M.S.? You should know him, he's also in business, in the distribution of Polish sand. Ultimately the same as Zdzisław Sztorm. Except it's mail order and on installment. And he's a fatter cat.

Angela has waterproof mascara. Zero runs. Protruding lashes. Legs spread. Dress hiked up. Arms braided into her hair. A dreamy face.

Yes—I say kindly and unambiguously.

To which she, like she'll burst from the pullout, like she'll fly off to the crapper. She's got to go puke again, this time maybe she'll puke out her stomach and her whole alimentary apparatus. She'll puke the whole contents of her absorbing-digesting cavity. Including her brain. She'll give back the world what she's owed it for all time, the debts she's run up in being born. With interest and penalties. With something extra for free. An alimentary puke plus herself packed inside. That's how I imagine it to myself. Meanwhile, I get impatient. I wonder if she's really so pretty. I wonder if she's a freak. Whether it's worth getting into that. Whether to get rid of her. To say there'd been such-and-such a call from the Advertising Office, from the Office of Processing and Transport. That I have to take immediate action to resolve certain issues. Regarding papers, business meetings where my presence is absolutely essential. I have to sign and seal this and that. A matter key to my company's growth. Rapacious early capitalism, I'm sorry, bye-bye, though it was pleasant, nice from my end, that she dropped by, here's her leather, here're her shoes: See ya, shiny black boots, you won't be seeing me in town for the next year. A conference of amusement-park manufacturers in Baden-Baden, a sand festival in Nowa Huta, the laws of demonic capitalism, that's the whole story. Something, however, is tempting me, alluring me. Being left to myself in the dark apartment deters me, terrifies me.

So fuck it all! and all at once. Fuck it! Lights out. Fuck it! after her to the bathroom, where there's echoes of Sodom and Gomorrah, a real call of nature. She's hanged half over the bath like a black dishcloth. She pukes without taking a break. Between one hack and the next, she says in a meek voice, almost like imploringly: Satan. Satan.

And then all of a sudden, totally suddenly, there follows a real explosion from God knows where. A real eruption of that girl. A considerable bang reverberates toward me. Or rather a noise, rather some hard tiles bought under the table from the Russkies, so-called glaze and terra cotta imported by Terespol for considerable money, now it shakes like a branch. Boom, noise, bang, an echo follows the clothesline, goes across to the neighbors, then sets the whole housing development to inevitable trembling.

I look at Angela, I look into the bathtub. Where, on the very bottom, a stone about the size of your average human fist rolls along down to the drain. That takes me aback, I'm in total shock. I'm terrified, totally torn out of whack. All my views on the human condition heretofore are trashed. A thousand intense questions to ask myself, to pose to Angela.

But I don't ask them in time, because right after the boulder comes the next heave. This time it's raining little stones in a row, smallish like gravel, but a bit of larger ones. Which is to say those common medium stones you might find at your foot without special effort. Holy shit. Fuck your mother. *Guinness Book of World Records.* Nowa Huta Katowice. Sandworks. Well, I'll be fucked. I'm getting the hell out of here. A young lady with stones inside. A young lady who pukes stones. And what's more. And I wanted to do her. To screw her. Into her abdominal cavity with a cobblestone. After that, after thinking all these words suddenly swarming into my mouth, I quickly cross myself. Something that'd stayed with me from my career as an altar boy at All Saints Church. A certain inclination toward superstition, toward blocking evil.

Sometimes a kind of thought pops into my skull, that things have gone well, that I'm not there anymore. That my altar-boy frock became too small, tight, before it was too late and the churches, the parishes, started swarming with armed pedophiles. Though maybe that's an unfair reflection. Since maybe, for example, if it hadn't gone down that way, but otherwise. Maybe now I'd be a different person regarding those, and not other delights. And now I'd have here some likable fucker, a Marcus, an Eric, a Max playing that game. We'd have fun, I'd show him the town from the balcony. And I'd have some peace, a clear conscience. Instead of pubescent Angela, full of real stones, a stone-swallower. Who knows what else. Maybe fire, maybe sand, as her close intimacy with Sztorm would suggest. And who knows what else more. But that's not how it is. Here's Angela, hung breathless over the bath. I'm waiting for an explanation. I'm waiting for your explanation, young woman. You don't eat meat, yet you eat stones. You're abnormal. You're really nuts. You're really psycho. Now explain it to me.

You like rocks?—I say to her like fucking pissed, basically scathing, because of the fact that she's so fucked up, that my life at this moment seems like a galloping shit parade, real bedlam. What, Angela, you like to eat rock, huh? Low-cal, I understand that according to your diet, that's a delicacy, to eat that kind of boulder. Poisonous, but fuck-all if it's not nutritious. Tell me what the hell's with you. Without the hysterics, without keeping it in the dark, you're a nutcase from the city of Nutland, and now 'fess up to it honestly at last!

* * *

But she doesn't answer. She hangs across the bathtub like a little blackened corpse. So in a night full of horror, emotion, everything next to this is a mere blip. Next to this Angela, I'm likely to have a heart attack, to have a whole-body attack. Even now, though she's totally inert, maybe even dead, on my end I don't have a single thought of the kind men can have toward women. Now, for me, she's neither a man nor a woman, nor even a fucking politician. She's a horrible death hanging over my bathtub, in my old lady's slippers, which she shuffles in through Zepter all day distributing and advertising cosmetics, therapeutic lamps, cookware. That's gross on her end, what she did to me. I wade with disgust through her inert extremities and pull the largest boulders from the pit of the bath. Then I chuck them through the window from this side of the sidewalk into the dark night, full of danger, hissing, cracking. A night electric with charge, a night under high voltage. From my end, it's rather unreasonable that I would hit someone or something living, walking by just then. Because amidst the dark chasms of night, a considerable bump and shout rings out. But then, no longer having the nerve for conflicts with assholes roaming around at night, I latch the window and go to the television.

Nothing on television, though in the wall cabinets I uncover some Bird Milkies—chocolate-covered marshmallows—which

I promptly inhale. Since during this night's events I've become categorically hungry. I meditate for a moment about my mother, Izabela from the house of Maciak, Robakoska by marriage. Who purchased those Bird Milkies today thinking about herself, yet this and that, she came home, let the dog out into the yard, the purse, the skirt suit, and then to wandering around. In a moment free from work she ate a quarter, and another quarter my bro, whom they menace with the slammer and hard time at every movement, at every step. The neighbors, our family, our cousins. Anyway, he's not so big on sweets. He's on an egg diet. That is, he takes ten eggs into his paw and eats up just the whites, tossing out the yolks and shells. Or depending on his mood, pours them into a bowl and leaves it for the dog. Since he needs a lot of whites to bulk up, milk with milk. And let him regret it, because those Bird Milkies are good. That's also the sort of product that could cause a furor on the tables of the European Union. Conquer the whole world, including Antarctica. Everyone will tell you, when asked, that there's no such thing as Bird Milkies. Since, logically speaking, it's been known since ancient times that no birds give milk, and if they did, it would have been industrialized, legalized, dragged into mass production a long time ago. And then you tell him: And that's exactly what Bird Milkies are. You just have to come to Poland, where there are still beautiful, historic facades in the towns of Wrocław, Nowa Huta, downtown Gdańsk. Which is the best, when it comes to sand by the kilogram at a worthwhile price. And the Western buck flies into your pocket. All the tourist groups show up. Chartering the bus—another buck. San and Jelcz, the worst, the cheapest, but exotic, domestic, guests from abroad like those kinds of throwback rides, those old-timey relics, pardon my saying. They go by Jelcz, PKS Bus Lines from Kamienna Góra, they love it, another buck, more dough. Instant soups, borscht, mushroom, onion, even Oriental—the driver pours it out from a handy boiler—still more bank. The interest blossoms, the register fills up. Get-to-know-you soirees for the tourist group with Bird Milkies on the tables, that's the culmination of the whole program. The whole stock of Bird Milkies available for purchase. Excursions to the Bird Milkies factory, getting to see how it's processed. A sham, of course, but the group likes it.

Then the population of our town is in the money. They fund the liquidation of the Russkies from these parts. They bribe the city workers to cross the Russkies off the residents' roster, off the personal data banks. No Russkies Day is an everyday occurrence, with fests, flares, anti-Russki festivals, flyers, colorful fireworks displays that spell out announcements: "Russkies to Russia—Poles to Poland," "Put the Factories Back into the Hands of the Polish Superworkers," "Tear Down Russki-Produced Siding," "Putin, Pick Up Your Lousy Children." But that doesn't much interest me anymore, that's no longer my domain. I make awesome bank, I'm doing business in the trade of white-and-red flags and banners. With which I fund Magda's elimination from town and live like a king, living among women and pouring myself glasses of wine in front of the television. Everybody's satisfied, though the Russkies least of all. With the rest of my funds, I finance the birth of a genuine leftist party. The first serious leftist-anarchist party. An anarchist wave to save the left. That's how I see it. The biggest facade in town, flags, standards, lawns. A beautiful European office block in bright colors. Me the general secretary, my bro the president, though whether he's an anarchist remains to be seen, we're still working on him. Mom for the accountant, elegant, though already older, with full authority, a separate office for matters of controlling the anarchy, a separate armchair, vertical blinds. And a lot of secretaries, the personnel and staff almost all secretaries. Gorgeous secretaries lying on the desks in office skirts rolled all the way up, in slit skirt suits, jackets, in tight tights, they all want it. Gorgeous cleaning ladies crawling around my feet in skimpy aprons. Amphetamine dispensers everywhere that work with a chip card to shoot a real load of speed right into your nose. Then, under such conditions, I can be the good Uncle Nails, take the Bartender for my driver, Lefty for tech support, Kisiel for inventory, Kacper for, let's say, for gardener. Anarchist secretaries put out right on the desks, the chairs, whoever's there, they brew good coffee with cream, deliver food on a tray. Magda for a cleaning lady, who'll wipe the filthiest dirt from the tile with her own tongue. Out the window, the most beautiful, sunny days. I'll issue decrees: This many banners go to Słupsk, this many badges to Pomerania, this many Arafat rags to the East, this many black shirts to the Szczecin area. The economy's in good shape. Everybody's living well, even the oppressed workers, to whom we toss what they need, inspiration for reasons to strike, for rallies.

But I can't keep thinking up these beautiful moments of the ultimate triumph of the left anymore, an ostentatious erection keeps swelling in my pants. So I say toward my loins: Well, George, you just know what's good for us. And that's how you smile. At me. That you like this plan, particularly the bit about the speed. And most of all, the secretaries strewn about the corporate carpeting. What, George? You want to go for a walk? Well, sure.

Unfortunately, you won't get ventilation so easily, even with that terrible fondness you have for sports. This lady we have here is seriously meeting her end. Maybe she's even dead. She's lying across the bathtub. She puked up a fucking stone. And it's possible she has a quarry in her bony little ass, asphalted, paved. You'll get chipped, and when a real chance for action comes along with some real piece of ass made of flesh and bone, even if it's Magda, you're not going to be so clever as you are now. You'll only be good for a contraceptive wee-wee through a catheter.

And speaking to myself like that in a half-whisper, half-aloud, since that corpse there doesn't hear anything in the bathroom, I put a fucking dent into those Milkies. And please, at the beginning, right away, like all my wishes were fulfilled while I waited, which never worked even in my shitty childhood. As if the good God, Lord of All Speed-dom, had mercy on my plight.

Because unexpectedly, between two of the papers that separate one Milky from the others, so that they won't stick together, glob together at room temperature, and so that they'll be elegant in general, I find a hidden stash of my White Stuff, of my Queen Mother of Speed. Anyway, a few bitty bags just for me. Which my bro evidently squirreled away in case of trouble with the police, if there's some harsh search of the apartment. And it works out perfectly, since a bad feeling in my bones, in my muscles, is already making itself known to me. Thus I make use of it quickly, in order to correct my faculties, my comprehension, my psychophysical cooperation. Since speed ain't no caplet of Tylenol, lemon tea, and two days in a coma. It's a continuation of the fun.

One, two, the Zdzisław Sztorm pen, end of story, no more tears. Right away the apartment's like whoa. The darkness is brighter. More transparent, more brilliant.

Also, I turn on the vacuum cleaner immediately. With the extension and pipe attached. So that Izabela Robakoska, née Maciak, won't find herself in a shithouse in the morning. Coming home after the weekend. Spent doing the books at Zepter. Then I go to the bathroom and the toilet. To see how things are with Angela and whether George is going to have some chance of altering his miserable fate. For the time being, no. Angela, clearly in a bad state, stone-poisoned, hangs across the bathtub with no hope of a speedy recovery. And I admit that reanimating the dead is not my strong suit. Like that once, when I endeavored to revive a woman who happened to be lying there, the outcome turned out dramatic. That is, it turned out that that woman was already long dead. It took me a while to get over that. Trying to chat with a real corpse. That was a terrible experience for me, when I went later to work, ate a sandwich with the same mouth I'd used to resuscitate that dead chick. But to the matter at hand. Angela's really fucked up. I try to nudge her with my foot, I try to rouse her somehow. But nothing, a corpse, death, total listlessness. Regarding that speed I found in the bowels of the Bird Milkies, that doesn't discourage me. Her head under the faucet, under the shower. That head's pale, anemic, totally done for, bereft of blood. The waterproof makeup is indestructible, like a tattoo. The face is pretty much expressionless, if it should show anger or joy, there are no traces of that on Angela's face. That turns me on. She could even be like that, saying nothing, not getting off the fucking subject, like she's wound up. In that silent state, I'd even be ready to show her some affection. If only to have some guarantee certifying in writing, with a seal, that she'll open her trap for every purpose except articulated speech. Then, sure, I'd buy her.

George wants something. He's fidgeting. I tell him: Hold on to your rod, don't you see there's a reanimation going on here? For now you can only dream about her, since she's puking so dramatically. Behave yourself now, and if we can only wake up our stone-puking Sleeping Beauty, then of course, together she and I will try to put together some entertainment for you that's more interesting than sitting alone in the dark.

Then all of a sudden I know what to do. Fast, skillfully, like the Boy Scouts doing their maneuvers. I pull one dose out from the Bird Milkies, though later the trouble with my bro's going to pretty much come to fists and kitchen knives. But no, I don't waver, since this puker's already cost me enough heartache. I take that other, blackish skull in my hands, squeeze open her mouth, and rub that shit into the meat set down around her teeth, good expensive speed, which she maybe isn't even worth. That's what I do, because my pal George demands his share, which definitely is owed him for all the insults and intellectual experiments perpetrated against him today. Speed, that magical welfare for the unemployed. And in a minute, after waiting a couple moments, while I'm rinsing her stone upchuck from all the terra-cotta tiling, she comes to life like some Russki doll running on new R6 batteries. She flutters her black eyelashes, from underneath which her eyeballs emerge. Which it's like she hasn't had for like several hours. She glances at me pretty sluggishly. After which she says in the tone of someone who's discovered America, sunbeams, and gas ovens all at once: Nails, is that you? Pretty much in a mumble. But I know that George is on the right road to consuming this at any rate accidental acquaintance. I take her under the arm and drag her to the pullout. She, scraping her crippled legs on the carpeting along the way, that if she had, like for example, her hands cut off, she could work as a mannequin in a fabric-store display. I'd drag her then, too, since I'm already dispensing with the formalities, whether the woman is perhaps dead but perhaps alive, or maybe just taciturn. Or undecided among these options. Fuck that. She's got female parts means she's got female parts, and suddenly there's no need for great de-

bate on the matter: Angela says to me: Get the fuck off, take
your hands away from me, I'm going home.

That is, the music box is playing, it's all good, an elegant
return from the land of the dead to the land of the living and
talking, a return, it would happen, in great staggering style,
fanfare, Auntie Amphie will put the dead on their feet. I don't
give a shit anymore about those boulders she rolled out of
herself into the bathroom fixture, I'm not going to discuss what
that was all about with this half-headed stress case. Because
her narcissistic, pseudointellectual career is not my priority
at the moment.

I'm not going to beat too much around the bush, and right
away I get to the key thing it's always been mainly about from
the very start, male-female acquaintance. Because such acquaintance clearly occurred. Though before that clearly documented
fact came about, there was a significant—as is known—stoppage. Just the kind of stoppage that, with the first aid I ex-
pertly applied to it, Angela's lousy ass came back to life. Or
rather her face, with its speech organ. There's no way for me
to mention all the words that came about, since she, right after
recovering her vitality, became very talkative on every subject. Lush gesticulation like an immense forest growing out
before my eyes from her arms, legs, parts of her face. A lot of
different words, a lot of conversation on her part. With whom?
Because maybe not with me. Multiple subjects. She was very
oral, speaking like that without stopping, chatting with herself about everything, about dogs, about animals in general.
Then she started in on Satan. That she's already getting tired

of that style, gloomy, deathly, that she would like to be totally more ordinary than she is. That occasionally she would like to be like her various friends from class, completely stupid normal girls, to school and back, no fun, no big thoughts about the bleak dimension that can envelop the world, no thoughts about death, suicide is unthinkable to them, since they're limited through and through, unreceptive to new trends. And to her, suicide is no big deal, a movement with a knife, a kilo of pills, and she's dead, and a picture of her in the papers with the sea in the background, with her makeup, in chain mail and drapery, obituaries in the papers, apologies, explanations for why so young and very talented an artist left us here all to ourselves. That's what she was saying, not skipping, of course, the culinary themes, that from birth she hasn't consumed meat or eggs, since they're products of crime.

That was a stoppage for me, since then I was watching TV, where there was absolutely nothing interesting. One porno in a thousand channels, German, and more like medieval sci fi. It was set in a castle, a guy in armor, and a German shit-eating glam-rock girl gave it to him in quite uninventive ways. Rather classic, raw liver and giblets, suddenly in place of the soundtrack that should have kept the whole thing together, Angela substituted her own dialogues in mono. Shit. Angela, what a time to pick, why be so slaphappy. I got fucking pissed about that. Because if I'm watching a movie, I'm watching a movie, and I don't want to chat away half the action and not know what's going on now, why are they fucking this way now and not some other way, for instance.

That's how it was. I asked her why she's so happy, told her I see her here in front of me and that she's next to me, which brings me great joy, pleasure. Then I tried quickly to grasp what had happened in the moment of my distraction and how much hard-core fucking there'd been. But despite these several assaults on the continuity of events, I always grasped what was going on. Because I have experience in this and most often, with a bit of intuition, can deduce exactly what's going on.

That's how it was. In a word, a lecture regarding tourist badges and discount cards for all the hostels in the Podkarpacki region. Another moment like that, and I'd put an open umbrella in Angela's hand and push her straight out the window, let her fly away home.

But that didn't happen, either. Now I'm turning over on that same smudged pullout, only I mostly remember to avoid that place where Angela made an indelible impression with her virginity, may it rot in hell. I turn over and ponder what happened later.

Later, things picked up enough that Angela stopped harshing my high, leering with her black eye at the wall cabinets, and would I show her some photo, from when I was a kid and butt naked. No way, Jose. I was never little—I told her. For real. I was born already pretty big and with hair, and then I just grew, I didn't even need to eat. You're bullshitting—she said, and plopped herself down on the foldout. Right away, George, but I won't say a word about that. Are you at all tired?—I asked her. To which she says that she's not, but that she likes to lie down in general, to lie and dream. Well, forget about whatever it was she was planning on dreaming about, about gardens or about a black badge for the blackest-dressed resident in the district, but I set myself down here next to her. She took a wallet with documents out of her purse. I started up. But nothing about that, that's my personal business. First of all, one mustn't scare this sort off, since thirty kilos of freak are ready at any moment to whip limber little wings from the wallet and fly off through the ventilation shaft to make a complaint at the Kiddy Police Station. But literally. With that sort of shit, there's no fucking around. So I play her cool, with no super-brutality. She pulls out a photo of a pretty depressing guy. Robert Sztorm—she says, and looks at it dreamily. Good, I think, let her focus her attention on something else. And I maneuver myself closer to her, but those are personal matters. To which she starts to drag out her varied collections of garbage, her letters to a friend from England who never wrote back to her. Because maybe it was the wrong address or the wrong language. Because, Angela says, there's a difference between English and slang. Slang is a language that gets used, too. And for instance that English girl spoke slang, and she didn't understand her letter in English. She thought that it wasn't to her, because Angela wrote the address in English, too. Or she thought, too, that it was a chain letter and immediately threw it out with the potato peels and used tissues. That's just how it might have been—I whisper in her ear, so as to interest her in other more important matters. She—nothing. If I were to take off her dress, she wouldn't catch on until she was being soundly fucked, and maybe not even then. I decide to go that route. With extreme caution. The whole time she, on the side, is making some puzzle out of scraps of paper, out of all kinds of shit. This is a leaf from a tree. This is a cornerstone. This is a cigarette butt touched by the mouth of the Lord God. This is her first communion, which she spit out after accepting it and dried it out, which she carries around now for luck. This is her first hair. This is her first tooth. This is her first fingernail, and this is her first boyfriend, Robert Sztorm, in profile with a hunting rifle on an excursion with the Gaming Society. So I keep at it. Stockings. Nothing from her, the lady speaking on the television's from TeleExpress, a talking head, and from the waist down the entire Polish army could be going at her one after another and she wouldn't bat an eye. That's Angela. Utterly engaged in talking. Let her talk. I'm going to be brief. She even worked with me in taking down the panties. Lifted her ass while looking at a vacation postcard she got from Hel from a girlfriend from Szczecin. That she's having a great time, in the fresh air a lot, lovely weather, sun, guitar, campfire, and a lot of good fun, and P.S., a song is good for everything. So it somehow worked out. I was afraid of how she'd react and that at the key moment she'd run off screaming. Tight but warm, one-two-three, my face in her wet hair, from when I washed her head of the aforementioned puke under the faucet, a formidable illness, and George is calmly singing his little ditty. She's so-so, it seems that she's even working with me, though I'm afraid she might do a number on me with some concrete or something. She talks about how she used to love collecting stamps, but now that seems infantile to her, which is what Robert told her, and how quarrels and feuds often sprang up between them.

And which I'm going to say a lot about here. Which I'm going to say, my future brats, mine and Magda's, or not her, it'll be someone else, they'll pick up and eavesdrop, and they'll find out what kind of biological configurations really sprang up. That I, their father, did not find them and their mother in a ditch by the road while on a sightseeing trip, just that I installed them in their mother's viscera with the help of my vivacious hose. And what will I tell them. That we're not people, just common coelenterates that join in a pair and perform lecherous movements. That in these actual seas of biologically active fluids, there swim tailed worms that then suddenly grow teeth, nails, clothes, briefcases, glasses. And though it's good fun, I suddenly suspect, basically, that something's not quite right with Angela. That I'm banging up against some kind of resistance inside her, some kind of physiological barrier on her end. Which will appear presently.

Because there suddenly rings out a bang, a snap, an explosion, because there's suddenly room, as if I'd broken through a passage to some underwater country, because Angela's screaming, recoiling suddenly, all her garbage with which she's assiduously covered half the pullout flies into the air. She's bawling, holding on to her little ass, shifting from leg to leg. Fucking hell, I say, and crack up, because though it's ended without finishing the fun, I get right away what's going on. That a little spring has popped up in our Angela, and that now a fine eager friend will come of her. That from between her legs of Zion soon will fall the symbolic shell, which she'll pick up and place in a golden frame that will hang over the pullout at her place. And which she'll copy and give to me in the same frame, that I might place it on my presidential desk, in my office for matters of public anarchy. And so that I might show it during business meetings to Zdzisław Sztorm, whose son did not accomplish this, but which I, Nails, Andrzej Robakoski, accomplished.

But it didn't happen that way. Little Angela stands over me pretty funny in her dress hiked up, like the shy princess of the Duchy of Hymen and, trying to drag her stockings back on, she says to me: I'm a virgin. And as a vivid illustration she immediately dispensed a sizable blood ball and a piece of raw meat on the foldout. To which I say: Chill out, woman, and I light myself a Russki LM Red from her handbag, since I have to make up for not getting off and for the premature demise of my pleasure. Though I myself am all fuck-bathed in blood, which I'll have to wash and scrub off in a minute, since I'm in a state of believing that by some macabre method I've been robbed of my sex and am now neuter.

How she looks, this Angela. Real despair, thirty-three kilos of steaming despair and a bit of hit-and-run, so that it sort of stings me that George is the perpetrator of all this embarrassment. So that I'm sorry, because it's already happened more than once that I suddenly go all tender-hearted and totally fall to pieces in that regard. Sometimes with respect to my dog, Bitchy, a pretty obese little faun. But I always stress to my bro not to overdo it with the yolks for her, since that's why she's overweight and gets indigestion. That's how I talk now, get over here, little Angela, it's your big day, Saint Angela's Day. Straighten out your little panties here, and you know, that'll heal before your wedding day.

But she's still so dazed, so turned around, as if at the least I had degraded her speech organ. I don't want to chat about postcards, I don't want to chat about booby birds, as if her teeth had locked together. At the same time, I wonder in a panic what more she can inflict on me here. Because I'm already starting to come down again slowly and pretty gloomily, which is why I'll have neither the strength nor the enthusiasm to clean up what she might still release onto the carpet or somewhere. Stones again, or else now some new turn in her internal disease, coal, coke, dynamite, brick, lime, Styrofoam.

So don't get all offended, I say to her, and buckle up my chinos, which are so besmirched, like if I'd been wearing them while getting a degree in heavy butchery and a land mine. So I get up from the pullout, take Angela by the hand, who seems to me a student less of economics than of elementary school, dancing at the carnival ball, dressed up for burning. That's my hallucination. Now I figure she's at most five years old, which makes me think my heart's about to burst and pour out all over my body. Then I sit her down on the pullout and say: Now wait here a while. I pull over a rickety little table, so that she'd be level with the tablecloth, Russki-style, stain-resistant fabric. I set out Bird Milkies, I set out a vase of fake gerbera, next to that cigarettes, total elegance, a voyage on the *Titanic,* pleasantry, the man symbolically extending his hand to the woman. She's still a little sulky, with her foot she gathers that whole mess of souvenirs from all her birthdays, kisses from mouth to hand. It's already almost dawn, Bitchy's howling bloody murder in the garden, she wants to feed. Bitchy, that fucking fat-ass. Angie, coming down pretty hard after the evening's ordeals, is looking unconsciously into the ashtray, as though in cigarette butts it augured her artistic future. Well, so I get to it quickly, so that she'd have some happy memories, before this falls completely to hell.

So, down to business, lovely lady, I say to her, rooting through the Bird Milkies with my fingers, so as to pour us some scrap of pleasure by way of consolation. To which she makes a movement with her head somewhere between yes and no. So I say: Today is No Russkies Day. So nothing doing, everyone's in the square. But starting tomorrow we're going to work out your career, my gifted lady. Starting the day after tomorrow I'm going to call here and there, the president, the premier, a photojournalist I know. That there's, like, a scandal. Someone's committed suicide. Clearly not true, but it doesn't matter if it's true. It's a matter of publicity. That's how we'll work it out. My plan for the day is intense, but a few meetings, a bit of extortion, you hear, Angie? Then it turns out that the suicide's been saved. A great talent rescued by evil doctors. An exhibit of your clothes, a press conference about what kind of music you listen to, what kind of hobbies you have in your time free from art. And then, suddenly, from one day to the next, you're not anonymous, the crowds want to see you and they want to have your personality, Robert Sztorm goes all soft. But Robert Sztorm at most can try to lick you through the crowds of bodyguards. And that precious thing you had that disappeared today. In *Filipinka* your photo in the very center of the cover.

Just not in *Filipinka*—Angela says hazily, unclearly, and something unknown belches up in her, perhaps a stone, or perhaps a piece of asphalt roofing, or perhaps some fiberglass insulation. It's her first documented sign of life in about a half hour. I think to myself, Don't let her die on me again here. So what do I do. I cut myself a line, Zdzisław Sztorm and atten-*hut*. Then I say to her like this, so as to dissuade her a little from suicide: And now, Angie, let's get to it. Death is unimportant, there is no death, you don't believe in death, since it's superstition. Infectious diseases—superstition; vehicular homicide—superstition; graves—superstition; misfortune—superstition. They're all ignoble inventions from the Russkies, which they spread about to terrify us existentially. Robert Sztorm is a puppet who's been bought out, also by the Russkies. Hooliganism and devastation are folk legend, there's no Arka, or Legia, or Polonia, or Warsowia. They're fictitious teams that serve Novosiltsev. Stás and Nel were likewise perfidiously prepared by Sienkiewicz, the Russki duke, for the needs of the film *In Desert and Wilderness,* real Greek myths. I, Nails, swear to you. Maybe the Russkies themselves don't even exist, that remains to be seen. Go to the balcony, out the window is a new, better world, a special world for our needs, zero coaxial leads, zero syringes, zero fires, zero meat. The All-Vegetarian Holy Aid Orchestra urges you to collect new stomach stones for Angelica, age seventeen. Hey, Angela . . . Angela, get off your ass . . . get up . . . get the fuck up!

Then I run up to the pullout, and goddamn. A bigger fucking shitpile. So that's why she was sitting so quietly, not a word from that reticent chimney sweep. Because she's all come out and trickled onto my mother's Bartek foldout, her totally brand-new-from-last-year sofa bed covered in blood, though maybe there's also a bit of me in there, I'm not without fault. So I go nuts. I'm fucking pissed. I'm about to pull the cord on this whole world, I'm about to yank out the coaxial leads, I'm about to tug on the handle, the emergency brake. I want to kill her here and now, though I'd have to ruin the whole sofa bed with this bitch's blood, to turn it over, slice it with a knife and gut it of its feathers, of its foam, the lining, the springs, drag everything out, trample it, destroy, kill, destroy. Goddamn motherfucking son of a bitch. Now, that's going too far, my dear, your whole career's down the drain before I had a chance to move a finger and mobilize my connections, fuck off, my star, here and now. Here are your beautiful shoes, your genuine Cossack boots from the Caucasus, here's your jacket, here are your souvenir wares, here are your internal stones. And Madame, we wish to thank you for participating in our program. These are the Gerd automatic doors, left, right, goodbye, the Number 3 bus will come pick you up shortly.

All women are a bunch of bitches. They don't leave on their own, they wait, lurking. Until I fly into a rage and blow up, and I have to kick them out, pull away from them like a fly from flypaper. I suspect that it's possible that it's just one and the same bitch changing into different rags, she's constantly attacking me, coaxes me with pleasantness, and then fucks up the whole apartment. Each day, each day she's new and still worse. I suspect that she lives somewhere here in the development. She knows I have weak nerves. She comes and fucks my shit up. And I kill her. But she grows back out of dog spunk and is already tight and ready the next evening. Russki droppings. Maybe they're Russkies and they're just euphemistically called women. And we men are going to drive them out of here, from this town, where they perpetrate misfortunes, plagues, droughts, bad crops, debauchery. They ruin the upholstery with their blood, which flies out of them like nobody's business, soiling the whole world with permanent stains. A real River Menstruation. Angelica, a serious disease. The severe penalty for lacking a maidenhead. When her mom finds out, she'll put it back.

∴

Bad dreams.

That Magda gives birth to a stone child, what appears to be a five-year-old girl with a nervous tic in both eyes. The kid— a stone monster neither Lefty nor anyone will own up to, Magda wants to sell it to the circus, she stands in front of me rocking the baby carriage, she says: It's either me or that one there, Nails, otherwise I'm selling Paula to the circus, choose, it's either me or her.

That in the mailbox there's a postcard from Angela, Hi Andrzej, I didn't know whether to write to you. I'm in hell, just today after coming home I committed suicide. Nothing special. We have a tape deck here, a common room. Though the counselors are nice, musical. I'll write more if I think of something. I have to go now because we have roll call. Then dinner, hide-and-seek, field games. On Monday, Satan's coming for inspection. We're going to check the tents, and there'll be storytelling. Kisses, I'll always remember you fondly, if you can, please send me some warm things (the nights are cold). Angie. P.S.: All best!

That the phone rings, that a huge phone rings right inside me, that I don't know where the receiver is, though I hear voices saying from everywhere, It's for you, Andy, some gentlemen calling for you, some gentlemen for you, Andy, gentlemen from a commission, they're checking whether your organs are fit for legal sale to the West, Andy, how are your nerves, the gentlemen are most interested in buying them, there's nothing to be afraid of, the date of the operation is set . . .

I wake up. Blind, deaf, mute, like a big mole dragged out of the ground, buried in a bloody pullout. Like half-alive, tossed into a matchbox and shut in. A massive delay. Ringing from everywhere. Ringing in stereo. The rest in mono. Seems that everything that was never in my head before is there now. Everything there never was. That total lack. The total silence, like a third conversant. The whole cotton ball of the world. All the ersatz, all the Styrofoam crammed into my head. I've gained weight during the night. I'm so heavy that I can't get myself on my feet. A concentrated solution. As if I'd gotten all tangled up in a curtain, as if I'd gotten all tangled up in a coat and couldn't get out of it, put my head into my sleeve and couldn't pull it back out.

As if that Angela'd gutted herself into me, and not into the pullout, so that now I'm lying here swollen, split, a heart split into two sides, a split liver, six kidneys, and several cinder blocks.

And when I get up at noon, I think for a second why my old lady hasn't come back yet from the Zepter Corporation. Though maybe she was calling, but I don't know anything about that. I wonder why I didn't pick up the phone. I can't recall. I wonder what the hell is going on here and whether it just so happens that all of a sudden I'm the only one living in this town, because the whole species has died out. And when I stand up, in front of me is a view of the whole apartment after the fashion of a battle scene, a landscape after the battle. I wonder whether there happened to have been a war here in my absence, when I was sleeping, a decisive battle, the central command itself. While I was sleeping, the Russkies had come into the apartment, forced their way in. They knocked everything over with their rifle butts, shot the waterfall portraits out of the pictures, the sunflowers, and especially destroyed the leather clock. They knocked the Mother of God of Lichen made of sky-blue plastic off the fridge, the head's gone, the holy water's scattered all over the place. They trampled the tile in the bathroom. They raped all the women, as far as possible, here on the sofa bed, set up their general staff here, a committee on screwing affairs. They brought in horses, ate up the Bird Milkies, smoked the cigarettes, fucked up the upholstery, and good-bye, see you in a future life in Belarus. They took my brother and my old lady as slaves. Me they surely killed, because that's exactly the impression I have, that that's exactly what they did with me, killed me with some heavy objects, blew me away, such that inside my head I still hear the distant echo of those blows, those shots. But why me, since my mother did pretty good business with them, siding, paneling, Zepter. Why exactly did they blow me away, why'd they shoot me in the head, so that now I feel like it's full of a feeling of scrap iron, of cranks spinning around their axis, a scrap yard, of warped slates. Where were they when Magda had her views against them and openly professed an anti-Russki ideology?

*   *   *

But something's changed, and I ascertain this when I open the vertical blinds. The world's broken out of its mold. The sun's bigger. Fatter, lardy, like a parasite gnawing away at us. It fucks you in the eyes. Without mercy. Aimed right at me, it shines right at me, like at the least a gestapo lamp, talk, Nails, you're going to let it out for us here yet, because if not, we'll turn up the dial and you'll die from this vicious, sibilant light, licking you clean with little white tongues. A bit of string is squeaking against the blind. The curtain's to the side. And there's a spectacle. There's a spectacle I never hoped to see in my life. Because there are no spectacles like that, those sorts of things never take place in the world. I can't believe what I'm seeing. I want to lean out the window from the shock, because my eyes don't want to open, and I see only as much as I can through the slits, the rest is dark. I bang my forehead against the PVC asbestos pane, which makes a sort of echo, a sort of reflux, a terrible echo that suddenly gets all the clearer. And I'll say further that the thing, with my eyes, what I already said, that during the night they grew some bonus skin, and in general I don't see much, but what I see, I see. And that's no hallucination in my skull, no dim flashback, since it's a reality show that I see now, Real TV.

Now there're hardly any colors in the world. None. A lack. The colors were stolen in the night. Or whatever. Maybe washed out. Maybe they washed out that landscape, that country scene out the window in a washing machine with not quite the right detergent. The kind of number my old lady once did on my jeans, too. So that one day I had normal blue jeans, and the next day they were basically white, white Big Stars with a blank white tag. I was fucking pissed, because in company, at the pub I'd be finished, What, Nails, have you come for holy communion, but you're too late, there is no holy communion, it's over, sold out, go home, you can come back next year.

It's not important what happened with my pants. What was, was. Only one thing's for sure. Whatever they did, whether it was acid rain or another ecological disaster with a tank of bleach, or that Lefty had an accident while driving his Golf, full of speed, the heap of houses. Basically a white wall run down with lime or some other shit. The house next door, the neighbors who made a real killing fencing the ripped-off cars the Russkies brought in, all of a sudden is also half white from the top down. Half. Half all white. Most often it's half of the houses. And what's on the bottom, on the street, what's more fucking obvious is red. Entirely. White-red. From top to bottom. On top a Polish pill, on the bottom Polish menstruation. On top Polish snow imported from a Polish sky, on the bottom the Polish association of Polish butchers and pig-stickers.

And somewhere where I'm not looking, some orange-clad worker staggers around with buckets of paint, with rollers, white-and-red warning ribbons flutter in the wind so that the crows won't land and shit all over the place. Patrol cars, some other cars, some wiring, scaffolding. Sick, it just looks so sick, Sputniks can take a picture of the city from space, fucked up.

And when I see this, bang!—I catch the cord and shut the vertical blinds right away, I go so far as to tear the string out. But this, I don't want to look at this. They couldn't talk me into looking at this porn with the help of white-and-red animals and white-and-red children, which degenerate city workers manipulate with our tax dollars. Maybe not my tax dollars. But my mother's, though I haven't seen her for a long time. And that I've been using a lot of speed, that even now I have that problem with my eyelid, that it pulls back and I see everything, but then it comes down and I can see only my skin from the inside. It's black, and that's as much as I see. But nobody will tell me that this town painted in our soccer-team colors, that this is just a blackout from coming down, that this is my trip manufactured by the speed's fermentation in my insides. Nobody's telling me that. Since if I were to just shut the blinds, then everything inside here's back to normal. I'll sigh with relief and run to lock the Gerd double doors. So that those sons of bitches wouldn't get in here, because then they'd fuck up my house with their lime, they'd destroy the wall cabinets, the carpeting, maybe even the blinds. That's it. Izabela'd never get over it. The ceiling paneling imported via Terespol. And here, a beautiful red matching her lipstick, so that in the evening she could lie with a hand mirror and check out whether it goes. They're not coming in here, and shit, perhaps they'll come for me, trample me into the carpeting and paint me white as well. For a moment I feel like a happy person and even think I might give Bitchy something to grub on. Because she's, like, stopped whining. But then I figure next that I'll have to go outside and then all over again it's that fata morgana, like a white-and-red plague pushing through town, a pox. So I sit down. Better not to go, because one can lose oneself in the carpeting. I look. I have to admit that at that particular moment I'm not thinking too much, not paying attention. Rather, I'll admit that I'm not paying attention to anything, because I happen to be sitting. I'm sitting. Some personal party is rolling in my head. Phones are ringing, Radios Warsaw and Moscow are playing at the same time, lights are shining, the electric train's going to China, going in through one ear and coming out the other, running down everything it encounters on the way. All my thoughts, my feelings.

And then, like in one second, my whole scattered life comes to me, that postwar portrait with blood on the upholstery, with blood on my pants making up some map of disease, actually, some board game, all the paths of dried blood lead unambiguously to the secret hell in my fly. These white stains on the carpeting are from Magda, when she spit out the toothpaste, and the red ones from Angela, who ran away from me, took a dump. Some candy-wrapping rain came down, a rain of pebbles, of milk teeth, as if Angela'd shaken out her handbag all over the room before she went to hell.

Here you are, Nails, here you are, and don't say I didn't leave you any souvenirs, here's my broken tooth, here's my split hair, here're my fake eyelashes, here're my still-bent legs, here're my hands, here're my stones, hide them away somewhere safe, dry them out, put them in books, in cellophane, in vases, in frames. And when you tread on the carpeting, you're treading on me. Since the fact of the matter in general is that I'm dead, I'm sitting in hell, it's a monstrous bore, Satan says that maybe they'll probably drag you down here as well. For now he bought me black hamsters, a pair, the male wants to screw the female all the time, I have to watch them constantly to take him off of her fast. I don't even feel like giving them water, I'm so bored I'm yawning more and more often.

While I'm thinking this to myself, at once these things, these postcards, all these gummy bears rolling out like some dexterity game, they're flying toward me, and I have to grab them. I gather them, though the way I picture it to myself I'm actually walking through Angela's flesh, that makes me weak, and I stagger into the furniture. Rolling papers pressed out into the shape of her black mouth, all that into the tote. Opaque. And into the cupboard. Under the secondhand duds, into the four-person tent, I toss in the ironing board so that nobody will ever snatch it from my family and get infected by the cadaveric poison.

Then the doorbell suddenly rings. Shock. Panic. To, like, grab my Adidases and hide in the wall cabinets, that like I'm not here. And all that shit on the sofa bed and everywhere, that cord for the vertical blinds yanked utterly out, the Bird Milkies eaten up, that blood trailing from the sofa bed across the carpeting, through the foyer to the door, across the steps, across the sidewalk, out the gate, across the asphalt to the bus stop, through the entire Number 3 bus to the driver and back to a seat, and to the exit, that's not blood, it's red paint used to paint the bottom part of town for the occasion of No Russkies Day, and which apparently trickled out of the pocket of some workman. That's what I'll say. The police and the sheriff together, the girl's dead, she bled out on the way, she soiled the whole town up and down, exactly on the day before the municipal holiday, No Russkies Day, she gave the whole town a bad name, that we don't live here like people, but like animals for slaughter. And you're responsible, sir, papers please, your mother's name, your interests, hobbies.

That's how I picture it, and I get the shakes. But the doorbell doesn't let up, so what do I have to do. Though I'm even wearing these stained pants, it's like that alarm sort of ringing, rather the kind that could kill a person if he doesn't open the door. So I walk half-blind through the foyer, with a feral eyelid batting like some strobe light, an eyelid like a separate animal gnawing at my eye. Sentenced to death, sentenced to death by the brightness, splinters of sun stuck into my eyelids.

Then I open up. I open up. I unlock the locks I locked earlier. A little pissed. Because it's overboard with the ringing, real ear-rape and ceiling plaster raining down on my face, real electroshock connected by a sparkling cable to my head. And I don't know how head-fucked you have to be to ring the doorbell to a stranger's house in such an assholey way.

I open up, and without looking up at all, I say: What the fuck?

Angela's at the door. Angela's at the door. Alive. Holding herself on her own two legs. She's standing. She stares by turns at me and at the middle of my pants. As if she didn't know that it's her doing, and that if she were a friend, she'd clean them, if she were fair. But she's not. She stands. In the background the street is painted white and red. Angela's face is like they've whitewashed it against bugs for the spring and drawn in her eyes, her mouth, all her small talk in black watercolor.

Like a potted plant that had withered and died. She looks as though a minute ago she'd dragged herself out of a river in which she'd drowned a month before. And in the meantime the dragonflies have shit all over her. I look at her. She's not pretty. Like a nun through the parks this time of year, she labors to support a man's face on a neck that's withering bit by bit. In her bony paw, crammed with some signet rings or other, she's also holding a withered homemade white-and-red flag. A paper flag. I bought it from the Russkies—she says anemically, just like she's reciting a poem about the Piaśnicki Forest at some state celebration. And she waves weakly. As if to say: It's not me who's shown up here. It's someone impersonating me.

I stare straight at her. Because she's alive, in one piece, she hasn't gone to hell, she hasn't hurt me that way, she's not the kind of swine that would lead me to the house of coppers and court psychiatrists. And of the goddamn devil: Nails, you killed her, you son of a bitch, my little tiny daughter, and she was so delicate, she loved outings, she loved travel.

Now I see that she's definitely not pretty. Rather, like I'd been visited by the charred remains of a chicken. From the Russkies, I repeat after her, holding the door firmly in hand so that she shouldn't by chance feel like coming in. A deathly notion. And I don't know if I'm just so out of it that she came here to take back her black virginity, which she left here yesterday. She'd died during the night, and now she's returned without warning. I don't know what to say to her.

Angela, you have a moustache—I put out there, staring at her, to get the conversation going.

A moustache?—she asks dully, raising her rotten hand to her upper lip. But that hand likewise withers and falls according to the dictates of gravity. A moustache?—she repeats indifferently.

Well, exactly, a moustache—I say briskly, because I feel that this subject gets to her. It's a neutral and cheerful subject, fun. I tell her: As you'll sometimes see, I look at you and I think to myself: it's a guy.

She, like, doesn't react. She doesn't laugh. Like she doesn't understand what a moustache is in Polish. So it's obviously not getting to her, this subject. Or else there wouldn't be an uncomfortable silence, like some wet laundry strung up between us, casting legs and sleeves into our faces time and again.

So what's up?—I put out there now, laughing reassuringly at her, I extend my hand, on which I also notice a little congealed blood, and pat her heavily, friendly-like on the shoulder, so she'll know that there's friendship between us, that we can always remain pals, that when we meet each other on the street, it'll all be good.

From that gesture on my part, she staggers pretty hard, raises the hand with its banner, waves it pretty apathetically, and says: I bought it from the Russkies. Lifting that drooping banner. I bought it from the Russkies, because it's cheaper. Boy Scouts also sell them. But they're more expensive. It's known. And from artificial materials. Nonbiodegradable.

While she's saying this, I don't know how long it can last. On her part, no smile, all seriousness. I calculate it quietly in my head. Maybe we've already been standing here an hour. And maybe half that. And maybe a second. And maybe I'm already dead. Maybe they're actually keeping me in some kind of crapper, in some kind of white-and-red detox cut out of ladies' magazines. Like it's all beautiful, and as soon as I move, that paper glue will go and spill out together with the entire stand, under which the fires of hell are blazing. Because that's a special hell for speed freaks. They shoot you these sick movies. And Angela, that's not Angela. It's some fucking cardboard cutout. Its mouth is moving, but you hear no voice. A black fish-hammer. A black fish-monster. A black origami crane. And now I submit my application for Tylenol.

For acetaminophen, understood broadly. For enlarging the extraction point. Because from her twisting stare, sort of piercing through me, my skull starts to hurt so bad that in another moment it would have to come unstuck from the rest, roll down the stairs and along the street to a manhole, and attain complete independence.

Your dog's died—Angela says vaguely, waving her flag. I say: Uh, what?! To which she says that Bitchy is lying there in front of the garage and is dead from hunger. Then I really jump at that, and it doesn't matter what mess of national colors I have on my pants, that matters least of all now. Because I'm horrified. Shocked. I take Bird Milkies, I take from the fridge whatever's there, a frank, a TV dinner, everything, and I'm off. Bitchy's lying on her back on the lawn. Which soon enough will surely need to be cut again. She's not very lively. Bitchy, Bitchy, I say, and I feel like crying. In particular because I see a little turd that had come out of her like a great black worm, which killed her and is now fleeing from punishment into the earth. Bitchy. So come on. Don't be a pig and hurt me so. Get up. I brought this here for you. You don't like beans, but perhaps, once in a blue moon, it wouldn't poison you to eat one fucking bean, the crown wouldn't fall from your flat skull, you didn't want to munch, so now you're dead, you see how you're going to fuck things up for your mistress as soon as she gets back, and instead of a dog's corpse here, the house all bloody, you see, we could all be fired from this, close this business down . . . so get the fuck up!!

* * *

Just as I'm screaming and even getting ready to kick her, Angela comes up. She lays her hand on my shoulder. She's solemn, with a flag in her hand. She says to me: Calm down, Nails. Your pain doesn't help anything. I know you're in shock. Just be calm. I know that you really loved Bitchy. But now she's dead. There's nothing you can do about it. Death walks arm in arm with us, blows mortality in our faces. Leaves pain and suffering. But the wounds heal.

And when I'm standing there like that, dumbstruck, totally taken aback by what's going on, that everything is suddenly falling apart and finally even my dog dies, slapped down like a rubber stamp on a package. That's when Angela takes a winter snow shovel from the garage and, with no further ado, starts digging a grave in the lawn.

I sit down on the curb, because I no longer have the strength for all that. Enough already, thank you very much, party's over, everybody home, your shoes are already waiting for you in the foyer, you can take what's left of the cake for your brothers and sisters. That's it. Today my last bulb burned out. Today I'm dead, today I'm watching as earth is scattered on the lid of my casket, and I throw a handful of it at myself.

Then I suddenly say to Angela as follows: The Russkies poisoned Bitchy. To which Angela says: Maybe so. At which I get fucking pissed, since it sinks in more and more.

For one Polish dog, two Russkies—I say—or three. For Bitchy, for one innocent, nonpolitical Polish dog, three Russkies into the sand. By firing squad.

At which point I take a stick and show where the Russkies are going to stand and how I'm going to shoot them.

Aggression always comes back to you. Man is a wolf to man—Angela says. She's even dug out a bit with her own uncovered veins. And the next thing I know, she's right in front of me and says: What's your real name, Nails?

I think for a moment. Is she totally abnormal?

Well, it happens to be Andrzej—I say. Andrzej Robakoski. And I'm Angelica. Angelica Anna—Angela says. I have a middle name, too—I say—but I won't tell. And I belch from hunger, since I haven't eaten for a long time. So tell me what it is—Angela insists, digging deeper. I sit on the curb and say that I won't tell. To which she asks why. I say because. But my mother is Izabela.

Then two drones come to the gate with paint. Dig, dig—I say to Angela, I get up and go to them.

Good day, Boss—they say to me, and speak well, though they're looking with surprise in the direction of my pants, with marks of indubitably organic origin. Pig?—they put in about the blood. These days, how much do you have to pay the farmer for an ungutted one?—they put in, pointing at that dried blood.

That's enough—I say, because I don't much feel like debating if it's gutted or ungutted, from a farmer, or from the supermarket, or from the sty, or wherever. Because it's got shit to do with them, they're my pants, and they have their own, so let them take care not to sully theirs. They see that I'm in no mood to chat about the weather and fashion, cosmetics. Are we painting or what?—one says to the other.

So, like, what are we painting?—I shoot back soberly. They look at each other and say that we're painting the house white and red, because that's the mayor's ordinance for the whole district. And what if we don't?—I say, which takes them a bit aback, they look at each other. It's not, like, a matter of not doing it—they say to me—that's up to you, whether yes or no. I'll tell you honestly how it is. You could say yes, in which case me and my friend here go in, cheers, elegantly, the full cooperation of city hall with residents of the Polish race, everything's fine between us, you're a bit overdrawn at the ATM, that deficit somehow disappears, you're behind on the rent and so forth, nothing big of course, because city hall can't afford any serious embezzlement. If your wife is giving birth, and at the same time, for example, the wife of some, let's say, pro-Russki anti-Pole who's gotten out of line is giving birth, well, then your wife gets priority and primacy in her birthing, and even a white-and-red rose by her bed. And that other one dies in the hall. Though you wouldn't even know it, since no cabbie will take her, and her car's just broken down out of the blue. Some V-belt, some, like, piece of shit, the exhaust pipe just happens to be blocked up with Styrofoam, but the car wouldn't run. Wouldn't run and that's it. Because the thing is, if you come down on no, I'll still tell you honestly, it's not like that decision doesn't have consequences. Because it does. It seems like nothing, but then it's everything. Now something of yours breaks, now all of a sudden your siding's gone, now your wife suddenly dies, even though she's never had a cold. Now something goes missing, like all of a sudden some documents with your first and last name show up not in the filing cabinet where they belong, only in just the one where they don't belong, so that all of a sudden you'll simply disappear from the world with your family, so that you'll suddenly disappear from this town, and your house will be carried away piece by piece to the outskirts, soaked in gasoline, paint thinner, and set aflame just on principle. That either you're a Pole or you're not a Pole. Either you're Polish or you're Russki. And to put it more bluntly, either you're a person or you're a prick. And that's it, that's what I'll tell you.

Then I look him in the eye for a moment, to make sure that what he's saying is for real. It's for real. He knows what he's saying. So then I turn toward the house. The siding is newly installed, elegant, white, a Western look, though it's bought from the Russkies. I look at it for a moment. Then I look at Angela, who's just now setting the shovel aside and dumping Bitchy into the hole. I think to myself: That grave's too shallow, it won't work that way, because soon it will start to stink, when it gets warmer and hotter.

My dog died—I say, showing Angela in the enclosed portrait of Bitchy's burial. The Russkies poisoned her—I add, so it will be known that I'm no fucking pro-Russkie anti-Pole and that I know how they herd about in town, those shitheads, and slip poison into the Poles through their Russki canned goods.

They poisoned her?—the drones ask, as though they no longer had any illusions about the depravity of the crimes that the Russkies perpetrate on this town's inhabitants.

Yeah, they poisoned her out of common spite, maybe they even starved her to death—I say. At that they point to Angela with a paint roller: Your daughter's surely suffering because of them? After looking at your daughter, you should finally state your position, sir, about the kind of political system you subscribe to. In a word, yes or no, Russki CD-bootleggers, Russkies who tunnel underneath our economy, Russkies who kill our dogs and yours, our children who cry because of the Russkies. Yes or no, Poland for the Russkies, or Poland for the Poles. Decide, sir, because here we're chit-chatting, and those motherfuckers are arming themselves.

I look at Angela, who, like a prematurely blackened five-year-old girl covered in grime, stares in my direction, waiting for me to return so that we can perform the rites for Bitchy's soul. Bitchy, a martyr for the defense of the purity of the Polish race. Murdered by the Russkies with particular cruelty for her Polish origins.

But then I look at the siding, new, worth a shitload of cash, entirely unused siding. Then everything crystallizes for me in a single instant, everything becomes clear. I won't surrender the siding, Russki or not Russki, it makes no difference. Angela, get over here—I yell. Angela trots over. They want to paint the siding white and red, I say to her on the side, under my voice. She looks me dumbly right in the eye, the left one, as if she didn't know what white was, as if she didn't know what red was and only knew at most what black is, like that's what I was saying: They want to paint it black, then she'd know right away what I was talking about. What do you mean, paint?—she asks, and all the same she's as dull as a plastic spork. Well, in the Polish way—I explain it to her like she's retarded—to paint it the Polish way, like for Bitchy, that the Russkies poisoned her.

Have you lost your fucking mind?—Angela says all of a sudden, like she understands what's going on.—You could paint over the siding if they, like, fucked your mom or brought some shady amusement park to town. Or if they, like, killed you and raped your corpse. So tell them that, for Bitchy, at most the fence.

And she's right, she's not such a dumb girl, she's got a head for business, how I'll take care of my own business, be it the sand, or the towns, or the Arafat rags, it doesn't matter anymore, I'll take her for my "calculations" department.

Don't touch the siding—I say to the guys without a hint of hesitation, without a quiver in my voice.—The most you can do is paint over the fence.

They look at each other, one at the other, they wonder where the hell to classify me now, for or against.

I wouldn't damage the fence, either—I say quickly—but it's for my dog, for the pain of my daughter, Angela, whom the Russkies wronged so badly as to slay her best friend. That's why I hate them, that's why the fence around my home will symbolize the Poles' declaration of war against the Russkies.

And then I even surprise myself at how clever I am, how crafty, really on a different level, because right then they take out the tables with the list of residents, they gawk at these tables under the headings: pro-Polish, pro-Russki, and they say:

What are we attesting? The second one, somewhat taller: Well, for me, he's obviously pro-Polish. Then the first, shorter: Well, Polish indeed, but what's his score? They look at each other for a moment. Then the taller one says: So what, we need a psych test. They pull their jackets back from their overalls and take the psych test out of their pockets. It's not long, but there's always a bureaucracy, three questions and do what you can. I look at them suspiciously, but I take the psych test, and Angela and I take a few steps back.

I read the first question aloud. The drones pipe in: In filling out the form, you are obligated to tell the truth or face administrative punishment. Okay, Angela and I say, and then we read: First question. Imagine that a Polish-Russki war breaks out. A buddy of yours tells you in secret that he/she backs the Russkies. What do you do? A) I report it immediately to his/her landlord and to the police. B) I hold off, I have pangs of morality, but in the end I keep the matter to myself. C) I back him up. I believe that the Russkies should keep developing their trade in fake cigarettes and CDs.

And poisoning Polish animals—one of the drones adds in passing.

Answer A—Angela says. Answer A—I affirm right away. So the drones mark you down for A and say: Good. Angela jumps with joy and pleasure at our getting it right. Then we read further: Second question. On the street you see a man who's hanging a red flag on one of the houses. What do you do? A) I promptly pull down this enemy banner. A—Angela says. Good—the drones reply. And the taller one adds: So we can move on directly to the key question, since there's no point going on with formalities, seeing as you know the correct answers. The shorter one says: Okay, right.

The third and final question. In recent days the salinity of the Nieman River has risen by 15 percent. I emphasize: by 15 percent. The natural environment of this region has been ruined, and the water of the Nieman has taken on an ultramarine tinge. Are the Russkies responsible for this situation? A) Yes. B) I don't know. C) Certainly.

C!—Angela says right away, the drones look at each other and the taller one adds: Nine points out of ten, very good in the subject of "armed struggle in the face of the race enemy." So we're painting the fence, which we have to do, we're not here to chat. So they jot down what they have to and make for the fence.

*　　*　　*

Angela and I go to finish up that whole mess with the dog. I'm standing, like, off to the side, thinking about Bitchy, that she was as she was, but it's a shame that she died. While Angela heaps on soil with her shitkickers, I watch as Bitchy fades out like the picture on a television with bad reception, like it's overgrown with garden soil. Hasta la vista—I say to Bitchy for the last time. You were a cool chick, just a little fat.

Angela looks at me quizzically, in case I'm talking to her, and fills more dirt in. Good—she says. Now we'll conduct the rites, a little hocus-pocus so that Bitchy won't end up where we're going to end up, Nails, and we're going to end up in the very middle of hell, at the very bottom of hell, crushed by debris, crushed by a cinder block. You'll witness it yet, as I perish under a boulder, under the devastation, the ruins. I'm going to watch as you perish, and that will be the end of it. So that Bitchy will never know as much suffering as we will in life.

Next Angela stamps down the earth, pulls up some grass by the roots, and plants it into the earth over the grave.

God would turn in his grave if he were to see this—I say, and I cross myself. Well, don't be so important all over again—Angela says, and grabs my hand, and I get shivers all down my spinal column, because it seems to me that it's an evil death, death from rabies, that's grasped me by the hand and is leading me to the other side of the river.

Have you lost it? Let me go, I say, slipping off toward the steps. Angela looks at me, a little surprised, and says: Yesterday you were more polite toward me, more sensitive. But if that's how it is, that's that, and if not, then not. We totally don't have to clutch each other's stupid hands. Each of us is a separate, independent, and free person. Regardless of what you think, I'm also independent, I'm my own separate, individual person. I want that to be clear between us. I'm never going to give up my friends, my hobbies, my interests. I want you to know that.

And now it's like this. No sooner had we gotten inside, put on slippers, house shoes, than the bell rings, one-two-three, like someone is going to start hammering at the door with his fists. The city police. Izabela as well. Joke's over—I think to myself, and if only it weren't fucked up that they're looking for my bro, if only it weren't fucked up that as a family we're all criminals, I tell Angela to pick up a little in the room, and I'll open the door in due time. I make it in time, because Natasha hasn't yet managed to kick holes in the shape of her shoe into the Gerd automatic doors. Though she wasn't far from doing so.

I look at her. Natasha's Natasha. I met her at a club. Though I don't know exactly what she's doing here, in this place, in my apartment, on No Russkies Day. This one time she dissed Magda, that's precisely when we got to know each other, when Magda came up to me to complain that some girl's starting things with her, and that if she had a real boyfriend he'd tell that bitch to fuck off. We'd been with each other for a bit then, me and Magda, we'd gotten to know each other a bit better, so I had to go, to chat. Natasha told me that she hates Magda because of her damn face and that if she crosses the dance floor it'll be ready-aim-fire on Magda. Then we got to know each other still better. And now she's standing at the door, she's staring at my pants, like in a moment I'd have an indicator arranged there, which I'd take, I'd shine on my lower belly and say the weather map. Today's weather will be decidedly red with gusts up to black, partly cloudy. Today's weather will be Russki. Red clouds are gathering over the city. No Russkies Day may be canceled, given the conditions.

I have no idea what she's come here for, what she wants from me. Her hair with a white streak in front. A sly look. A not so big hump.

You have a problem down there?—she asks me, regarding these pants, smiling lecherously, like I know something but won't say. Though she's a fine piece of ass. That, like, what. That, like, something's not right with my member, a terminal disorder of the member, bye-bye George, I've had enough of you, because of you I've fucked up my pants, and what, and that's it, attempted murder with a sharp object, worse, almost suicide, Suicide for Kids, a kit for kids over three, a potato knife and a small nonbiodegradable coffin for my George, on a chain. And for our first callers, as a special gift, a cover.

Nooo, a female friend of mine did that—I say to Natasha regarding these pants, though I hope that Angela can't hear and is just cleaning up.

Hah, that's some pig, not a friend, that made a pig pen of you, eh?—Natasha asks, she licks her finger and tries to rub off there, where it's needed.

A certain one. A certain perverted one—I answer. To which Natasha asks whether that's this girl's name, Perverted, because that's what she's asking about, a name and not a quality.

And she's rubbing me with the finger, looking at me cheekily, directly in the eye. To which I groan. Then she shoves me, cries that I'm a pig, just like all the others, that she came to me in friendship, and I blow her off with hard-ons, and do I or my bro have any herb, some blow, because that's why she's come.

Lower your voice, all right?—I say. Half a tone softer. It's just that my cousin's sitting here, I reprimand Natasha. No shit?—Natasha hisses, she comes in and, on the tips of her Adidases, goes to the room, where she peeks in. That's no cousin, she hisses toward me—That's some sadomasochistic Goth bitch. Shut up, okay?—I hiss at Natasha, and the two of us look through the gap between the hinges. Angela, on her knees, is quite anemically collecting pieces of paper and cigarette butts from the floor. Fuck, she's alive in general, did you dig her out of her grave, could that be a corpse running on DD batteries?—Natasha hisses, shoves the door, and goes in. Hello, Boss. I want to know your name. I'm Natasha, she gives Angela her hand and says: Nata. Nata Blokus.

Angelica—Angela says—but you can call me Angela, simply Angela. Just Angela, right?—says Natasha, and she pulls her pants up. Simply Angela—says Angela.

Those are cool bracelets, studs. How much did you pay for them?—Natasha says. Different prices. It depends which—Angela answers, raising herself from the floor. Because they come from different places, but mostly I bought them this

summer in Zakopane or on vacation in the mountains. Cool—
Natasha says. Fucking awesome.

I'm coming down really hard. I don't know if I mentioned this
before, but my skull's splitting, and maybe I'll be dead in a
minute. Angela was drawing the blinds. And there's no hiding it, and looking at Natasha, looking at Angela, I reflect on
the suspicion that it's white, fucking bright as hell, a special
hell for dealing, for speed, with a sun that never sets, with a
five-thousand-watt halogen right in the eyes, with some party
with a couple weird chicks, of whom one is probably dead, and
the other saunters around the whole apartment, picks up various things, with disgust, and throws them back down on the
carpeting. Like a one-person commission investigating these
here war crimes. Like a Vietcong soldier through the sugarcane.
She looks at the pullout under the quilt. Oh, I see that some big
slaughterhouse was at work here, Nails, you messed somebody
up here, a stray, perhaps your own dog, she says.

Then Angela couldn't get any paler, so she turns violently
gray. Plus she starts burping perilously all of a sudden, so that
she grabs her face, as if she wanted to produce the next wave
of stones that want out. I have to save her, since after all she'd
shown me and Bitchy a lot of kindness and cunning today.

My dog died—I explain to Natasha, pointing at the pullout—
the Russkies poisoned her. She suffered a lot in passing, her blood
got all fouled up. They gave her a charge that self-explodes
inside its victim. A land mine in her food—I say, sit down next

to Angela on the pullout, and hug her around the shoulder consolingly. She caused us a lot of shit, we buried her just now.

Natasha looks at me with a pretty uncomprehending expression, then she stands up suddenly.

Nails, don't get off the fucking point, because I don't give a shit about your doggy breeding, or how your dog croaked, dropping to the left or the right. Better, tell me where your stuff is, because we can always chat about the weather or hobbies, but not when I need that speed so badly I'm about to shit myself.

Then, since I don't answer, she goes to the kitchen. She starts to open the cabinets, slams the doors, bangs the pots, Where is it, Nails, the dope, where do you keep that dope, because I can never get anything out of you, you dickhead, you're so strung out that everything's already swimming around in your skull, you don't even know where the kitchen is anymore, where the bathroom is, or where you hid the goddamn speed, you don't even know what the hell your name was two days ago, back when you squirreled it away, Robakoski or something else.

Angela stays in the room, and I, as the lord of the house, toddle after Natasha, helpless in the face of her anger. As soon as she sees me, she says to get the fuck out of here, I'll look for it myself, it's not worth it talking to you, Nails, go scrape

those entrails off your pants, because you look like you gutted yourself at the very least. Get out of here, I say, because I
can't stand to look at you.

Well, so I walk out to the foyer, I walk for a bit, look around.
I'm having this trip that I'm the same size as a cotton ball and
that I'm rolling around the apartment, first over here, then
over there, that some violent cross-ventilation is carrying me
along. That's my sort of like dream, since it suddenly seems
to me that snow's falling on me from the ceiling, or hail, white
wrappers, great white mosquito netting is dropping down on
me. The wind is blowing through the rooms, it's carrying me
backward. The wind blows from above and carries me down
into the depth of the floor, to the basement, to the center of
the earth, where white wriggling worms crawl along under
my eyelids. I go into the kitchen and the dream blows away.
A rumble and ruckus, glasses shattered on the floor, my mug
with the little dwarf as well, the dishes dragged out of the
cabinets and spread out on the paneling. Natasha at the table,
what was there she's pushed onto the floor, she's propping
her head up on her arm. She's piled up powdered borscht on
the tabletop and, tap tap tap, she's cutting lines of it with a
credit card. She snorts it up through the Zdzisław Sztorm pen,
after which she sneezes something awful and spits red saliva
into the sink.

Fuck, Nails, things are going to end up badly for you today—
she mumbles. For your Goth chick as well.

She spits into the little load of borscht and stirs it with her
finger. She gets up. Goes into the room. Me behind her. When

she walks, that wind picks up and blows through Angela's hair, ruins her do. Natasha opens the minibar. All the bottles in a row. What she doesn't like, she puckers up and spits out onto the carpet. She's good at it. She can spit wherever she wants to. From nowhere she spits right in my face. So hard, all of a sudden, that I wheel back a couple steps. It was a martini.

You know what for?—Natasha asks, she hocks a loogie loathingly at my fly. You know what the fuck that's for? Because I'm fucking pissed today that there's no blow in the whole town, because today, on No Russkies Day, everything has to be peaches and bows down at city hall, fireworks up the ass, the mayor's, a healthy society with a grill on the balcony, with a single potted plant in the window. And fuck that, that instead of you being a friend and helping me find some amph in your own house, because it's definitely here and I'm not going to let it get away, I know it from Magda anyway, you stroll in like a Bulgarian truck-stop whore. Get the fuck out of my sight, or better, give me a smoke, because in a minute I'm going to fuck you up. Two smokes. Just give me whatever you have.

Then she turns to Angela: I'll keep it chill when I spit at you, because I see that you're quite delicate, and it could knock you down.

Angela looks at her, totally stupefied with surprise. You don't have to spit at me at all—she says to Natasha, sweeping her hair back. If only you would restrain your negative emotions.

Natasha looks at her, who knows what she's thinking. Nails—she says—how much did you pay for her? Because perhaps she was marked down for some sale. Then she spits at Angela very delicately, as she was warned, into her eye with loose white drool.

Then Angela gets up briskly and, holding her mouth, jets to the toilet. Out of the blue, Natasha lies down on the pullout and covers herself in the quilt.

Nails—she murmurs—Nails, enough of that roughing up. Let's sell that VCR to the Russkies, there'll be a bit of bank, so be a friend. Right away, we'll grab a taxi, go to Vargas and buy. Mom won't know anything about it. You, half the speed, me, half the speed, and a taste for your special lady, too. Well, stop gawking at me already, I look like shit in the woods today, and you're no better, come on, come over here and cuddle, better, tell me the first and last name of that skank you were humping yesterday, because I know you humped somebody, that bit about the dog's bullshit, was she at least pretty, with pretty hair, blond or black? Was it that one who's puking now?

Then I tell her, whisper in her ear, to fuck off.

She answers me in a loud whisper. What, you couldn't get yourself a decent girl without her period? Your hair's receding, Nails, I already see it right away that you'll be bald before long, you pig.

Saying this, she presses her lips tenderly to my lips, and when I'm thinking that all of a sudden everything between us is going good and that this is a cool girl, that I could dump Angela for her, she spits with full force into my mouth, all the saliva she had in her, maybe even more, her entire contents, all the bodily fluids she had there, since it's so much I choke violently.

From the toilet, there are echoes of vomiting.

Where are you going with that licker, huh?—Natasha asks, and would you like it if I were to plant my tongue into your clean mouth? Are you abnormal? Dog. Pig.

Tell me where you've hidden the goods—she says, sits on me, and tightens her grip around my neck. Because it'll be over in a minute, in a minute I'll pick up the phone and call the pigs, since you don't know, I'll have them come and give the place a good going-over. Shit, the way you look, you should see yourself. I feel like I'm at your funeral here. Nails's dead, Angela! And he was a good pal, a fun guy. They're not burying him in the ground because he has too many sins on him, he squirreled away too much speed at his place and didn't want to share. They're burying him in the pullout, so that his mother can visit him often, whenever she opens the pullout. He was a cool guy, we all mourn you, Nails, girls and boys from elementary school, the homeroom teacher, Angela as well, though she's doing pretty bad herself. That cunt Natasha, the one that strangled you, she'll get hers, but she was right about you being an asshole for not wanting to give her speed that time.

She's strangling me all the harder. She's strangling me harder and harder. For real, in a minute she'll kill me, in a minute I'll be dead. My whole life flashes before my eyes just as it was. Preschool, where I learned that for all of us it's about peace on earth, about the white dove made out of poster board, 3,000 zlotys a unit, then all of a sudden 3,500 zlotys, the obligatory naptime, peeing your pants, an epidemic of cavities, the Squirrel Club, brutal fluoride treatments. Next I recall elementary school, the mean homeroom teacher, mean teachers in their slutty Cossack boots, the coatrooms, the slippers you have to wear and the memorial room, peace, peace, the poster board dove of peace fluttering on an artificial cotton string through the hall, the first homo contacts in the PE locker room. Later, the cooler, Arleta, my friend's girlfriend, who was the first woman I had, on a class trip to Malbork, which I had enough problems with anyway, since she was too fast for me. Later, there were others in big numbers, though I didn't love any of them. Except maybe Magda, but it's over between us.

The Bird Milkies, you idiot—I groan from under Natasha's terrible embrace. She trickles out some drool from a great height right into my face: What do you mean Bird Milkies, fucker, you're about to have Bird Milkies come back out of you if you don't talk—she says, and presses into the contents of my stomach with her knee.

Your amph's in the Bird Milkies—I roar, and she lets me go, jumps back from the pullout, that thief didn't even take off her Adidases, and she dumps out the still totally good Bird Milkies onto the fucking floor, so that I have to pick them up. And a single tiny little bag of speed slips away. A line as fat as a worm comes out of it, and I don't even have the strength to get up off the pullout, I'm starting to see black, I'm looking at my fingernails. She's already bringing the Zdzisław Sztorm pen from the kitchen, but now she thinks for a minute and cuts three rows. I have principles, she says. One line's fatter, totally packed, the second so very thin that powdered borscht would do me better, and perhaps there isn't a third one at all.

And what the fuck, what am I, nobody?—I yell. I'm feeling the wounds from my clinical death from the strangulation that was brought down upon me. Right away, Natasha turns on her ass and snorts her fucking line, with my bit also, and with Angela's bit also, and before I have time to make my move, she says to me: So what? Not enough for you? Not enough? If it's not enough for you, go string yourself up.

Then, however, she goes completely soft and, her nose sort of sniffling, says: So come here, come, Auntie'll help you out. Hop. She drags me from the pullout, since I'm really enfeebled, though maybe that's because of the frequency with which I do speed. Soooo—Natasha says—come come, don't be afraid, a small pumping of funds into your nose holes and you're like new, Nails, brand new, still in the box with the tag still on. Yup. Snort it up now. Ooo. Now it'll be all right. Though there'll be impotency in old age.

As she helps me a bit in managing the line, she looks around and says:

What's with this mess, Nails, you need to vacuum in here, I really feel like vacuuming this whole swamp, you know, once and for all. But when I pick up the vacuum, I'm going to vacuum your shit so bad I'll suck up the carpeting, suck up the floor, suck up the basement, everything. The whole house'll fall to shit, all the Russki siding'll fly off with a boom. So it's better not to let me have it. Or give me the vac, but unplugged. And you, Nails, no, without that stuff, you have to get yourself together, such a big boy, and your filthy trousers, you look like the cashier in a butcher shop, when I look at you, it turns my stomach.

Well, so I pull my trousers off, since I already feel sort of better, a clearer picture, firmer jelly. Your legs are too skinny— she says, then she picks the pen up from the ground and looks at it and says: Zdzisław Sztorm, Sandworks, you know him?

I say I don't know him, though that Angela, the one puking so harshly in the toilet, she probably knows him. To which Natasha asks if I know what kind of guy he is. I say he's some producer of sand. She asks if he has cash. I say that maybe he does, maybe he doesn't. To which she says we're going to him right now, that we'll refer to my acquaintance with him, or best of all, Angela's acquaintance with him, she'll do her hocus-pocus and we'll fuck him over for some awesome bank, and then No Russkies Day belongs to us, grilling stands, we'll buy up everything there is.

And one-two she's got everything ready, the whole plan, I'm only the hired help here for doing menial tasks, nothing requiring thought, I scrub the pots, I shut the door to the john, where Angela's puking. Natasha's browsing through the cabinets, This blouse has to go, Nails, I don't know what your mom would have to say about it, but I wouldn't wear that to the basement. After which, on the carpeting, she finds the postcard from Angela's friend in Szczecin, which Angela, making her fast getaway from my being pissed off yesterday, tossed somewhere around the pullout, and she reads it aloud, with difficulty. Oh shit—she says—look at what that cunt wrote, I'm having a great time, I spend a lot of time in fresh air, lovely sunny weather. A campfire. Fucking A. Nails, you know her? That's got to be some rich pussy that went to a spa to treat her calluses, you think it would be possible to squeeze some buzz out of that? Get it? But nothing all bloody and brutal. The best would be a threatening letter. Professionally done, following a threatening-letter template. Your brother should have that kind of template lying around somewhere. One letter about how her end is near. Another about how her children's end is near. And a third about how she's already dead, already in the grave. Perhaps she'll pay money. But shit, you know what the meat and potatoes of it is? That she's from Szczecin. That'd take longer timewise, and we need that bank today, on No Russkies Day. Otherwise we're nobody here, zero position. That Sztorm guy's the only one we can fuck over, there's no way out, he won this along with his fortune, he's not going to slip out of this one. And then, Nails, you and me, we're going to do such a number on this town that neither the Russkies nor our guys will realize how they ended up without coin. We'll form a new system, today even. Everything somebody's got, cellular phones, wallets, house keys, remotes for their cars, right into the market.

Then she's making me nervous. They're both making me nervous. They snort my speed, they cause a riot. One's puking, the other's chatting me up, and I'm asking myself what this is, a two-person association for the psychological extermination of Andrzej Robakoski? They're valuable to each other, they should marry each other and it'd be an end to fucking things up, a female-female pair of children of war, some kind of speed-and-Tylenol company, puking stones, Natasha would take care of extortions, Angela would sow black tapestries all day long. And may they forget my cell phone number.

Cool it, Natasha, shut your cunt a minute, because I want to propose something advantageous to you, you know?—I say, a bit pissed off. Pay attention now. If you want, I'll sell you Angela. For real. As a slave. She's nice. She's social. She can recite poems. Things'll be good between you and her. She'll wipe your ass, she'll chew your food for you, when you feel like it, she'll puke up whatever you want her to. A stone. A baggie of speed. Acid. Heartburn. Whatever you want, just ask. She'll introduce you to Zdzisław Sztorm. She'll punch your stamp for you. She'll be your secretary.

Natasha isn't daydreaming anymore, she's looking at me like I'm retarded. Shit no, she says. Perhaps you're totally fucked up already. Shit, and that's it, I'm not going for it. You won't pull me into that kind of shady transaction. No way. Trade in living bodies is trade in living bodies. But like how would I settle it with her? That's tough on the coin, and then there's feeding her, inoculations, taking her for a walk, you think you're going to tempt me to do that? You led her here from who knows where, perhaps from hell, enjoy it now, but you won't drag me into any of those lowlife intrigues. Though I'll tell you what. It would be possible to get stoned that way, but I'd have to talk to Vargas. Maybe he could think of something, but that would be a bigger can of worms, like selling her to the West and so on.

As you wish, I say to Natasha, and I go to the toilet, because it happens that I've gotten pretty used to Angela, to the fact that she's living and is alive, and a situation that would have her, let's say, dead, that's unthinkable to me. So I go to the toilet. Angela's alive. In the traditional pose, she's hanging across the john and vomiting up what she had inside. There couldn't be much of it left after yesterday. It's ostensibly organic, white, just one single bit of gravel is swimming in the toilet, and there I recognize the gravel from the walk in front of the house. The rest—I don't know what. Lime for whitewashing, schoolhouse chalk, paint drunk down while the workmen weren't looking.

Is everything okay?—I say to her, nudging her leg. She's alive. She looks at me with the look of a stovetop-cooked chicken. I say to her further: You know what, Angela? Are you always like this? You know, with this puking. Because I don't know if you know. But sometimes that can end up badly. Everything's, like, fine for you here, you're puking peacefully, but at a certain moment it turns out that you've puked up your stomach. Or for instance you've peeled yourself inside out. Does that do it for you?

Angela wipes her mouth and looks at me in such a way that I wonder if it wasn't even worse and she hasn't vomited up her spinal cord along with her brain. After which she finally closes her eyes. I take her under the arm. Izabela could come back and, wanting to relieve herself, would stumble over Angela, so that right away there'd be crying and the grating of teeth over the mess in the house. I call Natasha. Natasha takes her by the legs. Let's take her to your bro's room, to detox, she decides. So we carry her. We lay her down on the couch. Natasha lifts Angela's arm. The arm falls down. Natasha sits with full force on her belly. In a second there's a gurgling, I scream: Be fucking careful!, but fortunately only a white bubble floats out of Angela, and it immediately bursts.

I don't know where you got her from, Nails, but I'm sure of one thing. That's a defective model—Natasha says. Even for the West, they wouldn't take her, perhaps for replacement parts. And they'd cut out all those guts as damaged, so there'd be no profit from it.

Then I get a bit nervous.

She's finally lost it?—I scream, because that's already taking me to the limit, to the complete loss of mental balance. She's finally totally lost it? Does she necessarily want to make problems for me? To bring the pigs to my place? Because it sometimes happens that when this house creaks because it's so full of speed. It happens to be plastered with speed. And that idiot's throwing herself suicide parties, she thinks to herself that here and now it'd be safe to shut the computer down, it's been a pleasure, a refuge for suicides, a house for a one-day stay for the deceased, she's found herself some people with inexpensive euthanasia, finally she should think seriously for once and realize what the agreement is, that indeed you can be in this house, but you have to be alive at the least, and if you want to shoot yourself, that you have to do somewhere else. Beyond the gate, but not a millimeter closer.

At this time, while I'm having this breakdown, this hysteria, Natasha, with a bored look, is conducting scientific experiments on Angela. She looks into her mouth, wincing a bit, feels around her teeth, then wipes her hand off on her own pants. She rummages through her pants pockets, rummages through her handbag and pulls out some papers, old documents, some scraps.

Why don't you chill out, because if it goes smoothly, we'll still make some kind of bank out of her, like you said to me. One piece of paper is a copy of a diploma from a summer camp in Bieszczady for coming in second in the race during orientation. Natasha tears it up right away, slips the torn pieces into Angela's pocket, and says: When this rotten princess wakes up from her eternal sleep, she'll think she got really fucking pissed and tore it herself. Then there are these two snotty tissues, which she uses to wipe Angela's mouth of sediment and that white poison, which she also slips into her pocket, and like some bigger trip to finish it off, some letters as well. So I think to myself, what kind of idiot is this Angela that, first of all, she carries unsent letters around in her handbag, and then she kicks the bucket next to Natasha, zero instinct for self-preservation, for real.

Yet what's been done can't be undone, Natasha tears open the envelopes with her teeth and flies off to the big room, so I fly off after her, sit on the pullout, and look over her shoulder. Natasha reads the first letter aloud and with difficulty. It's written as follows. To the management, dear sirs. I firmly and vocally register my protest in opposition to and against the resurgence of zoos and circuses in Poland. I vocally postulate that the animals be liberated from them and extradited to their countries of origin. I vocally postulate that underage children be liberated from any obligation to visit, under the auspices of an excursion, be it for school or on a Sunday, these places of torture, cruelty, innocent suffering. My motto in life is: If you want your kid to see pain, take him to the circus. I'm a student in the third year of the economics high school. My hobbies include, among others, animals. Together with my friends I've founded an organization for ecological animation, of which I am the director. We don't make threats, but we offer warnings. Respectfully, Angelica Kosz, seventeen, third-year student at the High School of Economics Number 2.

Her name is Kosz?—Natasza asks, staring at it dubiously. Then she picks the pen up off the floor and, in her illiterate handwriting, writes the following. Pee Ess. Suck our fucking dicks. Maybe I'd write more, but now I'm going to hell. Hastalavista, we're going to kill you.

After which she laughs satanically, and she seals the envelope back up with a bit of gum she pulled out of her kisser. Then there are two more. That same letter typed through carbon paper, of which one is to Jolanta Kwaśniewska, the other to the zoo in Ostrowiec Świętokrzyski. To the first one Natasha adds: Pee Ess. In case there's a resurgence of concentration camps to satisfy German tourists, my buddy Nails will kill you, your husband and kids. See you in hell. And on the other one she writes again about giving head. Then she goes back to my bro's room, and me behind her. Angela's sort of roused herself a little, and after a while I'm worried that she heard me and Natasha reading her correspondence through the wall. Whereas Natasha sees zero problem in that. Angela, turn on your side for a minute toward the wall, okay?—she says, and when Angela looks at her uncomprehendingly and uncomprehendingly turns over, Natasha slips those letters back into the handbag.

What, is something there?—Angela says, frightened, in a weak voice. Well—Natasha says, totally serious—a mosquito landed on your ass and wanted to bite you, but I killed the fucker. You have nothing to worry about.

Thanks—Angela smiles pretty hazily, like rarely changed water in a fish tank. What kind of music do you listen to?

A little of everything—Natasha answers, looking down, and I'm afraid for a moment that she's lost it, that she's going to take a speaker from off the stand and bring it down on her face.

But happy or sad—Angela insists, not realizing the threat.

A bit of this, a bit of that—Natasha says, I'm afraid she's gathering drool to deceive Angela. Different kinds. Both slow and sometimes fast.

And what kind of fast do you like?—Angela investigates, propping herself on her elbow, and then a wheezing, a coughing shoots out of her, and she spits a considerable white cloud of dust or powder into the air.

Different kinds, for the most part I like music videos most—Natasha responds. But not with some fucking lesbos singing about how if somebody's not screwing them at that moment, they're getting themselves off. I just prefer when men sing. Hip-hop, for example, English songs about how terror happens, that we live in the ghetto, you know.

I like that, too—Angela says. And what kinds of books do you read? To which she adds: Or newspapers?

To which Natasha answers: Ha, I could say a lot. A bit of everything. The TV guide. The teletext. A bit of adventure stuff, Conan the Destroyer, Conan the Barbarian, Conan in the Big City, I read that whole series once. I love posters. Jokes. Anecdotes. Programs.

That's cool—Angela says. Just like me. And do you like to diet?

At which Natasha sort of stares her down, freezes for a minute, and leans unexpectedly over Angela, such that Angela stops being able to breathe normally, and the purple shadow from Natasha's eyes seeps under her eyelids. I don't really know what to do so that Natasha wouldn't feel offended, because she feels free in my house and maybe simply wants to talk more intimately with Angela.

Who the fuck's paying you?—Natasha says into Angela's mouth. Fucking talk. Now. Chop-chop.

But what for?—Angela says tearfully, with surprise, since she's suddenly totally surprised, as if she wants to straighten out the whole situation.

For the fucking information, about me—Natasha says into her mouth.

What information?—Angela whispers.

I'm not asking what information, I'm only asking who, listen to the fucking questions. If you lie, you die. Who's paying you? Moscow?

Don't kill her, okay?—I say calmly to Natasha. Nails, go beat yourself off—she says, gets up, and comes up to me. So that I duck, since I'm afraid of this cold, rough girl. What the fuck, Nails? Maybe you're behind this, and your ass is listening in on me, and as soon as I turn around, she'll pull out a flashlight and shine it right in my eye? We're chatting here, the weather's nice, partly cloudy, culture and fine literature, and in a second she's going to call Zdzisław Sztorm on her cell phone and will sing it all to Russki intelligence, my every word plus her own impressions on the matter? Huh? Who's behind this, say it! Lefty? Vargas?

Do you know Zdzisław Sztorm?—Angela brightens up at once.

Sure. That is, like, no, I don't. But if I wanted to, I'd know him—Natasha says, then turns to me—You didn't tell her, Nails?

I didn't tell her what?—I ask, because I've lost the thread.

Well, that she has to give her ass to Sztorm, and we're going to split up the bank?—Natasha says.

No, I didn't tell her—I answer in accordance with what the truth is, since she's right.

Okay, since you didn't tell her, I'll tell her—Natasha brightens up, and she forgets about the whole deal with the intelligence. So listen, there's this project. A bit Nails's, a bit mine. This project, so you'd better listen and listen good. Because otherwise you won't be named Miss No Russkies Day, and you won't even be able to buy yourself a grilled roll. Nor will I, for that matter, so we're in the same boat. This is how it is. Now, with that bank you have in your purse, we're cruising by cab over to Sztorm's. Chill, totally laid-back, and maybe it's enough, certainly for half the way, and then we need to figure it out. The address is written on the pen you have in your purse. We'll go there, flirt with him. That, like, that we're from the organization for ecological animation, and would he give us some cash for protecting Polish animals from being annihilated by the Russkies. We have various papers, various stamps, folders. Then he says he won't give us anything, he's in debt, business is not going well, recession, unemployment, *Gazeta Wyborcza*. Then I go out, I say I have to go take a piss or puke, it doesn't matter, there's a good possibility I got my period or something, and that if I don't go, I'm totally going to fuck up his lovely armchair. And here's your role, the main attraction. It's all good, you lean over, you slide your tongue out. You recite a poem for him about animals. It doesn't have to be anything particularly romantic, it can be average, but it's important that it be from memory. Then he strips you and takes you, and the cash is ours.

Angela looks at Natasha with unconcealed surprise, with delight. How do you know about the organization for ecological animation?—she asks all dreamy, moved.

Natasha doesn't bat an eye about how she knows, though we both know how she knows.

I read it in the teletext or in some panoramic crossword, I don't remember, but it's not important.

Really? It's such a small world. I don't want to brag, but I'm the president of that organization—Angela says, delighted. We're fighting for animal emancipation and liberation, for their voice in the matter.

No problem—Natasha says, satisfied. The thing is, do you know some poem. It doesn't have to be about animals, any old poem will do.

Of course—Angela laughs, and from her teeth, which are arranged sparsely and pretty irregularly, like gravestones in a cemetery, radiates the glare of cadaverous happiness—I could even recite something from my own works.

Here, like as if she's been completely revived, she stands up and wipes a white coating and sediment from her mouth and dress, then she says: This one, for example. To Robert. That is, three asterisks, but to Robert. You understand. Like it was for Robert, very personal, though he's never going to read it.

And then she speaks in italics. A lot of words, and I'm in no condition to fathom them all, to understand whether they have rhyme or reason. She says to us, looking first at me, then at Natasha: Here's an epitaph for a withered man, your listless hands keep silent in your pockets. If you want to know, we were never here. If you want to know, we're not here now. This is the moment of silence honoring us. And even if we love each other, it's only separately. You're such a narcissist that you take only yourself.

Great—Natasha says and shakes her head with approval, and she even nudges me, so that I'd offer some praise for something—but that guy you wrote it to, he was a common fag, after all, a fucking impotent. If I had that kind of talent, I'd write that, too, the same identical poem you wrote. To Lolo. And I'd sign it differently. Natasha Blokus. I hate you, you meat-beating deviant, I won't be with you. But down to business. Now some shit about animals and we're peace out.

About animals?—Angela says with frustration, and she thinks it over a minute. I don't have anything about animals, perhaps something about matted, stuck-together wings, that one's sad and could fall under the category of birds. With regard to those stuck-together wings, it's very sad.

Natasha and I look at each other like some commission on animal competition. What do you think, Nails?—she says. I think that it's about time for me to get out of here, because I have the munchies, and here they're sitting and debating about literature. I don't say, however, what I'm thinking. I don't think anything—I confess, getting up. To my taste it's good, in particular you can emphasize that it's to Robert. That should get Sztorm utterly unstuck on the matter of ecology, because that's his son.

Okay, let's go—Natasha says and grabs Angela's purse.

But where are we going?—Angela suddenly asks, terrified, glancing at her purse and at her black dress with the white dots. Then you could see how Natasha was holding out with her last vestiges of strength.

To the zoo, to an antipolitical protest, you know? Give back the animals. Leave our bison alone. Liberate the janitors.

Then she grabs Angela by the shoulder and hauls her to the door. I toddle after them, because I feel like taking a piss. Stop—Natasha suddenly turns toward me—where are you going? I'm standing there and don't know what to say, because like what, now pissing is forbidden?

You're not going anywhere, Nails—Natasha says to me—you've already had your five-minute speed-rush today, you've already had enough. For starters, the plan had to be different, but now it's also different, as you see. Angela's with me, and you're staying home. Get yourself together, clean off those intestines so that you look like a decent human being, and during the fest, score some decent, unmenstruating ass that'll get you some speed. We're going, enough, good-bye, and see you later.

Arleta's drunk and pretty fucked up, she's a laugh peddler. A document shredder, whatever you say to Arleta a moment thereafter flies out of her mouth in the form of laughter, in the form of shreds, bits of paper, garbage, confetti, and is strewn on the wind. Video gaming, instead of eyes, two little neon lights flittering from under her eyelids, overgrown from smoking, two little dynamo-powered bike lights. In her snake-skin jacket, in a cloud of brocade.

She asks me if I want one of her smokes. I say that if it's Russki, then thank you very much, I'm washing my hands of that business, because I don't want to get tangled up in some Russophilia. To which she says that she never smoked Russkies, certainly not her, definitely Lefty, definitely the Bartender, but a girl like Arleta never had a lot in common with the Russkies, practically nothing, other than a couple times long ago and not really, since she was drunk and besides it was several years ago, when they hadn't yet dicked over the Polish CD industry, they hadn't stolen all the Polish sand.

So if she gives me her Carmens, I'll take one even if they don't have the excise band, because what else do I have to smoke.

Then we smoke, we don't say anything. No Russkies Day, a fest, a clang and cramp in the microphones, the Ladybugs dance troupe and the more youthful Fantastic Dance. Grill smoke has utterly engulfed the town, sacrifices of kielbasa, ribs, and animal cartilage submitted to the gods in the name of victory over the partitioners. The char will creep along the streets around the municipal amphitheater and sully the part of the buildings that's supposed to be, like, white. So now we're a state of the gray-and-red flag, a dirty eagle with a blackened crown on a red background. Angela wouldn't like it, though I don't know where she is now, she's probably pulling down her panties. A definitive rise in the level of carbon monoxide in the natural air, kielbasa its usual mother, subject to this holocaust, death everywhere, murder everywhere, hacked-up animals that, if they could, would cry out, but they can't anymore, their mouths have already been confiscated and packaged in separate packaging. Larynx of calf, ear, eye, minced, packed into twenty-decagram packages, next winter there'll be black snowdrops, the next winter all the lights in town will go out and everything will be in the dark. Pop culture will plant its own fake plants on the scene, artificial gerberas, artificial palms, dummy flowers potted directly on an infertile tray, in fiberglass insulation. Fireworks fly into the air, candy wrappers fly into the air, leaflets fly into the air, soap bubbles pop, the chalices turn over on the tables.

And the sky is like on the final day of the apocalypse, dark, drooping, that if I felt like stretching my arm upward I'd smash it all, the stitches would pop and the whole construction would crash the fuck down on the town, the branch offices included. With purgatory and the whole manufacturing backup system. That's what I'm thinking. And the umbrellas affixed with Coca-Cola logos are like leafy white-and-red plants calling to heaven for revenge, turned inside out. And plastic cutlery, plastic dishes fluttering through the municipal amphitheater in the same direction as the smoke, like on their own wind.

Suddenly Arleta says to me as follows. That if I treat her to a big soda and fries, then she'll tell me something she knows 100 percent for sure. I wonder if it's worth doing business with this kind of degenerate. I tell her that at most a small soda and that's it, that that's what I can treat her to. To which she says that it's information worth a kilo of speed and a rotisserie chicken, but she's giving me a deal because I'm her good friend, her pal, her friend's ex-boyfriend, her own ex-boyfriend to boot, it's known that the whole situation's changed and she'll tell me, just between us, for a soda and fries. So I tell her to tell me, and then I'll judge how much that information's really worth. To which she says okay, but so I won't be surprised and suck in a lot of fresh air, so that I won't choke. That in today's elections for the most likable girl at No Russkies Day, at six o'clock, Magda's going to win.

I'm cool. Total rigidity. Like what's the big deal, that it's Magda. Who is this Magda, anyway? Maybe I used to know her, but maybe I didn't know her at all. Maybe I used to have some points of convergence with her, but now I don't, because everything's deleted with that bitch, that fucking beauty queen, who I've seen more than once in these situations, in just panty hose, in broken fingernails, how she licks my pockets clean of traces from the baggies of speed, how she pulls her panties up, how she watches TV, puking on her dress, because shows of the reality-TV genre do that to her, that she can't pull herself away and go to the john. That if they had to show that on a projector now, that'd be an ultraviolent film restricted especially to adults with especially strong nerves, because the weaker ones would utterly break down into blood and bone.

So what?—I ask like all indifferent, so as not to give any impression about myself and to treat her to as little as possible out of pure malice. Because that's Arleta, and as soon as I buy her a soda, Magda's going to show up right away and say: Let me have some. Anyway, it's not for her, since that soda's from me. Since it's fake and poisoned, a black soda paid for by myself and my mother, and then Magda will come up and say: Give me a sip, it'll poison her, it'll be bad for her, she'll choke on that sketchy soda stinking of my money, she'll choke and stain her beautiful dress and no one will take her as their beauty queen. And she won't go to the West to have a career as a secretary, to have a career as an actress, because they don't let those coughers across the border, because they spread germs, the spoilers who don't have residency rights in the European Union.

But Arleta doesn't lose hope that she'll wheedle something out of me. I didn't get there yet—she says. But keep listening, because it's a whole story like there's never been in this town. She's going to win the election because she gave it up to one of the organizers. But it was worth it. Now she's supposedly going to get a mountain bike and a tiara and, you know, different chocolates, a voucher for some shoes.

By now it's hard for me to hold myself back, though I'm really trying not to get more pissed off. But in spite of my efforts, my attempts, I start to look around and I brush off some guy who's blocking me maybe sort of too strongly, some fucking pop with two kids who's buying them some kielbasa or other shit wrapped in paper. And indeed he tips over into the mud, but then he gets up, helped up by his kids, brushes off his suit pants and says to me: Well, pardon me, sir. The kids are both handicapped, one of them's wearing glasses, and the other, a female, is also abnormal, they're wiping the mud off his pants, they're all brushing off in the name of familial solidarity. So I say to him, already quite irritated: Why don't you watch where you're fucking going, and next time use contraception.

By that I mean those kids, between the two of which one has it worse than the other. Because what's the point of that dickhead producing that crap on a massive scale, what's the point of him poisoning society with such garbage, so I have to work for the medical care of these two duds.

Then he says that it'll be just as I say, and he stresses to his kids that they have to go, because it's already too expensive. Then Arleta, like, jumps up, flies after him at once, and calls out that I said that he has to buy her a large soda. He turns around conscientiously, the kids affixed to his pants, his glasses busted in a critical spot, and already wants to make his purchase when I say: Stop. Don't buy her anything. She's not worth it, she can go take a drink from the river.

Then he quivers all over, so that I wonder if his esophagus or some other cord or pipe hasn't gone bust from the shock. He looks first at Arleta, then at me, and then he rushes to drop this whole business in a rushed tempo. Arleta laughs, says: You did him good, lately this place has been full of some Greek-Catholic element that hangs around everywhere and breathes our common air.

So I don't give a shit what Arleta considers on this subject. So I don't give a shit what Magda's up to. I'm not, like, pissed off. But my leg is so much atremble that the swill is splashing in the chalices on the table. Then I look at the riffraff, the lumpenproletariat, which rolls by in a wave in front of the entrance, clasping white-and-red cotton candy and white-and-red hot dogs in their dirty mitts. And that fucks my shit up all the more, because first it's a lack of hygiene, whether it's white and red, or red, or something else, and then salmonella and worms in the aforementioned or other colors. And then puking, a white-and-red wave of puke splashing through town, a wave of puke clearly visible from space, so that the Russkies will know where our state is, and where theirs is, and how in Poland we're going to engineer a common campaign of solidarity against the predatory partitioners. Magda's not here, for sure she's sitting somewhere backstage or in a trailer and with lightning speed she's giving her ass to the sound guy, so that he'll turn up the volume when she'll have to say something, for example, what she likes to eat, what's her favorite weather.

But it's hard for me to restrain myself, because let her keep her mountain bike and good for her, and also her beach ball and a visor for sunny days, all the best, but after all she's not going to give it up officially to anybody in my absence. And then, unintentionally, I see before my eyes this, like, organizer. Minister Manager, Esquire. How he's an asshole toward her, how he's brutal, a portfolio in one hand, a calculator in the other, and that's how he does her, calculating the income and expenses of the Society of Friends of Polish Children, calculating the dollar exchange rate, calculating the alimony for Sophia, his wife of twenty years, counting the age of his children on his fingers. Magda asks if she's pretty enough for him, meanwhile he's signing for the receipt of certified letters from the district prosecutor. He says that indeed she's very pretty, she's so very pretty that she shouldn't turn to him right now, because he's messing up the receipts, he's messing up the calculations, he's messing up his game of solitaire, he's messing up his building blocks, shut up and concentrate on giving it up.

And listen to the best part—Arleta says, since she already sees what kind of impression she made and that I'm head-fucked with hatred and rage. Listen to the best part, because now it's about to get hotter—she says—because that, like, organizer, that manager wants to pluck her out of town and take her to the Reich. Maybe even me, too, if everything goes well and there's no trouble with the papers. Because I have issues stemming from sort of taking part in an assault, but we can probably come to an arrangement, that's what he says. That's the information. Magda's leaving. She's flying off to warm countries. Along with me, anyway. We're not going to see each other anymore, Nails, so for once you could be fair at the very end: a soda and fries, now. It could be just the fries, because I have the munchies.

I stand there for another moment. I'm standing there, and those words she just uttered are reverberating in my head like a radio broadcast direct from the scene of the accident, straight from the scene of the crime, and you can still hear the corpses' last sighs through the speaker, the last groans of the recently deceased, the rustle of their fingernails still growing. He's plucking. Magda. To the Reich. The manager. All the locks clamp down at the same time, a teddy bear for Poland slapped down in the passport, the gates crash down on the heads of passersby, Angela dies in half-coitus with Sztorm, spitting a small, black, charred infant out of her mouth, Natasha spits on the floor and her drool hangs halfway in the air. Arleta leans down and, collecting fries from between the boards, catches her fingernail on a strip of wood. She wanted to say to the Bartender: Thank you very much, but she ends up saying: Thanks. Because everything's suddenly coming to pieces for me, the whole fest arrested in half-step, at the word all the children throw open their hands and white-and-red balloons float into the sky, which for sure is visible from space, and the phenomenon's scale can't be overestimated. All of a sudden everything, as if it's stopped, the whole fest ossifies, the whole fest is lacquered with hair spray, the end. Someone was falling over, someone was laughing, on the stage an even newer band was performing a song still different from the last. And now it's the end, a period placed several times at the end of the sentence, the white-and-red flags are hanging at half-mast, the laces of Arleta's Adidases are untied. End of story, the roof of the amphitheater blows up and crushes the performers.

Hey, Nails, don't dick me over now, huh, Nails?—Arleta says.

I'm silent. I don't say anything. I watch. Watch. Not saying anything.

But Nails, I've got the Pac-Mans, if you don't get me something to grub on, I'm going to die of starvation—Arleta whines, and, seeing a piece of kielbasa stuck between the slats of the little table, she digs it out, again with her fingernail, and eats it, but after a second she spits it back out onto the table and says: That was something else, but I don't know what the fuck it was.

Well, go and die as quick as possible—I answer her pretty aggressively, moving more forward. Drop dead right now—I say. Because she's not going to get anything, she'll only lose what's left of her vertical posture and they'll have to make her a special casket for her bent-forward corpse and an additional vessel for her imploringly outstretched arm.

If you won't buy it for me, I'm going for Lolo—Arleta says in a huff.

But I don't care what more she has to say, what she thinks, who or what she will or won't bring down on me in the name of collecting her dues, because now, as far as I'm concerned, this one here can even place a call to Vargas himself and, like, tell him I promised to buy her some fries, but now I'm blowing her off, and to that Vargas can answer to me: If you promised, then be a friend and fucking buy it now, and then I'll say to him: I'm not buying shit, that's right, I'm not buying shit, not for her, not for you. Exactly, you can both go suck each other off, because now I don't give a shit whether I do good deeds now or not, what's the section where it says what level I'm going to after I die, up or down. That can suck my dick. But I'm not even going to debate whether there is a God or there isn't a God, because even if there were, He went to sleep a long time ago if He sent that shady manager down to Magda. Without wings but with a portfolio. Maybe not holy, but with cash. And it's the one moment while I'm raking with one hand through that riffraff, that she's whirling idolatrously around her royal kielbasa and fries. Maybe a couple people fall down, yet I don't see it, because if things get hairy, these people will put it all on Arleta now, because she's standing now and looking behind me, saying: Nails? Nails, I'm talking to you. Don't be a jerk, and buy me what I need, so I won't call our friends. Nails?

And it's already getting pretty heated, because my blow caused several people to lose their freshly purchased food, and now it's frothing in the mud, steaming. And now, Arlettie, though you're looking at it covetously, there won't be any food, in a second now they're going to grab you and kill you, and it's not enough that there's zero soda and fries, not enough that they're not going to give you anything, as compensation they'll even drag out from your insides what's left of what you were eating there, that fry dug up from between the slats. Because I'm saying see ya, though for sure we're not going to see each other anymore now, at least you're not.

And I calmly go. In the direction where I think I'll find her. I look around. White-and-red-swirled ice cream. Polish dolls in Mazurian and other folk costumes. Ten bucks—ten shots from an air rifle into a cardboard cutout of a Russki. If there was shooting into Magda, I'd pay for that. Fu—and there goes her shoe. Fu—and there goes her leg. Fu—and there goes her ass. And that'll be enough for me, let her stay that way, Magda missing the ass she couldn't give away to anybody, I wouldn't torment her any more than that, maybe I'd even take her in just like that, bring her to my place.

I'm walking. Totally calm. One foot after the other. First I have to push through the riffraff, and later it already knows its place and cowers in packs before me, steps out of my way. The squeals of the trampled, a dress torn on the fence, the packs falling over, kielbasa flying into the mud. Totally baffled faces gawking at me. I'm going. Calmly. Because I know what I have to do, and now no one's going to come up to me and say, Nails, Nails, chill out, everything'll be cool. Nobody's going to shove a cigarette in my mouth and say: Smoke, smoke, Nails, that'll do it for you, don't worry about Magda, she's like that. I take out a cigarette, I light it, though it's windy. And as I take out the matches, they move back even farther, they hold their breath, because they're afraid I'm going to light up everything for them. That I'm going to light up these pregnant women, their membranous skirts puffed out by the wind, those wrinkled suits, baby carriages full of children like some byproduct, their cotton candy on sticks. But I don't do that, because I don't feel like it. I know very well what I have to do.

And when I'm walking and I spot where the backstage areas are, the dressing rooms, I run into Kacper. Kacper. Who's totally out of place. Since I haven't seen him in several days. Plus he's with some girl I've never seen before.

Kacper's eyes are popping out from the speed, glazed over and shiny, like cabinet knobs, he's executing a superfluous number of movements. I ask if he's going to introduce me to his friend, because maybe I've seen her somewhere already. Then she says: Ala, and she gives me her hand with a gold ring that I notice right away. She studies economics—Kacper says, and puts his hand on her butt, so that I'm surprised he doesn't blow his wad from satisfaction. She gently but firmly removes his hand and says: But at the same time I'm finishing a course for secretaries in German. After that course I'll be able to work anywhere, in offices, in secretaries' offices.

I don't even have time to really examine her, because Kacper asks me where I'm, like, going. I say, like indifferently, that I'm going, you know, to find Magda. Then I see that he suddenly gets a little nervous, looks in all directions, takes out a cigarette. At which point she, this Ala, puts her hand on the pack and looks him in the eye as if she'd arrived here from a distant chapter of the Partnership for a Drug-Free Poland to execute the moral rescue of a victim of nicotine. Then he, it's obvious that he's totally pissed, but with the motion of a dog, he puts that pack away in his pocket and says:

Come on, Nails, come with us somewhere, we'll have something to drink, we'll chat about this and that, I'll tell you how it is with Magda.

Then right away that young lady stands at attention like she's been jolted with electricity and says: What, no way, Kacper, in that case I'm going back home. And it's like she's come out onstage at the schoolwide auditorium regarding the destructive effect of alcohol and cigarettes on fitness and sports eligibility.

I'm saying let's drink, I'm not saying let's get fucked up, that means let's get a drink, I'm just saying one beer in a 0.2L glass.

And that girl is wondering what she's supposed to say now, what would happen now in the script, and she finally remembers and says: But Kacper, you know, after all, that that's what they always say, that that's just a way of cheating yourself, a moral smokescreen. You know what kind of agreement we have, and if you take me seriously, then you should respect it.

Kacper looks at me apologetically and says with distress:

Nails, let's get a soda—then when the girl turns her head after some bird or balloon flying by, he performs a dramatic gesture with his hands and eyes for me, real theater, and from that message it follows that the girl doesn't put out and is unbending in general. But once we turn in the direction of the drinks concessions, she lets him catch hold of her little finger, and Kacper shows me with his eyes that maybe there will still be some happy times from her, from this Ala, that maybe he'll still get some good out of her, some pleasures.

So let's go. It's apparently contrary to my plan, contrary to my intentions at the time, but I think that if I have a little to drink, my whole plan will gain sharper lines, all of which lead to the dressing room, backstage. Okay. Kacper buys a small soda for himself, a small mineral water for, like, this Ala, and a brew for me. Okay. We sit down. He's all jitters, like he'd blow to pieces if he were to take one more bit of speed. He's bouncing his leg. He glances once at Ala, then at me. Ala says she has to go to the bathroom now and looks meaningfully at Kacper, so that he won't accidentally drink the whole soda in her absence, so that he won't get into a brawl. We watch as she goes off in the direction of the john. It's like this with her: first of all there's the turtleneck. Gray hair, mouse gray, clasped at the crest with a pin engraved *Zakopane 1999*. Around her neck there's a chain with a cross sticking out onto her turtleneck, which I noted earlier. Then: pants from a suit or from a dress suit, tapered toward the bottom, plus orthopedic sandals. She's a girl of the mother-hen variety. She'll tidy up, cook, convert to Catholicism. But not for Kacper, no one will convince me of that. And even before she opens the little door to the Porta Potti, she glances anxiously, and Kacper waves at her knowingly. And as soon as she closes the little door, right then he starts to pat down his pockets with excessive vehemence, pulls out a baggie, and eyeballs the amount to pour into the glass, which he half spills because his hands are shaking. After which he drinks it down ravenously, wipes up the leftovers with his hand, licks it from his fingers. Then he starts to pretend that, like, nothing's happened, elbows to the table, hands to the quilt, the wind was blowing but has stopped blowing, it was raining but it's stopped raining, free time, calm, nothing's changed, the world hasn't ended.

She's hopeless—he says to me suddenly, after a moment of silence. I've been with her two days, and she's already telling me to come to her house and have dinner with her parents. There's no talk about the giving up of the ass for the time being, I've already worked on that. Though I still had some hope that that will soon change, because if not, shit, we'll go to a nursing home for vacation.

Then he looks apprehensively toward the john, since she hasn't come out for a pretty long time.

She sure is taking a while—Kacper whispers hysterically, and I wonder if he's already lost it—she's fallen into the Porta Potti.

A second later, she comes out with a new image. A new hair color and a new face color. Hey!

After which, looking around, he leans way over the table and lights up one of my smokes. Wait, he says, looking around apprehensively. I have to keep talking until that pro-family cunt comes back: fuck.

Then he says a couple times: Motherfucking bitch, this sucks my fucking cock.

But a moment later, the Porta Potti opens up and out comes Ala, so it seems she didn't take too long, she's alive and doing well, she straightens out the elastic band of her panties and looks around proudly, extremely happy, a deeply evacuated princess. So right away Kacper shoves the cig into my hand, Take it, take it, fuck, take it from me as fast as you can. So that all of a sudden I have to smoke two cigs at the same time, so that it doesn't go to waste.

She sits down. And immediately it's: Pardon me, but I had to use the facilities for a moment. But now I'm here. You know, now that I've sat down, maybe I can tell you this story. That is, it's not exactly a story, it's a movie I happened to see recently at the Silverscreen theater. Actually, I went there with my parents and my sister, and my cousin, too, who was visiting us just then. She'd brought us a lot of meat products, but unfortunately, Mother had to throw them out, since there are a lot of cases now of salmonella, staphylococcus.

Kacper's bouncing his leg and looking everywhere all around him, sometimes he puts in, not looking at her: Good!

But don't interrupt—she says then, mildly offended—You never let me finish, even though we've known each other for several days already. But keep listening. So we went to this movie theater. Not remembering that I'd misplaced my ticket somewhere! My sister says to me: You know, Ala, you're a scatterbrain! Well, heck, then I got annoyed, because I really do happen to be absentminded. That's just my personality, and no one's going to be able to teach me otherwise. Then I said to myself: Jeepers, that ticket has to be somewhere. And just imagine, do you know where it was? I had it right in my purse, on the very top. There's that saying: hidden in plain view. Obviously apropos of nothing. So then we went into the theater. I've already been to a bunch of movies at the cineplex, but my cousin Aneta, for instance, she comes from a pretty small village, and for her it was perfectly exotic. I'm telling you, I was even embarrassed, everyone was looking at her. But that doesn't matter, I'm digressing. And then the movie started. It doesn't matter what it was called, you've certainly seen it. There was this woman and a man, anyway, you've certainly seen it. Various trials and tribulations, first she dumped him, then he went back to her, you know. It all took place in America. I think that the best part of the whole movie was when there was this car accident. That is, of a bus with a car. And they were the ones in that bus, but they didn't know each other yet. And they fell on each other, it was wildly funny, and even my mother was laughing, she thought it was really funny. The worst scene, in my opinion, was when the hero and heroine go to bed together. You understand. They make love. I felt really embarrassed, because I was sitting there next to my dad, and I brushed him with my shoulder. It would appear that he felt embarrassed as well. All the time it seems to him that I'm his little girl, that I don't know anything about the evil of this world, about the real quagmire. And you know how it turned out?

Nails, you know that Magda's leaving?—Kacper says pretty seriously, looking at me.

I'm sorry, I'm off the subject—Ala answers him—you're talking about Magda? I have a buddy named Magda, she's in my year, she's great with the macrostructures of sociology. Though she's a hopeless workaholic. Her name is Magda Stencel. Her parents are both in law.

No, we're talking about a different Magda—Kacper tells her slowly and distinctly, as if he knew some other foreign language that's spoken through the teeth. And I'm afraid that blood will be spilled in a second, that there's going to be trouble, because he's slowly losing his patience and good heart. Though she has a thoroughly innocent face, like there's a hymen imprinted directly on the face.

You know, Kacper, I get the impression you're not eating well—Ala says suddenly—you're sort of nervous, just eternally unnerved. Chill out a bit, because you're sort of tense, completely atremble. I haven't seen this side of you.

Kacper looks all around nervously and says: I'm going to take a piss, as though he were saying: May you meet divine retribution.

Then she looks shyly at her leather purse, takes out a Kleenex, and wipes the countertop clean of what had spilled from the soda and my beer.

Listen—she says to me—Andrzej, because that's what you're called, Andrzej, right? I'm Ala. I'd like you to tell me one thing, as a friend. Honestly. Even the worst truth. Because in my opinion, the worst truth is better than the prettiest lie. Does Kacper do drugs?

No—I reply. I'm watching as the kielbasa's frying, as the flags are waving, as the plastic cups are tipping over.

No narcotics, serious?—Ala asks, not completely convinced—neither hard nor soft? That's good, because I don't stand for that can of worms. I know that a few of my acquaintances from college have something to do with that stuff, but I wouldn't put up with it if my boyfriend wallowed in such decay. It supposedly destroys your mind, destroys your brain cells, then people are totally sick, physically and mentally wasted. They keep bad company, sell off all the stuff in their house. It's awful.

With my head I make a sign, somewhere between yes and no, that I agree with her.

To which she says: Listen, Andrzej, do you have some kind of problem? You look like someone who's depressed, down. Tell me honestly. Maybe I can help you, if I know how. I've just gotten through a transition myself, not long ago I broke up with my boyfriend. We were together for two years.

Flowers, kisses, you know. I left. Though he studied international relations, maybe you know him. I'll tell you honestly how it was. Because I'm an honest person by nature, spontaneous, and I value those kinds of people. Without complexes, without false taboos.

Aw fuck, I think to myself.

And it just so happened, she says, that when we'd been together for a year and a half, when we had that anniversary, he brought flowers, wine. I blew a fuse, because after all, neither he nor I drinks. Pardon me, but this is very personal. It turned out that it was all about the proverbial proof of one's love. I say, holy cow, after all, I'm not some loose woman. I asked him whether my affection, my being close to him, isn't enough, because if not, we don't have anything to talk about. We had a pretty bad fight. Can I call you Andrzej? Dammit, Andrzej, was that dignified, responsible, on his part? He was twenty-one, I was twenty.

Have you heard the legend about the apple that gets nibbled, that once bitten it rots, it gets all wormy?

Then something within me stops playing. Talk, keep talking—I encourage her, and I go to the bar for a minute. I ask them if they know where that boy is who was sitting with us. To which they say that he was sitting with us, and then he went to the Porta Potti, and when he came out, some girl was waiting for him and they both went off somewhere.

I ask what that girl looked like, the one he went off with. They, that she had long blond hair and a rather elegant low-cut dress with tulle, and a batting left eye.

Then I know right away: Magda.

And when I get back to the little table, totally beside myself, she's in the same position, like a hair-sprayed newscaster on the TV news, and she'll inform the entire nation, assiduously taking notes, that: Because I'm not a girl who's easy like the others. And I hope, Andrzej, that you agree with me on that.

Right—I reply pretty shortly and gloomily, because in light of recent events, I've gone minimal. Because I say no. That's right, no. She can tell herself what she likes, can start singing all the songs she knows, including Christmas carols, with a music video and the text running underneath. She can run down all her sins starting from the first grade in elementary school, providing the level of advancement as well as taking into consideration the ratio of their frequency to her increase in body mass. Because now she can do anything. She can describe the operation on her appendix and the stages of eliminating her baby teeth in favor of her adult teeth. Yes, feel free. And I'm just going to watch. She's of average prettiness, but

paper,
as stream of
consciousness

maybe if need be. If need be, I can turn my head and look somewhere else, just in case, at the furniture, the view out the window. She's probably been growing that hair since her first holy communion, and she's going to chop it off right after her wedding so that her relatives will get the message about her happy married life. Frankly put, a certain kind of disgust seizes me at the very thought, because I know it'll take some difficulty, some effort, for me to get some, like I'd have to put the moves on my mom or worse: make use of some unidentified domestic fowl, some undercooked poultry. Because this girl has a livid and undefined appearance, which disgusts me, which irritates me.

So because of that I become pretty cold and crabby, and with regard to those very reflections on the subject of her bluish look, I want to show her a bit of acerbity, acrimoniousness.

Do you live in a cellar?—I throw in, like not seriously. Because one way or another, either I'm going to beat around the bush, you're pretty and beautiful, or not, and that's how I'll have her, and it's inevitable, it's a done deal.

Indeed, Kacper took Magda away from me. And although it's absurd, though it's pure unadulterated assholeishness, no filler or additives, 100 percent sugar-free assholeishness with no artificial coloring, though for me it's a total shock, a downfall, the rape of my worldview, that's me and that's how I'll get mine and even a little extra. And then, in a whisper, I do some calculations on my fingers. He's waxing Magda's ass, that's plus one for him. But Magda gives it up to everybody, that's minus one and a half for him. I'll wax his Ala's ass, though for me that's minus one on account of her looks. But on account of her not giving it up to some dickhead of two years, plus for the fact that in the course of several days Kacper hasn't managed to wax her ass even once, for all that, it's plus three for me.

She looks at me as if taken aback and says: In a cellar? How did you get that idea? My dad's a teacher, and my mom's a teacher as well. We live in a one-family house nearby. I'm glad that I don't live in a big development. It's maybe a little infantile in general, but I raise budgerigars. This intelligent and social bird comes from Australia and lives there in large flocks, in Poland the budgerigar is the most popular parakeet. It's smallish, not difficult to breed, and you can easily teach the male to mimic various sounds. You really have to clean the cage every day, monotonous as that may seem.

Then I, while listening to her sea yarns, resolve to go for the concentrated attack, the air raid, the air drop. So I say to her that she's very well read, though when I utter this, it sounds a lot like I was saying that she shouldn't be offended, but I want to kill her.

Thanks—she says—thanks, Andrzej, but I'll say to you as a friend, regardless of how you feel, let's just be friends for now. I don't want to get to know new boys before everything's sorted out. But that doesn't mean that we can't be good friends.

By the way, I sort of have a little question, have you seen Kacper anywhere?

Then I whip out stones and anti-chestnut rifles, a heavy-armored, vengeful invasion force tramples Ala full steam right in the middle of her foot, in its orthopedic sandal.

You see . . . —I'm saying, looking first at her, then at my own empty goblet. And though she's one of those kinds you shouldn't touch with a stick through her clothes, because you, too, could catch that serious illness through her toxic turtle-neck blouse, as well as some incomparably worse syph, I know that I have to, because that's my relationship to her as a male of reproductive age. So I say to her, pretty sad and all embarrassed: You see, Ala, can I call you Ala? It's hard for me to say, but I have to be honest with a girl like you. Kacper is wanted for sexually assaulting women. *The Vampire of Zagłębie II,* an erotic film from the U.S. of A., period, the end. A total aberration, an unnatural bending of his George toward women as defenseless and pure as yourself. That's all I'll say, because it's not a topic for a chat over beer and salted pretzel sticks. This is no joke, it's not a reprimand from the supervisor and an administrative fine of ten zlotys paid in installments.

I see her all-out shockedness and the sudden atrophy of her face toward the floor. So then I keep going with the triumphal ride of the man-man army over the fingers of girlish illusions. The flagpole pounded into her orthopedic sandal, the international George flutters proudly in the breeze and shows his fuck-you.

You know, Ala, I'm sorry to say it. Like that Kacper. But ten years of a suspended sentence, the collection agency on him, an irregular attitude toward his military service, alimony payments all over the country. Producing shady bastard kids at every step. Wherever he goes, he'll make a stray kid like they're carbon copies. Full steam. You saw when he went to the Porta Potti, that he was looking at you in that way, that from the moment I first saw you, I sensed that he wants just one thing from you, and you and I know what that is.

And after the presentation on martyrological matters, a poem recited about the victims, you may be seated, smoke peacefully. Totally satisfied with myself, I pull out a smoke. But totally stricken, she looks at me like she'd maybe read in a wall newspaper posted in the stairwell, when she was on her way home, that tomorrow she'll die by her own hand and there's no reprieve from the decision. Suddenly she laughs in capital letters and says something to the effect of my being truly tasteless.

You can laugh, but I'm serious—I affirm pretty gloomily. There's proof, there's a lot of proof, a lot of women cry over him late at night. At least ten in this town, a hundred in Poland, including fifty Russkies. Because he's a common pervert, forgive my saying so, a carrier of effectively concealed deviations, like, let's stay friends, let's stay friends, but in reality he's all about one and the same thing, anyway, you know what.

You're just joking, maybe, Andrzej . . . you're screwing with me . . . —she says, though it'd be better if she wouldn't say that, because when she does, she becomes pale, and then she looks even worse than ever, like her ID photo's been thoroughly washed and rinsed of her facial features and identifying marks. With her Zakopane 1999 pin like warped by a staple, which is holding on with what remains of its strength.

So I'm telling you, and you can bet on this like on your first and last name and your mother's maiden name—I say to her sadly. I know this firsthand. It's good that he left. We're alone, we can have a calm conversation. And let him set up his factory for out-of-wedlock bastard kids somewhere else, in a stupid, easy girl, not like you. Because he's not worthy of you—I add with regard to erotic fantasy, because I know I've pressed the right button and the domino's fallen.

Enough already!—she says and looks ahead, drinking from her bottle of water, though she drank it all a long time ago. If I were to tell my mom that, I'd be forbidden from leaving the house until I was twenty-one. No, from even looking out the window. I still can't believe that that scumbag wanted to wrong me so perfidiously, maybe even take me off to Germany. He was tender, pleasant, toward me. Sure, a couple times he tried to give me a cigarette. That should have made me think, because after all, women don't smoke. Tobacco smoke kills unborn children, it kills blood cells in the blood, it wrecks havoc with regard to your respiratory system. The statistics speak for themselves, and I would advise you as well, Andrzej, to toss that filth into proverbial hell. Put it out before it puts you out. Forgive me, but I'll tell you a certain anecdote that should give you a lot of food for thought about your position. My dad used to smoke, too, and for him that was a mistake. He went along like that for twenty years, until one day he got sick. Out of the clear blue sky. And nothing helped, not cupping glasses, not vitamins, finally they had to give him antibiotics. From that time on he said to himself: No. I won't poison myself anymore, I have a wife, I have two magnificent daughters. And he quit. From then on he eats fruit drops every day. Mints. Mom's not pleased, because it gets pretty expensive. Even buying it wholesale.

Then I look around for a moment, it's four in the afternoon. So we'll still have time to come back here before the lights go up and Magda says what she thinks on the subject of her favorite weather. And then everything will already be over, after the whole shitty war for the lust of thy neighbor's wife, for George's fitness and for fluency in the shutting of eyes. And the result of that war is already known to everyone. I—plus two diopters and Kacper—minus half.

Then I take my hand out of my pocket, and I, like, just happen to reach over the table, I just happen to, unintentionally, brush Ala's hair out of her face. Right then I pretend to catch myself in that rather subconscious movement, and I withdraw my hand, furtively wiping it clean under the table of all the germs and protozoans that might have passed to me from this girl and creep all over me, lay slippery eggs in my jeans. From which gold-rimmed glasses will hatch first in a few days, then a cross on a chain, and finally a turtleneck shirt will crawl out, which will spell out death and my immediate demise.

Let's go back to my place—I say pretty sullenly, since that story with the bloodsucking germs and the insects is bugging me, and as if that weren't enough, it occurs to me what a truly satanic party I have in my apartment with the oral, the anal, and the blood, and I start to think about whether Izabela hasn't happened to come home and die upon seeing the pullout. So: Or maybe your place is better—I add quickly.

⁘

And whether Ala's really a virgin, I never found out firsthand. I'll talk about the reasons why later on. I also never found out if she's a woman at all. Because I rather suspect that she's not. She's something in between. Poultry. Domesticated fowl. A potted plant. An animal, typically shade-preferring. The kind that uses makeup powder, and between her legs it's stitched overhand so that no pervert would be able to take a swing at her holiness. Because she's probably a saint. Because she commits no sins. She doesn't drink alcohol and doesn't smoke cigarettes and doesn't have intercourse before marriage. For just these outstanding merits, she'll soon win a medal and the diploma of the Society of Friends of Abstinence for her unwavering opposition to people committing sins. For just these outstanding merits, she'll go to a separate heaven for non-smokers, where she'll get her own armchair in the common room. She'll sit there like now, legs crossed, and flip through a women's magazine called *Your Style*.

You know, Andrzej?—she's going to shout downward toward hell, where I'm going to sit and smoke cigarette butts, the stubs people toss aside, because I don't have anything else left—this periodical's extremely interesting. Really up to snuff. It has interesting articles, interviews, crosswords. You should read it and judge for yourself. It's ostensibly a magazine for women, but in my opinion, men can find a lot of interesting things for themselves, information, remarks. I'll toss you down a couple issues, and especially my favorite one, the May issue. They've printed a very cool and engaging memoir. The author's name is Dorota Masłowska, and she's sixteen years old. Besides the age difference, I think I could get to know her, be friends with her. She's an interesting person, original, artistically talented, she makes things and writes. At her age that's baffling, intriguing. Sometimes she'll write something and even want to laugh or cry. She also has a sense of humor. Although at the same time I believe that she's a person pretty much lost in the contemporary world, she's going through a rebellion, she's starting to smoke cigarettes. I think that if we were to get to know each other and become pals, she'd have a chance to change for the better, get herself together, and her life, her feelings would become easier. Because whatever you think about me, Andrzej, I know how it is—I wasn't always the way I am now. I used to clash with my mom, I wanted to be someone else, oh, I even thought about slicing off my hair, about totally changing my personality. But my mom remained my friend the whole time, she was strict sometimes, but I think it did me good.

While she's saying this, I'm sitting on the sofa bed and gazing out the window, to which she's Scotch-taped little horses made out of green tissue paper. Besides that, she's got glassed-in wall cabinets that keep the preserved corpses of stuffed animals, of the doggy and teddy-bear variety, in great condition.

On two planks attached to the wall, there's a movie poster for *Good Will Hunting*. She has a lot of keepsakes as well, a shatterproof porcelain mug marked *Sagittarius*. And when she sees that I'm staring at it, right away she explains it to me like she's talking to a dumbass: I got it for my eighteenth birthday. Although I don't believe in horoscopes, I think they're superstition, stupid fun for simple, internally undisciplined people. And I also got this chain as well. From my godmother.

Besides that, she has two parakeets, which both strike me as the spitting image of her, and since I'm pretty bored, I say stingingly:

Are they both named Ala?—and my allusion, my joke, really makes me want to laugh.

Of course not!—she says, walks up to the cage, and gives a little seed to each of those two starved motherfuckers. You don't give animals people names, don't you know that animals don't have souls?

Actually, I don't have a lot to say on that subject.

Are your folks home?—I ask her, because as necessary, I want to get things going with her already, I want to get down to business on her bony ass, I want to get it over with already, I want to have the points I've won and that are owed me and get the hell out of here, so that I don't pass out and miss the elections for the beauty queen.

No, my parents went to the church fair, and then to visit my aunt and uncle—she says, and right off she waters the flowers with a handy watering can, the various cactuses growing at her window. Then, suddenly, as though frightened: And why do you ask?

No reason. I answer cunningly: Nothing at all. I'm asking because I don't want to cause any trouble.

No one does—she replies with concern.—But don't worry, you know, they're really cool, despite appearances. They let me do everything. They're lovely, simply wonderful, they're my friends. I think that you should get to know them. They could help you for sure, they could come up with something for your problems and worries. They're, like, mature, serious, but sometimes I get the sense that they're a couple of teenagers in love. They ride bikes together, hand in hand, go to aerobics together, take walks together.

Then I, while she's saying this, picture to myself what that has to look like. That is, her old lady. First of all, she sleeps in her glasses in order to have a good view of what she's dreaming and not miss the appearance of Saint Amol from a headache. Needless to say, there's no talk of being touched by a man above the elbow for the sake of the inviolability of the person and the dignity of a woman. In my thoughts, I don't even bother with the man, since I have a certain respect for him. Because he had to invest many frustrations into putting together this whole stable of two unsuccessful daughters, driven to all means by a periodical for self-teaching teachers or some other women's magazine. Stifled, castrated, pushed to the edge of the pullout.

And then I begin to sense defeat. Because in this whole situation I'm overcome with impotence, an internal restraint is telling me, Stop, red light, hands away from the pan. Don't touch, because you'll get burned, don't touch, because you'll be infected. Don't use those towels, don't sit on that toilet seat, read the fact sheet before use. And while she's sitting next to me, she's cleaning her glasses with the hem of her turtleneck, after breathing assiduously on both lenses, I'm thinking, utterly drained of power, how to get all this going on. She's sitting pretty close, and I'm supposed to have a reaction to this other, meanwhile on George's part, it's the pits, apathy, George doesn't even want to look in that direction, he's pretending to be asleep, but actually he's rather trembling and sniffing around for a way to escape his destiny, down one of the pants legs. While his destiny is effectively smothered as well, tightly, between two thighs, closed for business, lights out.

Whereas she suddenly unwinds, who knows what or why I, instead of being satisfied, am revolted.

What do you think about politics, about this Polish-Russki war?—she says from up close, looking me in the eye. I immediately notice that she has sickly yellow teeth. I don't want to fall straight into armed conflict on national or nonnational issues, so I cunningly ask what she thinks on the subject. So she says:

My dad, who's very prudent, anyway thanks to that we always had different meats under the Commies, a big selection of different kinds of meats, cleaning detergents, he says that one shouldn't have any binding opinions in this matter. And he's right about that. Because now all of a sudden everybody's important, broadcasting their opinions, and then there won't be wise people anymore. And he's right on that. So when someone asks you who you support, I'll give you some good advice, Andrzej, refrain from any kind of ostentatious display. Because you can lose big. Are you taking me seriously?—she asks suddenly, looking at my mouth.

And why do you ask?—I say, sort of terrified, because I want her to get away from me, to leave already, no points, but mentally healthy, right out the door to dust off what remains of her feathers, her hair, to give Izabela my jeans so she can clean the dust off with a wet sponge.

To which she says: Why do I ask, why do I ask. Since, you know, it's not because I want to flatter you somehow. I was just thinking that we can go see my sister for a few days at the regional hospital. She's just given birth, it's already a year since she got married to Mark and the wedding, which was really nice, which had a really nice atmosphere. She's still in the ward, because little Patrick's probably caught jaundice. No one knows, hard and fast, how. Mom suspects that it's the fault of the doctors, who are incompetent, don't have goodwill toward their patients. Sometimes people even die because of it, killed by their doctors, who are the ones who are supposed to help them, the patients, the most, since it's absurd, paradoxical. Besides that, when it comes to so-called corruption on a common scale, doctors don't have a speck of loyalty, a speck of motivation to perform their professional duties. You can read about it in the current press, in the weeklies, hear it on TV shows, it's simply everywhere.

I keep quiet and proceed in such a way as to have the least contact with her surface. I feel all-out defeated, minus ten points and the discreet pattern of her spittle on my face from when she was talking to me. Her orthopedic sandal imprinted on my face. The heavy-armored army retreats in a panic to the deepest interior of my pants. A total withdrawal, a total rout.

So then I just become barely talkative, since my loins have already gotten word that this is the wrong address and that there will be no propagation of the species. George also wants to blow this party, because he knows there won't be any contests, no fitness games. So I start to shift, like, farther toward the blinds, so that she won't happen to imagine to herself too much that I want to be friends with her. So I try not to let her be too offended by my emigration, but perhaps she is. So right away I try to squelch the whole situation so she won't feel particularly hurt and it won't be like we don't have any topic for conversation and we just sit there ostentatiously not saying anything. So I ask her if her sister's heard of that disease gestosis. She says that indeed she has, that it's a troublesome complaint among pregnant women.

Then I get up from the sofa bed. I walk a bit toward the window. Then I walk a bit toward the door. Because I'm on the edge of what I can take, and I'm giving fair warning that if in the next few minutes I don't get either some brew, or even a bit of speed, or even just a Rubik's Cube to twist around, then first my nerves are going to start fraying, then they're going to get all fucked up, and I'm not responsible for what will happen after that. If only she would turn on spider solitaire on her computer for me or maybe put a calculator into my hand, then I'd be able to calculate those hundreds and thousands of points I'm behind because of her preposterousness, because of this person's generally fucked-up character. Because it's probably an infinite number that, it so happens, can't be counted in one's head. For a minute I think about what would happen now if God had even a speck of decency, of honesty. Because if it were like that, and not otherwise, if he had even a smidgen of goodwill, just a smidgen of logic, he'd have inserted a scene into this script so that now I'd have Magda, since from the very beginning she was purchased as a present for me. But no. Even in the ostensibly honest kingdom of God, there's corruption, confederation, kicking you when you're down, covering up the speed-filled trunk of your Golf from the police. There's even sleaze, dealing and prostitution are openly supported, as is the export of Polish girls to the West. God Himself poses as one of those, like, great extreme leftists, everybody gets an equal amount, no more, no less, just the same. And suddenly he slaps me on the paw, Give Magda back, Andrzej, go have fun with something else, now we're giving Magda to Kacper. And after that to Lefty, let him enjoy himself with something normal, since that boy spends too much time in front of his computer, since it's bad for his posture, his scoliosis. And you, Andy, don't worry, they'll give her back to you, right, boys? Swear to God and cross my heart. You have a good time with Ala now, she's a little not right, I'll say, busted and out of order, but that doesn't mean you can't have a good time with her, to want is to be able.

Fuck you, I'm not having that kind of fun—I say under my breath and look up. But it's not even the sky, it's a ceiling with peeling plaster, and that's not even a doll eager for fun, just a prematurely deceased TV host who's furthermore wearing gold-rimmed glasses and leafing through a periodical, sucking her finger.

If only she'd give me that calculator I was just mentioning. Then I could have a moment's worth of entertainment, addition, summing up, first all the digits from left to right, then from right to left, and finally multiplication. I'd calculate everything. In relation to Magda. Her height. Her age. The length of her hair. Her life expectancy. Kacper's degree of slant relative to her. The level of speed in her blood. The percent of her satisfaction. Certainly low. Certainly negative. The speed with which the Russki army is approaching the city. The amount of kielbasa sold. I'd count it all if she'd give me a calculator.

But she doesn't. She sits, gawks a little at me, and with her other hand she fixes something in her teeth. And it doesn't even cross her mind that in a second it'll be no more. That the fate of her horsies stuck to the window hangs in the balance, as well as that of her glass wall cabinets, since any minute now I'm going to light everything up, including her hair, which I'm going to trim anyway, not to mention trample to a pulp with my own feet. Finally this is how I put it. Because this is no joke anymore: Frigity-frigity, what do you think of me, Andrzej, am I pretty, am I ugly, is she like me. Because I am good by nature, but I'm also not a walking CARITAS shelter for listening to contraceptive chat from self-help books and not even get anything out of it, no pleasure, only melodrama and melorecitation, and long conversations about art, poetry, and protecting a conceived life at sunset.

And you're rather economical?—she says then, as if to say down with my thoughts, as if to kick me when I'm down, and take that, and that, you didn't want to talk about the weather, you didn't want to talk about gestosis, so we're going to talk about economy, yes, Andrzej, the jokes are over, roll the camera, hello, ladies and gentlemen, and welcome to our program, my name is Alicja Burczyk, and right now I'd like to list for you all our products now on sale, which we can buy in order to manage an economical and functional household. Because it's not as if by buying all the products like crazy, tossing them into the cart without rhyme or reason, we could manage the house modestly and safely. Shopping is an issue that requires precise consideration, planning, and calculation of everything, both for and against. Let's see, this meat looks good, apparently, but please just look at the price, it's horrendously high, especially since next to it there's a perfectly similar piece of meat, produced only a few days earlier, but still perfectly good, and it costs half as much. The first task is which meat will you choose, Andrzej, because perhaps you'll prove so extravagant as to choose the more expensive and, as a result, certainly the less tasty one. You don't have to answer, it's just important that you agree. Now we'll take the cart to the next area on our board. Before us is a shelf with textiles. Your task, Andrzej, is to choose the most sensible socks. Indeed, they're pretty durable, but for the price, you can have three pairs that are less durable but still good. Perfect, I recognize that movement of your head as assent and, as such, the correct answer. So let's move on, the next area shows a shelf with alcoholic beverages. Your task is: not to buy any alcohol in order to have more cigarettes. If you do buy it, you lose the prize automatically. If you don't buy it—you'll go on to the next levels, which are just as magnificent and full of emotion as this one. And we know that you, as a serious and reasonable person, will concur with our common choice when we all stand up and all together, in a single voice, loudly proclaim: Out with alcohol, shut down the tobacco factories, prohibit the sale of alcoholic beverages with more than 5 percent per volume, Andrzej, you're fidgeting uneasily, for sure you can't advance to the next board, which shows a fruit counter. Basket A, that's expensive fruit imported from the distant West, coated in a thick layer of poisonous pesticides—germs spread by the blacks who touched them. And now let's look into Basket B, that's Russki fruit, a little cheaper than ours, but they're doctored fakes, certainly empty in the middle. Whereas in Basket C, there's genuine inexpensive Polish fruit, even the bruised Polish apples taste better than the apples of the putrid West, it goes without saying, Andrzej is prudent and chooses Basket C, that's a magnificent, correct answer, assuring us all of a good time together in the next rounds of the quiz show.

Can I go take a leak?—I ask pretty gloomily, then I jet quickly to the john. I run the water loudly and, hoping that no one hears, go through all the cabinets. The narcotics level in this house is as follows. One nervosol. And one box of Tylenol. So I hastily dose myself with both these super-hard drugs, because I've suddenly started to dread. That I'd maybe gone nuts or something, that I'd gone through too much speed in recent days, a short on the circuit boards, a mess in the cables. Yes, yes, Andrzej, now Tylenol, nervosol, and then the station, I hear it right away and look around, but it was only an echo bouncing around my head. Impotence, zero interest in the woman sitting nearby, so maybe it's homosexuality, and just when I think that, I look right away into the mirror to see if maybe I have physical traits of faggotude, but I can't see anything, not one trace.

A moment later, so as not to arouse suspicions, I'm back and sit down in my place. The fun marches on. Welcome back. This board requires you to buy the shoes that are most sensible for you, Andrzej. And here we've given you a selection of fantastic and functional shoes from CCC, a company with outlets nationwide. They're shoes for all kinds of weather, as they're all equally practical, equally easy to use, you just put them on and go, for work and around the house, for skirts and for pants. For pants—I answer quickly, so as to have the right answer behind me as quickly as possible and not be accused publicly of faggotude and other tranny stuff.

That's it! It's all the hotter, there's more and more emotion, because it turns out, Andrzej, that you're just as you should be, economical, practical, and now for the next round of our program. These questions are controversial, maybe even embarrassing, whether you opt for yes or for no, you run into a classic six-person family from God knows where on our game board, and now how do you act, do you shove your egotistic, hedonistic, self-loving shopping cart to the side and make room for the real values, or will you push it against the stream, jostling God's children and knocking them over, stomping on their small, defenseless feet, knocking the inexpensive and comfortingly sweet heart-shaped lollipops out of their hands? Will you run over the feet of that man who works so hard to keep his crops alive? Will you give up your seat on the bus to a woman with a child in her arms? And even if you don't answer, your face speaks for you, that you're a decent person and would like to have a lot of children in the future.

And now we move on to another category, for which you're maybe better prepared, because maybe this is your hobby, the thing you're interested in, let's get to it, even if you're timid by nature, get focused now, the question is simple, a warm-up, since everyone, both myself and the studio audience, we're here with you and keeping our fingers crossed that you'll win on this program, so we'll ask you another question. This time on the subject of psychology, because I'm very interested in that, what kinds of interhuman correlations there are, how we can change ourselves, work on ourselves, fight against our weaknesses, cure our lives of anxieties and imperfections, and become conscious of our feeling of personal worth. Because I see in you that you're tense, hardly free, maybe that's why you won't manage to give answers to such truly elementary questions, maybe you're em-

barrassed because of me, and that can't be if we're to remain
real friends, because in such a situation we're supposed to be
open with each other, honest, spontaneous, not hide anything
from each other, our greatest weaknesses. Because I'll tell you
now, as well as all the physical persons watching our program:
a friend is a person with whom we can always remain ourselves
without suppressing our emotions, and do you have a friend of
your own? Write us about it, we'll await your responses on
postcards until the end of the week, valuable prizes are waiting, a subscription to my favorite magazine. But returning to
our show: maybe a different question now, posed in this way,
since that one was formulated in a way that was too difficult
for you, why are you so taciturn, is it because of the presence
of my person, do I embarrass you, if you like I'll leave, and the
television audience will close their eyes for a moment, and you'll
be able to prepare yourself freely for the given topics, you'll
figure out what you think about them, you can make notes for
yourself, the skeleton of a statement, and we'll have a conversation later, during that time we'll take a break in the taping,
our audience gathered in the studio will stand and we'll all take
a second and raise our arms, take a deep breath, and screw in
the little lightbulbs, while I'll stand up from the armchair, oh
yes, I'll take off my beautiful glasses, which were relatively expensive, even taking into account that it was when I was still in
elementary school, but it was sort of a purchase for all time,
I'll set aside my favorite magazine, which by the way is spon-
soring our program, and I'll tell you something, Andrzej, completely honest, that I myself am the prize on this program, if

you'll answer all the questions correctly, if you'll acknowledge that I'm right, if it turns out that you have the same interests, then you can kiss me, on the mouth, but very delicately, because I have very sensitive lips that crack right away, peel off together with their skin, I tear them off in pieces, I tear them off with my whole face and all my innards, but that's nothing, in the end there's nothing to worry about, because a second later I grow even better ones, with even longer hair than I have now, and the cross I have on my neck, oh, you see, it's growing back even bigger, as do my orthopedic sandals as well, my feet, and my hands. But we're returning to our program, I'd like to welcome all of our television viewers and our studio audience.

And we will begin this round with a key question, thanks to which everything hasn't been lost just yet—you can still even make it to the final, loosen up, because this is the last question and your fate hangs in the balance, will you get the main prize, or do we have nothing to talk about and then the end—everyone in the television audience gives you two thumbs down and, at the signal that will appear in the corner of the screen, spits at the television, and we don't want that, so take a deep breath, spit out your gum, the question is: What do you study?

What do you study, Andrzej?—Ala says again, putting on her magical gilded glasses, abracadabra hocus-pocus, and I study economics, I love a good book and a good movie, I don't listen to music of any kind, I'll meet a nice cultured boy without addictions between the ages of twenty-five and thirty for the purpose of a serious, cultured relationship.

I keep quiet. Quiet. She looks at me searchingly, don't you know the answer? Concentrate, you know for sure, after all, for sure, what you study, otherwise you wouldn't be here, since we all study something and we're not embarrassed about it, we admit it rather openly, think hard, since you certainly remember.

Fine, since you can't recall, first hint, listen carefully: so it's a course of study . . . connected with administration . . . with management . . .

Administration and management!—I say instantly and press the appropriate button on the sofa bed so that that answer won't haul ass off the screen before I have a chance to select it. And I look to Ala uncertainly, is that the correct answer.

She stares sort of searchingly, is that your final answer, do you really want to go with that one, are you sure, do you really want to go with that one.

Then I, already totally exhausted, repeat, Administration and management.

Oh jeepers!—she says, it probably turned out that the answer was correct. I was supposed to study that, too, my parents had already chosen that course of study for me in elementary school, but I didn't get in because there weren't any spots open, anyway my mom says that it's not because there aren't any spots open, only that I didn't get in because of the corruption, the cronyism, the incompetence of the ruling elites and the bad situation in the country, and besides that, my mom says that economics is good, too, and even better, more lucrative, it has greater prospects, and I definitely don't want to scare you, I don't want to worry you, but administration and management is a subject area totally doomed to collapse, after which you won't find work in any self-respecting enterprise. Anyway, that's what I always say to my bosom buddy Beata, who got in back then and thinks that now all of a sudden the world is lying at her feet, all of Poland, Russia included.

I'm going back to the fest—I say to that, not taking any resistance. Because the show's already over, and whether I won or I lost, whatever would happen, I'm donating the main prize to benefit orphans, to benefit the Polish Society of Polish Administrators, to benefit my best buddy Kacper, let him have that prize, by all rights it belongs to him, maybe he'll have some desire for it. And fuck if I'm not hundreds of points behind in my calculations, in my scoring, so that now I'd have to screw Magda a thousand times in a row plus Angela as a virgin a few times, too, in order to get back in the black with those points and not lose face.

Okay—Ala says, and is glad it's finally game over, end of airtime, and with that, the *Cook With Us* show has reached its end, our baked swan is ready for your consumption after removal of the fabric decorations, for the moment it still looks pretty unappetizing in its turtleneck blouse, but it tastes excellent, though it's a tiny bit stringy. It can be served at banquets and family cookouts as well as at official formal receptions.

It's a shame that you have to go already, it was nice talking with you, you're a cool friend. Wait for just a moment, I wanted to show you photos from my sister's wedding, it was a very pleasant reception, very tasty though modest dishes, a very pleasant, familial atmosphere. Sit here and don't touch anything—the baked swan says, and smoothes out her turtleneck, straightens out the positioning of the gold cross on her breast. And goes. And I don't waste that moment in time of being totally completely alone with myself, eye to eye with the potted plants and the wavy parakeets in her room. But after taking the aforementioned special medication, I feel sort of calm, calculating. Because I haven't mentioned it yet, but fuck that system, and I'm not going to cooperate with that system, no public interviews, I'm not going to take the floor as a participant in any "Pardon me's" about poetry, of this one thing I am certain. And that's my take. First I put a potted plant on the carpet, I whip out George and piss brashly into the flowerpot, though I let it out unevenly because of my nerves about being discovered, and I don't always get on with it ideally, such that some of it lands on the carpet. It doesn't all go in, so what's left, what remains, I put the parakeet cage on the floor and relieve my urine onto them, on their birdbath. So that in the meantime they're tearing their crooked snouts and fleeing among the rods, they're so afraid that Swanny's not going to come running, having learned of their torment by their calls. Calm down, fuckers—I tell them—a bit of urine from a normal person will do you better than a hectoliter of psychically sick water from Mother Superior.

But then they're like abnormally tearing their muzzles more and in a second will start trying desperately to fly off to warm countries for help, for reinforcements, because that freak raised them in such a manner that they don't know how to behave decently in the company of an average person, they're just set off and ready to jump on respectable, mentally normal people, they're clearly inclined to do me some harm. So then I'm looking at them like that, how they're completely stupid like their bitch-mother Ala, surely they studied economics, or: that one on the left banking and estate management, that one on the right finance and finance. Your mother's fucked—I tell them quietly, like it's a secret, and with a whisper, I spit on one of their heads.

Okay. Then, totally laid-back, I stick a couple things into my pockets, stuff that's lying out, a pen after the highlander style in the shape of an alpenstock, a gold ring with a little stone, and a glue stick, because that can always come in handy. Those are the consolation prizes provided by the host on the show, so that it won't be that I'm so drastically in the red, because it, like, so happens that the points are deducting themselves from me with every moment and are depreciating in value more and more, but that being the case, I should get some benefits from this whole event. Then I arrange everything the way it was and in a whisper, totally conspiracy-like, I open the door, and right away it reverberates with a substantial, drawn-out groan.

Are you going somewhere?—Ala calls out from the abyss, from such distant, nonexistent rooms, from the book club where the shelves are filled with, in alphabetical order, albums, literature, texts, photographs, a picture of Ala and her sister welcoming the parish priest with bread and salt, in Kashubian folk costumes, as well as a diploma for finishing elementary school, with a score with a red banner as well for exemplary work as class treasurer.

But when I hear that she's somewhere certainly far away and won't be able to run up here before I get out, I run down the stairs, grab my Adidases in hand, and run out of that house, smack into the gate. Where I'm breathing heavily and slip away, since when she ascertains my absence as well as the occurrences that went down in her personal ecosystem with regard to the flora and fauna, it'll be bad, maybe she'll start chasing after me or, even worse, will want to show me those pictures.

Some random bus came along just then, so I get in, though I have to admit that I feel weak, like sleepy, that I could ride like that on that bus without end, and no one would reproach me for not having a ticket because they couldn't even kick me out, I'm so heavy that that whole business would come apart in a second. Accordingly, we're moving slowly, most likely because of my weight, the weight of my hands, which are so heavy I can't lift them, they just hang there. I'm afraid that in a second they'll fall onto the floor along with the rest of my body, and nobody'll move them from there, lever them off. We're going slower and slower and the city is moving just as slowly, as if it's drifting closer and farther away on a wave on the sea, remote-controlled by bored town councilmen, drunk as pigs. There are clouds over the town, like ominous, drawn-out eyebrows. God's peeved, God's cleaning house. But for that Ala, if she were here, it wouldn't be so bad, I have to admit. Even if hellfire were falling from the sky, she'd show her student ID plus pull out her cross from under her jacket, and the panicking crowd all trampling each other would part before her, O student of economics, cultured, most obviously a Catholic, though she's with some sleepy boy, surely her own handicapped son, but in that case it's all the more necessary to help her raise him from his seat, unstick him from the leatherette. Parting, letting her pass, maybe they have important things to do, they're all going to check out the latest book by Bolesław Leśmian, they're all going to pick up their vouchers for potatoes, the fire will wait, the fire won't go away, stand back and let her through.

That's just what I'm thinking to myself, that I've fucked up in not taking her with me. Because now she'd lead me somehow or at least arrange my hands in alphabetical order, and in that very state I'd surely get to the Urals and no one would even wake me for the Christmas holidays, my mother all desperate because she bought me a present and suddenly it's confirmed that *nyet,* no Andy here, though a few months ago she called the apartment and he was there. And now all of a sudden he's not, for many months he's been riding an uncomfortable PKS state-owned bus to the end of the world, on funded research. I think that she'd be the only one to remember me in that situation, she'll send me a toothbrush, some spare socks, jam, needle and thread, and wishes for a lot of good cheer. And while I'm thinking that, I think about how my life's fucked up, that I've lost in so many things, and what's more, the devils have taken me with them as a keepsake, and meanwhile I'm not entirely sure whether maybe I've already died or maybe not, because the bus is definitely moving, but as if through a fog, through smoke, which is spreading inside. And my eyelids are closing automatically, wherever I look gets covered back up a second later, yet I always manage to notice that everywhere it's full of smoke, and the passengers are like as if devoid of borders, they spill out all over the bus, it being a rather warm day. And I also notice that their voices reach me as if through cotton, from behind a wall, from warm countries, from the other side.

And just then, when I'm thinking more and more slowly, more and more in capital letters, in increasingly blurry handwriting, I hear the following. Have you heard?

I hear that question. It's pretty clear, repeated several times over the background of the internal combustion engine, in which some particularly loud wind, or rather a cyclone is blowing.

No—I plan to say back, but it turns out to be a particularly difficult question on this quiz, because I can't move my lips at all, one way or the other, because they're sort of like covered in concrete, utterly cemented with flour paste or some other plaster, one set of teeth sealed to the other and affixed with a seal, top secret, do not open. While the one thing I still state is that I don't have a tongue in my mouth, it must have slipped out of me on some bend, it's rolled under the seats. While some meatlike creature is making an appearance in the tongue zone of my mouth, a gummy snake that I can't steer for shit.

Have you heard?—someone keeps saying to me, the echo reverberating, and as a bonus something's tugging at me from one side, some bonus auxiliary wind into my left shoulder.

And after a lot of struggle I succeed in pressing the right button, such that I truthfully say something sounding similar to no, but as though it were from a mouthful of undifferentiated potatoes, spuds. And right off I feel this dread that maybe now I've crossed into the realm of my garrulousness, my straightforwardness to the next level, and I shouldn't have said anything that might make them switch off the camera.

And that's a fact. Just as I say no, that whole carousel starts spinning anew, the wind tugs at my shoulder, the engine whirrs, and next, the next question sounds off, You haven't heard? You haven't heard and haven't heard, if you didn't understand the question we'll ask it again, and again, and finally until you answer, until you answer, and you can die, but the audience wants to know, you've heard, you haven't heard, the audience wants to know the truth.

And fully trusting my skills of articulation, I try to emphasize once again that no, but then it doesn't work out so well for me, but somehow otherwise, less comprehensible, maybe I even say something intermediate halfway to yes, because I don't know yet if I'm just hearing a buzz, and the smoke is thicker and thicker, less and less transparent, and that's what I see the moment before my eyes ultimately close.

⁙

And then there's a long break worse than snack time, and if I had to represent it graphically, I'd have to paint the whole sheet black and a few white ellipses at the top. Because I wake up just as I establish that I'm definitely walking, though maybe I'm rather rolling like a buttload of stones enshrouded in a rag and pretty much shit-sticking together, but able to fall to pieces at any old time. In any case, it appears that I'm in motion. Or it could also be that this street is moving along in my direction, rewinding here before me like a fucking white-and-red tape packed with flags like some birthday cake, a torte made for me by my mom, Izabela, on the occasion of my return from an inestimable darkness, where I was quite clearly in some kind of convalescence, rehab. Because that's the only way I can explain it to myself. I'm bringing various touristy mementos, kitschy commemorative landscapes in which you can see that very darkness caught in the daytime as well as at night, in profile, and from a bird's-eye view, and which always looks the same and is categorically black. I also have some photos taken with my own camera, me on a background of darkness, in which you can't see me, but I was probably there. Izabela, I'm also bringing you a little darkness in a jar, too, a regional specialty, a little opened, because the food wasn't so good, like low-calorie, not very nutritious.

Suddenly a burping rings out, and then I notice that the force that's driving me is Lefty, holding me up all friendly under the arm and by the belt. We're moving along, and that street's standing in place, with the small exceptions of passersby—I establish that as well. But how I got here, my recollections are really crystallizing pretty slowly, but surely it was one of the levels of the quiz show, would you prefer to go to heaven or hell after you die, for sure I recklessly chose the incorrect button and thereby the wrong answer, but now I'm already coming back with everybody to the studio, everything in its place, I'm not scorched, I can even walk with some difficulty. But for a moment I'm afraid that it was that question about homosexuals and now because of that, there's this embarrassing situation with the arm and his hand on my waist.

What are you sticking up against me for?—I say indignantly, unanimously affirming that I can speak well enough, though for example I don't have saliva in my mouth anymore, a total meliorization of my mouth, a draining of the wetlands, through which I feel a certain grinding in the hinges.

And then, totally beyond my control, I set a storm going, you wouldn't believe it, but on the part of my friend Lefty. Who then suddenly enlightens me about everything in a sort of vulgar and insensitive tone, that he doesn't know what I popped, but it must have been a load. That it was a crazy trip, the moodies and suicide, simply haloperidol, going to the other world by bus. And he also says it's good that he happened to be going in that direction as my friend and colleague, because I'd be in deeper shit, a side street, detox or even complete death, because I was already in such a state that three random passengers and one female passenger had to help him get me out of that bus at the appropriate stop, an awful shitstorm for the whole town, and I also fucked up his cell phone with my drool, which I was tracking onto everything, like I was just exhaling that drool. And finally he even underscores, as an example, how for my sake he invested a whole dose of speed onto my gums so that I could walk like a person, and I bust his balls about some gay inclinations, because if it were up to him, he'd sooner take a cat under the arm than me, because generally I'm not his type. And furthermore, while he was dosing me up, I fucked up the entire sleeve of his jacket around the elbow with my drool, which he even displays for me with these wet stains, but it looks to me more like at the least he overdid it with some hand washables, and now he's filming some sick movie for me.

I'd like to respond somehow so that he'd fuck off, because swallowing down some nervosol with Tylenol for frayed nerves still isn't a sin that I'd have to confess at the Last Judgment before Uncle Lefty, who isn't without sin on this point, either, because he likes to get seriously fucked up himself. But I can't say anything, because the whole time he's talking all kinds of shit that I don't quite understand. That something somewhere, that if they'd known I'd react that way to the news, they wouldn't have said it at all, just don't say a word, nothing to talk about.

Like, to what news?—I say to him suddenly, taken aback.

What, you haven't heard?—he asks me then like he's talking to an idiot—you haven't heard that Magda didn't win the beauty-queen competition?

Then I start to get it, that in town there's been some hocus-pocus during my spiritual absence and that not everything from that mélange is quite clear and logical to me. Get the shit kicked out of you for a moment, vanish for a moment, keep that whole business to yourself, and in one minute there's one big shitstorm of epidemic proportions.

What do you mean, she didn't win?—I say—That, like, she didn't win like she was supposed to win?

Supposed to, supposed to, but the fact that she was supposed to doesn't mean anything. The shady manager got screwed. He had debts to some Sztorm guy, he's some, like, big shot, he has shares in sand and a magazine, *Polish Sand*. And Natasha won, she came with Sztorm in his car, and there was also some metal-head cunt with them who got the title for Miss Audience Choice, though it's a hundred percent certain that no normal guy would allow himself to screw her when sober.

*   *   *

To which I keep quiet, because when I screwed Angela, I was on speed, and in that case the equation balances out, but that doesn't mean that all of a sudden I have any desire to discuss it. Because I don't, because let me emphasize that right now I feel categorically bad, particularly because the nervosol is sort of repeating on me.

So we go to like the amphitheater, like in that direction, but somewhere else. Because it isn't like Lefty's the least bit peacefully disposed. I even suspect that he skimmed off some of that speed for himself, that he borrowed quite enough for himself when he was reviving me from that wholesale apathy and stupor. And praise and respect to him indeed for having saved me from my demise, but he must have given himself a good bit, because his eye is fluttering, as if batting his eye were his obsessive neurosis or as if he'd taken part for instance in professional eye-batting, the one who bats the fastest wins. Eye-batting as a skilled trade, eye-batting as his favorite occupation in his free time as well as a progressive addiction to eye-batting.

He's all nerves. Quite clearly he's ready to fuck somebody up, perhaps even me. Even besides the fact that first of all he's my friend and buddy, secondly that he screwed my girlfriend and not just once or twice at that, and thirdly that he lost his whole dose for the sake of my demise, so it won't pay off for him to kill me now, because then he wouldn't get the amph back, a total waste and no profit from a serious investment. At any rate I try not to walk too close to him.

*   *   *

My mouth's really fucking dry—I tell him, my voice extracting itself from among the heaps of solid-state drool. And if, for instance, I didn't have so much culture, I'd spit like an asshole, but I don't do that. Because I dread that my drool would fly out onto the sidewalk no less than in cubes or more likely in sheets, maybe even in coils. I wonder if that's not the fault of some kind of shady amph from Vargas. Because that dude always keeps his doses inside his shoe with who knows what other kind of junk, and in these times it's not hard to get poisoning that way. Maybe in a minute now I'll be in my death throes, because I spit out all the water I had in me earlier onto Lefty's jacket and now there isn't a sad-little drop in me, and the powdered blood is sifting left and right from one vein to the other.

So fucking drink, don't talk—Lefty tells me as great advice for living, a maxim and a proverb for my whole life until they stitch me into the tapestry. Well, I'm not going to drink from a puddle, right?—I answer him sullenly, because I'm also in no mood for jokes, word games, and riddles. Then he shows some moderate mercy, because here, as never before, he sprang for the speed, and here and now he's the master of ceremonies, here and now he's cranking it up, so we're going to McDonald's. And we go in like a two-person team playing for Our Lady of Amphetamines. A big soda—I say to the cashier in my pretty rough convention, enough that she peeks out suspiciously from under her supercorporate visor, after which, at the sight of us, she's equally inclined to seal the register with Velcro. And she goes to the back suspiciously as well. Lefty is pretty much perked up, so that the whole time he starts talking all kinds of shit in the cashier's direction, though generally speaking, there's no chance of her hearing it in that corporate hinterland, especially since her corporate ears are muted as well as plugged by the corporate visor.

What the fuck, pour that soda and cool it with that express masturbation through your apron, because Nails's thirsty, and if you don't, I'll come back there and help you, but you wouldn't want that. And while he's saying this, I realize that he's right and makes a lot of sense in being so rough and cold toward the cashier. Because the truth is that at the very least, twenty groszy calculated into one of those sodas for both her work and the courtesy of her service and it can't be that just now she has her period, makes faces, sulks around, and does a feminist soda-pouring over a half hour at a gram per minute when I'm really thirsty now. So now I'm fucking pissed along with Lefty, and we stand like that as a pair and say across the empty counter: Come on, you Babylonian slut, don't suck Babylonian cock, just hand over that soda, because we're going to sic the capitalists on your mongrel children, so that first they'll gnaw on their little hands, then their little legs, then their little dicks, and finally they're going to gnaw away at you and things won't be so easy for you anymore with the grip, you're going to fucking poof away in a cloud and perform miracles, cure the faithful of the runs.

Of fucking rashes!—Lefty roars, so that everything shakes, the wind blows, and ripples, rifts, appear on the cardboard clown.

And when at last she obediently appears and carries the soda in one hand, and also as she, somewhat frightened, gives it to me, and she says four zlotys forty groszy, her hands shaking, Lefty suddenly gets all fucked up and says to her without warning: Hey. And when she raises her head timidly, he adds: Osama's going to fuck you over anyway.

Then I'm listening to what he says, and I think that this is my good buddy, cheerful, with a sense of humor, and that we can't allow Brussels to fuck us in the ass. So I catch the thread and say: Osama's going to fuck you up for sucking off those Eurococks.

Both Lefty and I are dead serious just then, Lefty's eye has even stopped running, since if it were running like usual, then the whole situation could be taken for a stupid joke, but it's not.

And thus consternation on the part of the cashier. Quiet. Her hand trembling on the corporate walkie-talkie. Give me that—Lefty tells her in a rather vulgar tone, nodding toward the handset—I always wanted to have that sort of shit for my first communion.

And as he's saying this, a wind flies from his mouth and blows through the cashier, scatters her hair, undoes her apron. She sways a little, like she would at least have to break into tears, and in a minute it's possible that she'll cry even more bitterly: I won't give it to you, I won't, it's mine, I got it from the boss. But that doesn't happen, she unfastens the handset from her belt as if in frustration and gives it to Lefty according to the order, with a face like that of a slaughtered animal.

But it doesn't end there, since Lefty is quite obviously totally wound up, he's completely engaged, and now he's decided to utterly fight against all the fingerprints of Euro-American truck-stop whores on Polish soil. And now get back there—he says to the rather unnerved cashier—and dig up another one of these devices for Nails. Only one that works, and nothing shady, otherwise you die.

The cashier looks at him and once at me, she has acne. She's looking at us as if she's just at least been smacked, just been hit with a branch, and now she can't snap herself out of the shock. Then she goes to the back and doesn't come out for a long time, and she returns even paler, carrying a walkie-talkie in front of her, throws it on the counter, and hastily retreats toward the coffee machine.

Then I take what's ours as well as my soda, and since she's so shocked, I don't even pay anything especially, on the house, Babylon's treat, a big sale offered for the occasion by the U.S.A. And before we leave, Lefty spits right in the clown's face, telling him: And he'll fuck you up, too. Osama in person. And to the unfortunate cashier: And you, for fuck's sake, have more sex. And take off that apron. Because you look damn awful.

Then we leave. Friends. The Armed Brotherhood of Saint George attacks the world. Warning, they're armed and dangerous. Armed with a pocketknife, armed with shortwave communications. Armed with amphetamine, armed with adrenaline. They trample the lawn, they tear up the flowers. They're denting the sidewalk, they're tunneling under the world.

Cool, huh?—Lefty says to me as we're walking, and he shows me as he presses the button on his walkie-talkie. Fucking awesome—I say back to him. Then he tells me to go over there and stand next to the street, and he'll stand over here, and we'll talk to each other. So I do it, because it seems to me like a great idea.

Then it turns out that these are no artificial walkie-talkies, fakery, Bartosz toy store, little policeman set, that these are professional walkie-talkies, like in movies about narcs.

Hello. Hello. This is base. Over—Lefty says in a serious and focused voice, and I have his voice in stereo, because in the first place I hear what he's saying normally, and secondly I hear it in the receiver as well. I like that a lot, that shortwave's cool gear, even more fun than a cell phone, and though there are no dexterity games, it's cool gear, handy for getting to know new people in every situation, for ordering yourself speed right to your bed.

What's the password, what's the password, over—I say, sipping my promotional soda with gusto and keeping an eye out for enemies.

Birds fly in flocks—Lefty says. That's the password he, like, provides. So I say to him, all pure acrimony: Boot error. Incorrect password.

And I stand there and am pleased with my prank, the soda's good, cold, promotional, and free.

Then, totally without my expecting it, Lefty abruptly switches off his receiver. Suddenly he yells: What did you say?!—but in an aggressive tone.

Then I disconnect, too, and, pretty offended, say: So what the fuck, you gave an incorrect password!

To which he says: What's fucking incorrect, what do you mean incorrect, you didn't like something about it? That's what they said in elementary school, maybe I don't have a screw so loose yet that I wouldn't remember.

Upon which he throws his walkie-talkie on the lawn.

Perhaps it's just the wrong fucking password, huh?—I tell him, totally knocked off my balance by a shot of adrenaline. What, are you out of your fucking mind with that, like, keycode?!—and in a rush of anger I tear the antenna out of my walkie-talkie and throw it on the lawn.

So what the fuck's your password, toss it out there, what the fuck's your motherfucking password?—Lefty screams bloody murder, all serious, red in the face.

It's fucking something else!—I holler, when my weakness suddenly totally withdraws, and right off I feel fucking pissed to the limit with this whole situation with the walkie-talkie. The principles are simple, either you know how to have fun or you don't, either the password's known or it's not, and if not, then you'd better not start.

Then Lefty picks up his receiver from the ground and turns it on again. This is fucking base—he says into the handset in, like, a calm tone—I'll give the password: Nails sucks Moscow's rod. Nails sucks Moscow's rod. Over.

Then I get completely fucking pissed, because think what you want, but no one's going to insinuate that I have pro-Russki tendencies and get away with it.

Warning—I yell into the walkie-talkie, so that it'll be heard clearly despite the torn-out antenna—connections cut, alarm situation. Lefty's a fag, a homo, and a eunuch.

Communication cancelled—Lefty yells into the handset then—The correct password is: Nails's a motherfucker, and his mother takes off her panties for the Russkies.

I can't stand it anymore. I can't stand it, mentally. I'm thinking about killing him. Serious. Because my mother, well whatever, you can say anything about her, but that she'd wear some kind of panties, that's just base slander, she's a peaceful person by nature, of the mother gender, she's not a woman who's been fucked, and certainly not pro-Russki, and no one's going to say anything perverted about her, and especially not Lefty. Okay. If that's how it is, all right. Were we friends? We were. But we're not anymore? No. That's it. So I grab the walkie-talkie and say, since this isn't a joke anymore: over. Over.

And then I chuck it with no scruples. Arka Gdynia Football Club, you fucking pig.

After which I finally sign off forever, though I've already broken that handset and in the end, why the fuck turn it off, perhaps for effect, to make my point. Lefty stands in place, he drops his shortwave in amazement. He's standing there. His hands are swaying back in the wind. Shock, frustration, chaos, panic. I wonder if I might have gone a little too far now with the strength of my argument.

So then in a second it could be such that the action's already going fast. One-two-three, hocus-pocus, a leaf in the face, because it doesn't take much to piss Lefty off, so like on *Dynasty* the camera would do an about-face, because it would be a live show exclusively for viewers after one in the morning, parental guidance suggested. Now they'd show a flower bed, a tree, a total idyll, a quiet village is a happy village, McDonald's at sunset, if I could, I'd buy Izabela that kind of blown-up photo-wallpaper so that she could sit on the sofa bed in the evenings and gaze at it. While in the back from off-screen, where they wouldn't be showing anymore, there'd be total hard-core violence taking place between me and Lefty, tooth and nail, pulling of hair. Of which there isn't any, but that could maybe be done with special effects. Because me and Lefty are so fired up to beat the shit out of each other that we could go mad, and no nunchakus, technical tactics, or professional boxing, just an eye gouged out and the liver and an ovary pulled out by the throat. And I admit that I'd have shares in that business as well, because I'm fucking pissed all the way down the line. I'll even go so far as to say that I might be the one to throw the first punch, since I'm of the opinion that it wouldn't make much sense to foster great expectations, "Lefty, it's not what you think," "I totally don't see it like that, those are Kacper's opinions," or any other shadinesses. Arka Gdynia

Football Club fucking pig and that's it, once it was said the lock was opened, Lefty would get a couple slaps on his trap, I'd get my own, too, by return mail, because he's a big boy and mightily hopped up on speed. And we'd kick the shit out of each other pretty hard like that for about an hour, I'd be on top and say: Arka Gdynia Football Club fucking pig, then he'd be on top and say: Lechia Gdańsk Football Club, you fucking *Scheiß*. And maybe the whole story would end there, we'd mutually fuck each other's shit up and then there's just the afterlife, which we don't even know if it's there or not or if there's yet a third possibility.

Yet as I mentioned, that doesn't happen, oh no. Rather, totally the opposite. Because just as he's supposed to come up to me and get down to fucking me up, all of a sudden Angela appears. Angela. Out of the clear blue sky. Complete nonsense. She rides up suddenly on a Mountain City–brand mountain bike. It's a nice bike, the stolen kind you can easily buy off the Russkies. Silver, fancy-schmancy, with balls in the spokes. She rides up from the direction of the amphitheater. With a tiara stuck on her head and a matching Miss Audience Choice 2002 sash, she curves in a circle around us, she has one hand on the handlebars, and with the other she waves and greets the crowds, performs the gestures of passing out autographs, she puts on black glasses from her handbag to drive away the crowds. Then I, as well as Lefty, right away immediately forget about our task. Because she's like a black queen, a triumphant queen riding a bike, she has a crown and a sash, and boxed chocolate in the corners of her mouth, her black hair is fluttering like her personal banner, because she's the one who's probably won that war.

She wheels around, she's arrived by bike straight from abroad, from cold countries, from black countries, to deliver us. She's brought us costume jewels, she's brought foreign candies, oranges, and cartons of milk, and a bundle of good foreign-made amphetamine in packs of two fruit-flavored fizzy doses. She came to take us away, me on the rack, Lefty on the frame. And then what? Then nothing. Right away Lefty and I forget about everything that had divided us, we walk quickly toward her, arm in arm we paw the bike, which it turns out quite clearly that city hall treated her to a stolen one.

Natasha told me to have a ball—Angela says with pride and makes sure that the wind hasn't knocked the tiara off her head. She has dark streaks at the corners of her mouth. Today she's going to puke fuel-grade coal.

Let me ride—Lefty asks, and folds his hands as if in prayer, God, be nice and let me have a ride, to which she says fine, but don't break the gears or the bell, because then Natasha will fuck all of us up together.

And while Lefty's riding, before I manage to chat up Angela, the what and how, how did it go with Sztorm, cool or dumb, from around the bend a blue police car comes from out of nowhere with the window slightly open like a Last Judgment with door-to-door service. Then everything seems suddenly clear to me, because right away it occurs to me that that cow from McDonald's called the pigs as revenge. She was offended for sure when Lefty told her she looked bad. And then right into the handset, Hello, two dudes here are calling me names, the crown's fallen off my head, my corporate visor's fallen off my head, get them, Officers, and throw them into the quarry. And a second later, the pigs tore themselves away from their important earthly duties chasing down the drunks and pro-Russki riots, Hello, hello, this is Wildcat, boys, we have a case, attempted soda-pilfering at McDonald's, we'll go to the scene of the incident. And they arrived here presently to save God's world from the anal sex terror.

Fucking hell—I say, because suddenly everything seems lost to me. Because I'm aware of how it's not going to be easy now, hugs and kisses, don't spit, don't curse, and don't write with chalk on the sidewalk. That there's going to be harder-core badness, if only it were the one walkie-talkie with the torn-out antenna, if only it were the other one that's now fertilizing the lawn, if only it were that spit-on clown, that would all be all right, we could still explain all that, smooth it out, and wipe clean what's gone down. But no. Because the cashier pissed her corporate panties from grief, McDonald's was placed at risk of serious financial and moral liability.

For which I, and Lefty here as well, and maybe even Angela, too, are going to buy the farm.

But Lefty doesn't know yet, he's confidently riding the bike in circles, turn the dynamo on, turn the dynamo off. And when he rides up to us, right then he, too, sees what the situation is. And I'm sure he has dope on him. But it's already too late. The little car drives up. The little window rolls down. A dickhead in a black firefighting jumpsuit with the face of a serial killer with a life sentence and the death penalty around his neck drives his state-owned black ass in that wagon like he was at least on a road trip or something, elbow cocked out the window, it's all good, maybe even a drink and a fold-out bed. Dude next to him's the same, only more so, since in the bounds of his job, his super-serious duties, he holds the steering wheel. They pay him for that, anybody would want that, you hold the wheel, you get a shitload of cash plus a free bulletproof jumpsuit for working in the garden or in the veggie plot.

And he says to us: You got ID? There's no hello, no fuck off, zero culture, pure assholeishness with no artificial colors.

It's like the moment of death, you're already dying, no forgiveness now, and you know that you still have all this dope stuffed into your pockets, all this sin jotted down in pencil in the margins, and exactly, no smudging, the teacher's taking your paper away, time's up. And that's exactly this moment, fun's over: Documents, please, we're not fucking around with the likes of you, we have here an extra-special machine purchased by the taxpayers, we put your ID card in here and it comes out the other side in ribbons, and you're GONE, sir, you don't exist, zero benefits, zero social welfare, you don't have children, sir, you don't have a taxpayer identification number, you don't have you. To hell with this sir crap, you're gone, you prick, you've disappeared, you can go home, though surely your home is also gone, it's been voided.

So we stand and look at them. Then they're already more vehement. The little hatch opens and they get out, they stand there shoulder to shoulder and say to us: Documents, but in such a way that you can say only one thing back: Just a sec, here they are. Plus get down on one knee, kiss the family signet and the watch in turn.

Lefty and I look at each other. Yes or no. We hand them over or we don't. We're going to lick these dickheads' ankle boots full-on with our tongues, or not. This happens fast, these are fractions of seconds crumbling like glass under our feet. That's enough. One look and I know that it's not going to be good. The black pigs of the gestapo race are impatiently tapping their man-skin shoes.

At that very moment Angela's bike falls over.

Documents for the bike—they say to her a second later, when they see it, pointing at her with their shortwave—certificate of right to own a bicycle. It's their professional conditioned response, they teach them that at the police high school, they show them a person, drool flows into their traps, the right lightbulb lights up, and they say: Documents, and you show them a bike, it's the exact same thing, drool, lightbulb, and just a different password: Documents for the bike.

Then Lefty and I look at Angela. Because suddenly we realize that the whole incident was personally provoked into occurring by her. It's not our fault that she rode up here on a bike, made tracks on the sidewalk, O please, great adherent of the cult of nature, and without scruples she destroyed a beautiful, corporate, totally innocent lawn. Besides that, that amphetamine Lefty has in his pocket, that's from her. She snorts like a dragon, she's already dropped down to thirty kilos, because she already does half a kilo a day herself, and she needs more and more, anyway you can see from looking at her that she's practically made out of speed, and the rest is drawn on her face with coal.

So she rode up here now while my friend and I were standing here drinking sodas. We told her right away not to ride on the lawn, not to destroy the greenery. Nothing from her. She crammed her amph into my friend's pockets and said: There you go, boys, the first dose is free, you'll see how you'll like it, all your problems with school and your parents will disappear. We didn't want that filth, that cesspool, but she insisted. And from Lefty's look, I see that in the matter of testimony, we have complete cooperation and understanding.

Angela says to them, though evidently scared: But I'm Miss Audience Choice.

They look at her, then at each other. We can check on that— one of them throws out. So they pull a black gestapo knob on a cord out through the window of the patrol car, and one of them recites to Angela that poem he learned in his first year at policeman's night school. Last name, first name, birth date and residence, house number, parent's maiden name, shoe size, number of windows in your apartment. It's an oral table for Angela to fill out. Then everything happens in turn. We already know, Angela Kosz and so on. Weight, twenty-eight kilos. And so on. Then they convey what they manage to remember to their gestapo radio. And in the hinterlands of that whole system sits Big Brother, he smokes a cig and replies. He confirms that there's an Angela, that they have her in their notes. Then he confirms the data she provided. And at the same time he adds a little bit from his own archive. That she's been seen in suspicious company, that she's under suspicion for the iconoclastic besmirching of the Number 3 bus, as one town resident reported, she's the leader of the ecological opposition who rats out the municipal authorities to the government and the vegetal organizations regarding the sewage. Denomination: satanic anti-Russki fundamentalism, this year's Miss Audience Choice for No Russkies Day. All that flows out of the receiver, that radio broadcast in Angela's honor, and Lefty and I are looking around, combing back our hair with our hands, 100 percent innocence, we don't have anything in common with her, we're even a different gender.

Then for a minute these policemen hold a meeting in full gestapo confidentiality. And right then they say what Lefty and I least expected. They say: Please ride on, ma'am, and be careful, because the roads are slippery from the paint, and don't have any more conversations with any suspicious types. And could my friend and I trouble you for an autograph.

But that would be no problem at all—Angela smiles, and the lights flash, the red carpet unfolds like a tongue chucked out at me and at Lefty from the mouth of that system. With which she cohabitates on favorable terms.

And our friend would also like one more for his wife and kids—the pigs say, and they give her the pad they use for writing out tickets.

His wife's name?—Angela says professionally, and she signs everywhere in sweeping pictographs: Miss, Miss Angela, Miss Audience Choice 2002, for Aneta and Wojciech with the best hugs and kisses miss audience choice Angela Kosz. Plus, as I'm looking over her shoulder, I see that here and there she adds "Satan 666" and "one race, a Polish race."

Whoa—I say, no longer paying mind to the police listening— When did you become such a radical, huh, Angela? Perhaps fame's gone to your skull.

What—Angela slings back, well look here, how she's made herself so glib all of a sudden, she said three sentences about her favorite kinds of vegetable and now all of a sudden she's gotten the honor badge for "chatting" from Scout Master Sztorm sewn onto the sleeve of her dress—the Poles have chosen me, so perhaps I'm for the Poles, and not for any Russkies, it's logical, right?

After which she says in the direction of the policemen: Just a moment, and she takes me aside.

Don't you understand, Andrzej?—she whispers, full conspiracy—Either Poland or an increase of the U.S.S.R., and then the end is near. And Sztorm enlightened me about a couple things. He says that when I represent the national right, then I'll have my own soiree at the cultural center, and maybe I'll even be printed up in *Polish Sand*, we'll have to see. That was a big break for me.

And what, does your friend favor the Russkies?—that pig asks suspiciously when he sees our ongoing case confidential and the strictly secret manner of our conversation, a cord drawn from ear to ear, top secret.

Andrzej?—Angela says like an idiot, as if she didn't get anything in general, that he's gripping his paw around his pistol. Actually, we've known each other for a pretty short time—she adds without rhyme or reason. After which, seeing what she's done, she takes the bike, blows me and Lefty a kiss from her hand, then waves to the policemen and presses down on the pedal.—When I know the how and what about that reading, I'll let you know!—she calls out, riding away like a streetcar named desire and ringing her bell.

So now it's just us. Then, in a single moment, things get not so nice again.

Maybe a little autograph?—I say to sort of loosen up that tightening atmosphere, which is stretched so tight between them and us that in a second it'll burst, and that if we stretch it harder we'll get seriously bitch-slapped.

Maybe a little dick?—that one pig says and spits, completely not covering up his intentions anymore. To me, into the trunk—the second one says to us, taking out his club.—We're going to the station.

I, like, stand there, I glance at Lefty. Lefty's totally breaking down, he figures that these are his last moments in fresh air, so he tries to take as much as he can into his lungs and his mouth. He's looking around the whole time, he's sizing up a way to bolt, tears are welling up in his eyes. His eye's going like crazy blinds, like a broken shredder.

But Officer, sir, like, why?—he says tearfully at last, because he hopes for sure that we're chatting here, the weather looks like there'll be a storm, and a very successful fest, and in the meantime, snap—all of a sudden all the speed will disappear from his pockets. If staying here is forbidden, if standing here is forbidden, then we offer our deepest apologies. We promise that we will never behave in such an assholey fashion again. It's happened once—true. But Officers, sirs, you know how it is. How a person's walking, he gets winded, he stops, he drinks. All of a sudden he gets caught up in conversation and forgets that he's not allowed to stay here. But Nails and I are already on our way . . .

We're on our way to fuck up certain characters . . . —I add, because despite their whole coldness, maybe besides the garden shears, they keep some sort of official heart there in all those strictly confidential pockets in their garden overalls. That is, no—I explain and gesticulate, because I catch on that all these dirty words are going to be blacked out. That is, we're on our way to show how to take a long walk off a short pier to these, like, hotheads . . .

. . . from Kazakhstan—Lefty perks up and strikes up some rightist sentiments. Because they came here, probably, some fucked-up excursion, to make measurements for the future displacement of the Poles, to loot Polish abodes . . . we're going to give them a good flaying. And since we've stopped catching our breath, because we're in a hurry, so that they won't leave . . .

But the pigs are not entirely compassionate toward this sad yet pro-Polish story, zero sympathy, zero understanding for the patriotic spirit, total coldness. One takes me by the arm to dance, the other Lefty, the gentlemen ask the gentlemen, holy rites, at the same time shoving us into the patrol car, and he recites to the first one: Fucking get this down, yeah, and no slacking off. Multitudinous insult against a policeman. Vulgarity and abuse. Unprecedented wholesale destruction of the greenery and the public flowers of government property. Effort to establish cronyism and attempted corruption, pro-Russki opportunism.

And before we can get a handle on what's going on, before we get the general idea that the good times are over, they slam the fucking doors right in our faces, and the light goes out, the air supply is cut off, and no, the end, there's not weather, there's black weather. Yet before they manage to lock the padlock, Lefty manages to scream desperately in retaliation, in a voice broken in two:

Fucking shitbrick LEGO men. Fucking LEGO cops!

At which they are also completely unperturbed, the gestapo paramedics. Write this down as well—that one says in response to Lefty's words in a tone of "You do X to us, we'll do X to you even worse"—both under severe influence of narcotics with no possibility of establishing contact, broadly understood. Severe hallucinations, screams, probably, broadly speaking, mental illness with metastases.

And before we drive off, they light themselves yet another cig. I've never had it so very bad before, because it occurs to me that I want to smoke so bad that in protest, I'm ready to take Lefty like as a hostage. Besides that, I'm thirsty, I feel more and more bad. And if I find a company pen on the floor of the wagon with the inscription *Polish Police Association, Inc., A Subsidiary of Zdzisław Sztorm Enterprises,* right away I'm going to stick it out through the grating in the wagon and shank one of those pigs in the back, begging them to give me even a little whiff of cigarette.

Upon which he abruptly moves to the side like he's been stung and says to the other one: Aw, fuck. Now write that down so you don't forget. Unprovoked aggressive assaults with the use of a sharp object.

And it ends with that. He puts out his as yet unfinished cigarette, tosses it, so that I can see that wastefulness perfectly through the little window, fucking gardener's dog, he doesn't smoke it down himself, and he doesn't give it to someone else. And we're off. Lefty in despair, crying. Those others like that. One turns the wheel, the other peeks in to see that we're not up to anything. With his eyes Lefty points toward his pocket, where the speed is blazing with a dry white fire, that we're finished, and he most of all. Well, then I don't know what to do anymore, so I yell: Look out, fire!

Despite the glass, it's like they hear, so they look back at us. And then I say: On the right! Pointing to the right. And in a fraction of a second, while they're looking to the right by pure stupid reflex, before they manage to figure out it's a ruse, Lefty manages to pull the speed out of his pocket and skim it under some blanket, and with his other hand he crosses himself. That's how it happens.

Well, and then everything is one-two-three. We get out. We walk docilely without even handcuffs, because we've already been schooled, that whatever you say or do, there are countless paragraphs for that, your every word is turned inside out and used against you.

*   *   *

Fuck me—Lefty keeps repeating—fucking LEGO cops, fucking LEGO cops.

Then there are various holy inquisitions, first they take our mug shots, in which I think I have to look pretty bad. And then room twenny-two, and Lefty to another one. But I've been assigned to room twenny-two, toward which I'm led by the arm by a pig, I even hear how it's broadcast over the short-wave: I'm taking him to twenty-two, have Masłoska write down the testimony and get this mess over with.

I'm already completely indifferent to what they do with me, but something there seems weird to me, that name. Because I've heard it somewhere before, I'm not sure where, but the hope rises up in me that maybe it'll work out, if I get something going between friends, put out my hand here and there, say something nice for me and Lefty as well and everything will pan out somehow, work out, they're still going to kiss our hands before we leave, and they'll outline the traces of our shoes in red marker, here walked Andrzej "Nails" Robakoski and Maciej "Lefty" Lewandoski, martyrs in defense of the anarchist revolution in Poland, wrongly accused and arrested in a raid on the fifteenth of August, 2002, at eight o'clock in the evening. And in the station in general, they'll fucking break ground on a museum sponsored by city hall, my jeans in a display case and a jacket on a mannequin, on the jacket's lapel decorations for fidelity to anarchist ideals, for the overthrow of fascism, for opening up a can of whup-ass on the fascist tourists. And the still-stained pants as a relic of Miss Audience Choice of No Russkies Day, crowds will come, place their hands on the glass, and all their ills will be cured in a few days, a rash, and acne, and Down's, all of a sudden *all* their ills will go away, and those girls who've already lost it and would prefer to have it back, they'll grow back what's needed and can calmly get married with no pangs of conscience, and when they're filling out the census and inventory, they can mark off ten points out of ten in the "purity and innocence" column. And then I'm not going to laze around, I'm going to get myself some fucking pimped-out disguise and I'll be the boss of that whole operation. Entrance—ten bucks, cure—fifty, Bird Milkies—a buck apiece, forty for the box (fifty groszy for the bag), excursion to Bitchy's grave—thirty bucks plus the motor coach ten bucks per head, advice from Ala—twenty, though in the final tally, I don't know myself how much, because her advice really isn't worth shit, and I don't want to drive people into charlatanism and New Age cult prophecies. Just into the anarcho-leftist essence of all-everything and onto ships of freedom sailing the sea of freedom.

And when I think that to myself, I imagine I'm seeing it through my soul's eyes, and all of a sudden the door opens. And some guy comes through it who, as a matter of fact, has nothing to do with this whole business, because, like, he's typical of the many extras working on this movie. But right away I notice him, that something's not quite right with him and that he has a direct connection with this room, he came in smiling confidently, full of optimism and back straight, and if he leaves with progressive scoliosis and a hump full of water on reserve for a moral hangover and everything, his whole change was a matter of his entering that very room twenny-two. The lamp in his eyes, mental torture, does he confess or not to the fact that he has kin among the Russkies, we have proof, we have your pictures, and here he's supposedly a patriot, and automatic-pencil refills for the kids were purchased from the Russkies, that's it, for that a lamp in the eyes, for that he gets scoliosis. Behind the typewriter sits some shady typist, and she notes down everything he said, but such that if it fits the form, no matter how the question might have been preconfigured, she'll write in: Yes. Yes: he fosters a pro-Russki orientation, yes: he favors annexation, yes: he swears on Poland that it wasn't the Russkies who raised the salinity of the Niemen. And all just because "no" doesn't work on this typewriter, actually that character was eliminated from the font. And even before the war broke out, they'd ripped it out already, while they were interrogating artists about their pro-Solidarity inclinations.

But so when I hear "Next" and straggle in, I ascertain that actually we can't accuse that typist of falsifying the results of the moral elections from Martial Law, because I calculate in my head that she didn't even know back then what's yes and what's no, because back then she probably wasn't alive yet or she wasn't even in the picture. Because to my eye, she's at most thirteen years old.

Hello—I say up front, so as to be polite towards her, that maybe she'll learn to write "no" all of a sudden. She doesn't reply, so right off I begin to suspect that there's a lack of respect between us, in particular that she has a taller chair than mine. A second later, that pig comes in behind me and says: Masłoska, as soon as these testimonies are done, you have to take them to the chief with some coffee and cake, that's what he says, and you have to come in yourself for a serious conversation that'll take a long while, that's what he says. To which Masłoska says out loud: Yes, Sergeant, and at the same time she mumbles something to herself, some vulgarisms, something about the Polish Boy Scouts. While I'm listening to what she says, while she's gawking like that at those keys and aiming at one after the other with one finger, and gnawing at the fingernail of another, it seems to me right away that I should sit down fast behind that typewriter and note down her case history. Her mental case history, anyway.

Last name—she says. No big deal. Robakoski—I say. First name? Andrzej, a pleasure to meet you, I add, and yours?

Dorota—she says, and looks at me strangely, enough that I get this trip in my skull that, like, she knows everything about me. But what's going on. I look at her, have I maybe met her somewhere before, at some disco in Luzin or in Choczew in the summer, but it's hard for me to figure out, because she has a blue jumpsuit on, an outfit under the title *Driver, Neoplan Bus,* too big besides. She's sporting a watch set to the wrong time, written in pen on her left arm there's an L, as in "left," on her right arm an R, as in "raw pussy," which she examines over and over while she's writing or doing whatever.

Your mother's name—she mumbles to herself—yeah, your mother's fucking name . . . Ma . . . ci . . . ak . . . Iz . . . a . . . b . . . ela . . . and one L, and married . . . Ro . . . ba . . . kos . . . ka . . . fuck.

Then something nudged me. Something touches me with a great finger, eh, Nails, wake up, some big-ass trip is going down before your eyes, this typist is sitting here, you don't even know yet whether you'd like to screw her or not, and all of a sudden she knows your mother's full name. Wake up, Nails, because something's going down here that you don't know about, all underground, somebody's secret, clairvoyant eyes are hidden in the walls.

You work? You study?—I chat her up, to pull out a bit from this sick movie I've been caught up in, and I ponder over whether this might happen to be the start of some tortures.

That one keeps writing, she has such slow ignition, and when she says: What? to me, right then all of a sudden, I'm so afraid of her, because she looks rather abnormal, like she's totally not from the same housing development as I am, but from another one. So then, like, it's the realization of a text spoken by her, on her part, the girl has at least this advantage that she understands Polish, though most likely she's speaking some internal inland dialect of her own and of which smoking cigarettes is also a part. By the by, while she's writing like that on that typewriter, she's most clearly engaged in some big lexi-cal skirmishes with herself in her thoughts, some midinterior domestic war and fratricidal butter-and-bread-knife battles, some internal calculations with her own irrational numbers. But so she communicates in Polish okeydokey too, so she to me: Yeah. And this, and that, too. All. The answers. Are cor-rect. You've won. The prize.

Then she takes, plucks, the letter N from the typewriter and tosses it to me. But it doesn't reach me, because surely the angles were off.

So then I've already decided not to let it go, because the thread of friendship has been wound around us, and who knows how it'll be, one word leads to the next, I saw a cool movie yesterday, then she'll unwind, give me her cell phone number, I'll borrow Kacper's Golf, so I'll come pick her up, we'll go somewhere to the lake or out for coffee, tea, and all of a sudden it'll turn out in the meantime that the letters N and O have turned up and at once have started to work, and like crazy they crowd under her fingers in the appropriate configuration, the configuration "no," pro-Russki?—she puts down: no, alcoholic?—she puts down: no, guilty?—she puts down: NO.

So I say to her: So where do you study? School, economics program, extension?

To which she tinkers with something there on that machine rather aggressively, bangs her hand on it. NO, she answers somewhat dissatisfied, like regretfully. Then that pig barges in again, says to Masłoska to hurry up with that coffee and

cake, because the chief's getting bored, and to learn some
new jokes and tricks, because supposedly the chief's already
gotten bored with the other ones. And she also has to quit
smoking right away, because it makes her cough or something, and that unnerves the chief. Again she says: Yes, Sergeant, and grumbles something to herself under her breath,
again some curse about the Polish Boy Scouts and concentration camps.

Then she taps out something more like she were playing on
some keyboard instrument in a retro band, and then all of a
sudden she shoves that typewriter away with such a fuss that
the machine barely misses fucking my shit up, and various
papers, sheets, fly out like her white, fucked-up domesticated
fowl, which she feeds with sandwich crumbs. I've never seen
such a hothead.

You have a cool space, cozy—I put in faintheartedly, so that
nothing even worse should enter her head, for instance to kill
me, stab me with the points of pens and pencils, because you
can see from her that she's capable of it. By the by, she's a
redhead. But her roots are showing. All the flowers on the
windowsill are drawn fat-lady style, the Russki-produced vertical blinds are withered fat-lady style, plus the glass is overgrown with minute, torpid aquatic animals, plus scattered
around the desk there are various charts she's making the
whole time, even during her conversation with me. And while
she's sitting there, I just manage to see that the vertical line Y
signifies total fucking pissed-offness, and the horizontal line
X the flow of time. The function is growing. Now, in propor-

tion to the current hour, the level of total fucking pissed-offness is very high.

So she lights up, she even gives me one so that things will still be good between us.

And where do you study?—I insist.

Extension. School. Elementary. Teaching—she says in this tone of "I'm leaving my pawn here, you keep playing by yourself." For people. Without. A high school diploma.

And what did you do, vo-tech school?

No—she says—I did. High school. But on my exams. They flunked me.

Oh, for Christ's cock—I say to that, like, that I'm outraged, that I'm behind her all the way, walking shoulder to shoulder to the National Ministry of Education building to roll out the right in wheelbarrows—but what for?

What for?—she says bitterly.—Because I have morals. Unfavorable. Negative.

Then she starts to, like, tell me something. That she, like, won some contest there, something, some magazine, *You and Style,* or *Woman and Life,* that she like won it two years ago, but they just printed it now, because earlier they had a lot of urgent ads to print. And if I didn't lose the thread, it was a matter of their having printed her like diary or memoir. Fucking A, what a story—I say, so as not to be taken for an idiot, that like I don't understand, and I shake my head with despair. So shut up—she's like embittered and taps top speed with her pen, who's going to tap faster, her, or me with my foot. That's just a sneak peek, and now for the hard core that happened after that.

And she goes on. That one of her teachers or something like read this diary, and then when she went to take her exams, this teacher was basically unpleasant toward her, hostilely and prickily disposed. Because it came out that she'd written something in her diary that wasn't right, that she smokes, for example, that various things of an immoral nature had taken place in her life, and that teacher had intercepted that diary and had read it like an asshole. That's how I understand that whole story.

And I flunked—she says, banging her head on the desk—I flunked in religion.

Serious?—I ask, as if I'm like interested, because you have to be careful with freaks, you have to tiptoe around them, not make a peep, you're completely normal, just a bit different from everyone else.

Serious—she says in a depressed voice, and she wraps her face desperately in typewriter paper.—Serious, my oral exam in religion. That woman asked me if there's a God. And I just became a nervous wreck, finally I took a shot at answer A, there is. But she was so harsh on me for that diary, for everything described in there, smoking cigarettes, flashing my panties, that she flunked me, she said to the committee that I was like copying, that she like didn't know it herself, only I was copying from somebody. And she flunked me.

What a bitch—I say forcefully, so she'd know that I'm right there with her and inclined to show up with my crew at her teacher's place in the housing development and take a piss on her door, and make her kids understand that they're not to show their faces again, not in the stairwell, not in the yard, not on the jungle gym.

Then she sobs, sniffles, asks if I have a tissue.

Don't cry, you have such beautiful eyes, I tell her. But when she raises them from the desk all of a sudden, right then it's error, short circuit, wrong password, wrong voltage, explosion, system overload. Because right then it suddenly terrifyingly occurs to me that even if I really wanted to, I could never wax her ass, a complete ban, a red light plus a buzzer abuzzing, contact on pain of death. But why. Because just then there's this feeling akin to my old dream, which I remember well, but I'm not going to talk about it here, I'll just say that my bro and I are in the starring roles, but in this place the faces are blurry and the voices are digitally modified, because this is a big-time purely psychiatric iberration from the norm, a deviation in the wrong direction, some kind of sick movies of George flying off of poor-quality film, some subconscious hard-porn thriller unwinding from the reel through the dream. In a word, an incestuous perversion performed in the comfort of our hearth and home on the family pullout. Then I wake up terrified, desperate, and for the whole day I can't look at my bro from disgust, that he and I, you know. And right now I have that same feeling of terror and a desire to escape from this girl, because at once I take on the conviction that she's my like some kind of maybe genetic sister or mother, though maybe I've barely ever even met her. Because think what you want, but I like different women and girls, but I'm totally not perverted like that, to postulate intrafamilial intercourse. And in particular, taking into account the way she looks, pedophilia.

And she looks frightened about this as well. Leave me alone, Nails—she says, grossed out, then she corrects herself right away.—I mean, Andrzej.

But I've already heard everything she said, she said "Nails," which deepens my paranoia. Because if these are some latent tortures supposed to bring out my hidden pro-Russki Oedipal complexes, I'll surrender, and as she pleases, she can write down everywhere in advance: yes, yes, yes, as long as she lets me go, you can leave now, Robakoski, I'll write down everything for you here myself, as it comes to me, but for that you're freed, no more screwing this sick movie into you, and here's a Danish for the road.

But no.

Ultimately, things aren't so bad for me here—she sighs, pointing with her free hand to her ruined princedom of drawn blinds and expired flowers, a princedom practically without windows, where there's one time of day: night, and one time of year: November, and it's strange that bad weather doesn't rain down from the ceiling, hail with snow, and that she doesn't sit here with an overcoat pulled up around her face. You know, it's not bad, because not long ago I got my own chair—she says—my own typewriter . . .

Which is surely another segment of these like confessions, but supposed to reveal my pro-Russki, anti-national unpatriotic dallyings.

Because I was supposed to like go to college—she drags on. For Polish studies, because, you know, I was always good in Polish, in grammar. I liked diagramming sentences most of all. Besides that I wrote poems, various creative writing. A few of my friends and acquaintances even claimed that it was pretty, that I could even win some competitions with them. Because, you know. I had talent, I knew how to use the lyric subject appropriately, as well as an epithet where necessary. And they maybe liked it, but at the same time I heard opinions that you could see the influence of a phrase by Świetlicki redone by Dąbroski . . . , you understand yourself how that got to me, I was thinking that I'm writing about my own feelings, but it turned out that I'm writing about feelings Świetlicki and Dąbroski already had. And that's how it looks, that's all there is to say. Then I didn't get my diploma and everything fell apart, Mom fixed me up with a job here through her friends. That's how it is.

Don't fuck around with me too much here—I say, because I'm slowly losing my patience for her duplicitous confessions here, for her false, hastily assembled testimonies to my death, which she thinks up while you wait, so that for my part I'd maybe say something, Don't worry, Dorota, my life isn't easy, either, I broke up with my girlfriend, I got caught up in thieving, big-time troubles with the pigs, because in the depth of my soul I have Russki paneling on my house, and my bro deals speed, to say nothing of my mother, who, between us, imports tiling "on the side," and so on, one word leading to another, that bitch would like never tap out anything on her typewriter, she'd press a pedal with her shoe, and as a result it would come to light that I've been set up for a sentence of five-to-life and exile. Though she's like nice, open, she looks thirteen, and she'll only get younger before she disappears. She'd like even gather the crumbs from the table and give them to me, she'd like even read my fortune from the rotten tea leaves, where she's breeding invisible but effective animals. She pretends to be my great friend, right away we're on a first-name basis, though she's thirteen years old max, so right away we're on a first-name basis, right away she knows my nickname from who knows where.

And even if it's not how I think it is and she won't be a bitch and squeal on me, then she can always take me and describe me in one of her writing projects, and it's up to her, using my real name and personal data, not to let this pro-Russki out of his house and into the town for shame for the rest of his life.

So now—I say all serious, because the fun and games are over, so I even shove the desk with both hands to provoke the spectators' awe. How do you know my nickname? And no funny stuff.

To which she gets a little mixed up, she sort of doesn't know what to say. She looks around for a place to hide from my wrath, maybe in the drawer, go ahead, I'll drag her out of there by her hair if I get fucking pissed off enough. So right then she talks.

How do I know your nickname? Well, I know it, there's no hiding that. And then she pulls out some folders, files, the whole mess, her whole breeding operation for documents, white birdies ironed out completely flat, clasped into bundles. And she starts reading to me what she's mastered fluently despite her obviously being a child. "Andrzej Robakoski, pseudonym 'Nails,' mother's maiden name Izabela Maciak divorced employed officially to promote Zepter hygienic products by Zdzisław Sztorm state ID number, that's not important. Seen today fifteenth August 2002 at the fest at the municipal amphitheater under the banner 'No Russkies Day' with a certain Arleta Adamek pseudonym 'Arleta,' suspended sentence for complicity in a beating paragraph number, that's not important, at a hearing on twenty-second February 1998, docket number one three eight three one one, beating number one thousand seven hundred and eight, indictment number, that's not important. Suspected of instigating the fall of city resident Adam Witkowski and knocking him into the mud, as well as provocatively destroying his property in the form of normal kielbasa in colors demonstrating pro-national sentiment. The victim, Adam Witkowski, testifies . . ."

Enough—I say, because my head's starting to spin. Because it can happen in the bath as well, and even my dreams are perhaps under perpetual surveillance. Is there more?—I add weakly.

Then she shrugs her shoulders, opens some drawer, and right then I say: Fucking A, because before my very eyes there appears a picked-over KGB archive like the kind in American movie thrillers, where these like individual animals, pressed flat and clipped together, are the files, a real laboratory, where surveillance and brainwashing flourish on a massive scale.

But before she can close it, one of those pigs comes in and says: Masłoska, keep it short and get to the chief, he's waiting for you, he's got zero company, he's all shit-pissed about it. That's the first thing. He's ordered that you comb yourself properly beforehand, and he was complaining in general about your roots showing. And the second thing, leave that hotshot alone now for a moment, because there's this thingy that the chief ordered in a strictly urgent manner. Apparently some Kazakh spies who came here on an excursion got it in the face from those returning from the fest—this pig explains—but there's no evidence and zero witnesses.

So she quickly changes the sheet of paper in the typewriter, and next that guy dictates to her from a sheet:

"To the embassy of Kazakhstan in Warsaw—write 'embassy' in lowercase. It should be more in the middle. And now, indent. We are informing you that City Hall—tap that out in capitals—does not acknowledge the assault that allegedly occurred on the part of native Polish—Polish capitalized— residents of the town on the sightseeing group from Kazakhstan. Regretfully, City Hall—big letters—denies that the alleged riots occurred, and four Kazakh citizens were roughed up and in-sulted regarding their origin (they identity themselves as having unsubstantiated Polish roots, most likely falsified, investigation ongoing). We express our regret over these unsubstantiated attacks on the part of Kazakhstan, and likewise over the toler-ance and support of espionage. We are grieved to announce our severance of diplomatic relations as well as an absolute ban on coaches and sightseeing groups from Kazakhstan entering within the city limits. From Kazakhstan —that should be capi-talized, and underneath: signed, City Council Chairman, Inde-pendent Contractor— Master of Science in the management of natural resources and water conditions—Roman Widłowy."

Then Masłoska pulls the paper out of the typewriter, blows on it, then in the space for the signature she puts in a sweeping signature, "Roman Widłowy, M.S.," and slams it with the appropriate rubber stamp.

The pig takes it from her, checks if she made any typos, if everything's all serious, and says: Write up this hotshot and go see the old man. Then he leaves.

What are you here, the chief's piece of ass?—I ask her straight out how it is. Because she's so sheepish here, a thin little voice, great satisfaction with the title to her own swivel chair, shyly clattering on at one letter per minute, and for sure she pilfers the chief's Order of the General on the sly, his compass and trouser stripes, and covertly runs the whole enterprise, smoking his cigs.

Yeaaah—she says, full of bitterness—quite the contrary, that veritable Landau's killing me. Every fifteen minutes he calls me because he's bored. He orders himself to paint landscapes, his own portraits *en face* on like a forest background. It turns him on that I read various books. He orders me to state the title and author first, which he notes for himself. For that he promises to like take me into another room with horizontal blinds. And like a uniform in my size, but not quite, because of like the budget. I always have to tell him everything, the basic framework of the book I'm reading, okay. The whole world represented. He notes everything for himself in a calendar, and then he learns it by heart. Then when there's like some scuffle with Municipal Sanitation, some sort of protest by the anarchists, he lashes out through the microphone with literary references to the right and left, and he fakes being educated. Truly. On that basis, anyway, he started the All-Polish Reader's Club, the so-called APReC, at the Regional Headquarters. He draws cash from it. He's presiding there. In my free moments I have to write him papers for their gatherings, get it? For instance, this last time I wrote—here Masłoska whips out some lined sheets—"in recent weeks reading in the service of order has increased by 25 percent. Fantasy and adventure items are lent with greatest frequency. The Soviet literature shelf enjoys the lowest level of interest, there are sporadic and quickly detected cases among the lower-level personnel. Whereas the most borrowing has been recorded in the section of Polish Romantic literature, in light of which the APReC committee has decided to purchase new reissues of Mickiewicz and Słowacki."

That's the sort of stuff I have to write, and sometimes I deliberately make mistakes. For instance, two days ago I even ostentatiously made several anti-systemic orthographic and punctuation errors, the police masked as Babylon. And no one even picked up on it, surely those club types generally aren't listening while he's reading, they just munch on pretzel sticks on the sly and rustle about with their papers.

Then she shrugs her shoulders and says to me: Because they all really couldn't give a shit about all this here. Because there really isn't any such place, so what's the point in suffering, what's the point in taking it seriously, doing your best, being motivated to fake it the best? Then she knocks loudly on the wall and says: After all, there isn't even any reinforced concrete or brickwork in the walls, Nails. Check it out for yourself, it's old newspapers packed together. It's all makeshift, Nails, none of this is here.

While I'm looking at her, I start to feel weak. Because it's already way too much, an ostentatious trip put provocatively before my eyes, if I have to look at such things, then perhaps I'd prefer to start going to church. After all, either she's so out of it that the connections have snapped in her skull, or she's damn schizo, the doors of perception popped out from their frames fat-lady style, and she walks around the station like that, cursing her utterly sick movies about plastics. And

like what does she have to do, type—so she'll type, they leave
her alone, sometimes at most they pour nervosol into her tea
so she won't do too much auguring of the chief's going to hell
for embezzlement.

Don't you understand anything, Nails? She's still striving to
explain it all and is still surprised that her schizofied horoscopes aren't making an impression on me, I'm not coming to
any meetings of that cult and want neither the uniform nor
the candy she's pushing on me, The first dose is free, she says,
it's a fucking awesome drug, it seems like nothing exists.

But she goes on with that movie of hers: Perhaps you don't
believe that this station exists? I don't want to tell you anything, but it's been substituted here. I'm part of the setup here,
too, and this uniform I have on—here she shows me how her
sleeves are a meter too long, they go down to her knees—it's
all borrowed shadiness, fiberglass, paper. And out the window there's no weather or landscape, there's just set design.
That if you hit it harder, it'll fly apart and fall over. That
doesn't really happen, just, you understand, it's written. In the
charts, in the tables, in the files, in the lesson plans . . .

Okay, okay—I say, and I shift my chair back, so that this
psycho won't hit me yet from here or there with some bar,
won't jab me with a pen to emphasize the expression—I understand everything. I don't exist, you don't exist, we don't
exist, that's already settled. And now that's it with the coun-
sel regarding the meaning of existence and the essence of all-

everything, because we're having a chat here, and the Russkies are arming themselves. Ask me what's needed there, and I'll get the fuck out of here, because I didn't come here for psychiatric electroshock, but for honest authentic testimony. Either I testify or that's it, I'm not joining the cult, I have enough things to interest me in my free time.

Now Masłoska takes in some air to say something more to me and explain her delusions.

A second later, she's ready to drag out the chart, the pointer, and show the increase in her delusions in relation to the amount of tea consumed. The amount of tea increases, so sound, light effects appear, origami giraffes fly before her eyes, thank you for today, miss, it was nice, but you should have a decent nap. And she knows about it, she's letting go. And good, because one more word and I'd use my cell phone to call the hospital, so they'd come, bring the whole building with them, and instantly hook her up with some haloperidol.

But perhaps she understands my furious unmoved standpoint, she says, Okay, Nails, there's nothing to talk about. Have it your way, I'm leaving you a free hand. I could disclose everything in your testimony, your extreme leftist views, and even go so far as to make a note of your participation in an association of the militant godless. You'd be on the shit list all over town. But no, respect, whatever views you have for yourself over there, here I'm going to write down your category: radically anti-Russki with right-wing tendencies. For "individual achievements in the advancement of Polishness," let's say . . . it's not important, I'll put down something, agitation activity, propination of the peasants . . . I'll think of something. And you, you can leave if you want, you're freed, drop in again sometime, we'll play checkers, I lose my head over checkers.

Right—I finally say in a like rather friendly convention, because generally she was a nice girl, emotional, though perhaps straight-up-and-out fucked up. Something still isn't certain for the time being, will I survive our mano a mano, I'm standing here for a second and for instance, before I manage to leave, she could get me with a knife or an arrow pulled out from under her desk. That's why I don't mess with her, and I say out loud that I wish her all the best in her new path in life, that she'll get some totally new, decked-out letters for her typewriter that haven't existed until now.

Which I wish for myself—she sighs, rearranging papers—because I'm already freaking out here. Now finally, think about it, there are these matters of pro-Russkiness, collaboration with the enemy, sowing ferment. One, literally one was about attempting to extort amphetamine, so that I nearly pissed myself with happiness that I can write down some new words besides "pro-Russki," "pro-Polish," and "yes." But it's endlessly some sawing a chain off a barrier, some soiling of a flag, some trade in non-Polish tea, I'm already literally starting to wig out that I'm writing a book about it.

Right, well, write it—I say to her at the end—the best, a remembrance. Under the title *I Was Fucked Up*.

And saying this, before she has a chance to kill me for it, which I'm sure she's planning, I flee from the room in fast-forward mode, I slam the door. Because I still have to go back for that lost shortwave, which I won't give up, and I will get it back. Because I like it, it was a lot of fun.

And as I'm running out into the courtyard, not stopped by anybody, right away I want to check if what she was saying might happen to be sort of like maybe the truth. And I have to check, because otherwise it'll turn out right then that all of them here dicked me hard. I run up to the wall and knock on it at first lightly, knock-knock. And indeed, to my shock, a sound reverberates like as if I hadn't knocked on a wall but was just playing around in the Styrofoam while unpacking a TV. Styrofoam, cardboard, and fiberglass insulation, that's what this town's built out of, you were imagining it, Andrzej, my mother says to me from over the stove, frying up a kielbasa, you were imagining you were alive, you dreamed it up yourself, you had erotic dreams about yourself. After all, you can't possibly think that that really happens, after all, this town's made of paper, I myself am made out of cardboard and go to work in a make-believe car, and when you look out the window while I'm driving away, you don't get that it's a Matchbox car purchased at a kiosk. That's right, Andrzej, delude yourself, cooperate with the photomontage that Masłoska cooked up for your needs, stick your head in that opening.

And I'm not going to take any more of this sick movie. Such mental assholeishness like they're practicing on me, unknown enemies from beyond the other side of the river, they pull the strings in this whole theater, they carry out animal experiments on me, out of my tissues they're manufacturing creams with elastin and collagen, they're cultivating me for shoes and handbags. I won't endure this uncertainty, I'm all trembling with outrage, with despair. And right off I accelerate from some distance, I take off and smack right into that fucking wall, with my shoulder, with my whole body, the head included, I smash this whole business. And then I don't know anymore what's real and what's paper. Darkness rings out again.

⁝⁝

And further, it wasn't as easy as they show in animated cartoons about the little red rag dog in the black square. That *tralalala*, the doggie's going full fucking blast on the floor, asscrashes into the edge of the cupboard and sees stars, a lightweight, then he stands up, shakes himself off of what befell him, and tears ass farther, flicking his tail. And that if he smashes the vase, that's cool, because a second later, the vase will glue itself together, Mr. Editor will already take care of it, so that the tape will run backwards, he'll press REV, before Ola-slash-Ela comes back from school and gets peeved at what he's done, you little silly, what a mess, a veritable Augean stable, just wait until Mom comes home, she'll scold you.

But there's nothing like that, on this device there's only the PLAY button, pressed down now for all eternity, rooted in the casing. And the movie keeps going. But of one thing I'm sure, please, sir, this machine of yours is broken, sir. Some tiny element, some screw's loose, the tape's snapped and flutters in the air.

Ultimately, I don't want to be accused of, you know, lying. Because they're all going to say: Right, Nails, bye-bye, go to the community health center to get treatment for your mythomania, and we'll file your regular-patient card and pay your Social Security taxes for you. Because those kinds of things don't happen, say it yourself, who pukes stones, since that's basically impossible. I understand that once Kisiel maybe drank down a beer with cigarette butts, so he swallowed one and threw up two, but that's physically possible. Whereas you're blurring something here, you're making something all shady, and your trip just doesn't click, you have your slates all warped, a warning trip, man, you can no longer distinguish between what's really happening and your hallucinations. Right, Nails, that all sounds cool from your side, we love you, high regard in the housing development, but we don't believe in it, it's not like that, let's be adults.

And I'll say: I'm not going to prove anything to anybody here. Shit. The end. I'll swear no oaths to the white-and-red flag.

I'll say it straight up: That unfathomable night descended probably by the resolution of the fifteenth of August 2002, on the occasion of my collision with the wall of the headquarters of the Polish Police, Inc., the account of which I am rendering in full to myself and honestly telling from the top.

And this is no hocus-pocus, a finger stuck in my eye by the distributor of the land of Oz for Poland. It's a loss of consciousness in a classical version, which you can read about in any Polish Red Cross sympathizer's handbook. And if you also include in that other chemical factors, poisoning with poisonous American Tylenol and disorderly co-reactions with the other medications speed and nervosol, then perhaps it's logical that things aren't going so well with me, and my brain-slate's not so much warped as broken into two pieces, and it's not like there's a short circuit in my connections, Kasia Kowalska takes speed or doesn't have speed, just the ultimate system crash of nervous installations. And even speaking logically, that wouldn't be possible under such natural circumstances for me to simply hammer my head into that wall and whatnot. He went to sleep for a few hours, woke up in excellent form, brisk and full of strength for a new and better day, and he started to rearrange the furniture.

And furthermore, I'll say: Because I definitely lost consciousness, but it's not such a common loss of consciousness, that the darkness, you look to the right, you look to the left, and nothing. Just various dreams, wild and vivid trips that there's no way you can get out of so simply, say good-bye and slam the door. It won't work. The party's cranking, and you're at this party, hooked up to the ceiling by a thousand cables and no retreat.

I'll only say that in relation to what I said earlier: it was an all-out, really an all-out trip, the biggest trip of my life, and if I had bad dreams before, they were never on that level of bad.

There's always some vessel connected with reality. And here the jar full of trip is twisted carefully shut and heat-pasteurized.

So this is how it was and I'm telling it straight up, without any great theories, metaphors, or an explication of the most difficult terms: an emblem factory. A guy unscrews the eagle's head, another removes the contents, screws it back on, a third presses and glues on the crown, a fourth glues it onto a red background. Full cooperation, productivity at a hundred emblems a minute. The sounds of total slaughter, the pressed eagles yell to heaven for revenge from the production line, Leave us alone, we don't consent. Then it turns out that this film's popped out of the projector. Masłoska stands under the screen, she waves her pointer. There's an audience. Doubled, because it's reflected in the windows, two times as much audience, more and more audience. Who are they?—Masłoska yells at the agitated crowd, whipping her pointer at the screen. Mur-der-ers—chants the furious audience. And what do they do? They mur-der. And what do the eagles feel? Suf-fer-ing. And what else? Pain!

And round and round. Just then none other than Kwaśniewski and Jolanta Kwaśniewska appear on the screen dug out from the newspaper, at hand, by the hand, in a forest and on a walk, what a trip, the audience has already seen it, has already associated it, and all of a sudden yells out: Stuff the president, stuff the president! The crowd goes crazy, destroys everything it comes across, and right then from neither here nor there I hear a yell rising up above the others: Stuff Nails! And the crowd's already picking it up, all of a sudden I do, too, so as not to re-

veal my own views, I call out together with them: Stuff Nails!
Stuff Nails! And just then Masłoska's taking aim at me with
her pointer, I see its tip, which is aimed at my rib cage, to which
I say: So, what, Masłoska, after all, we're friends, right? After
all, we're girl-buddy and boy-buddy, what's with you suddenly,
you don't like me anymore? Since I offended you back then,
well, my bad, well, I wasn't even talking seriously, well,
Masłoska . . . don't move . . . stay there . . . but I have a hunch
that my end is near, that it won't be long now, that something's
pulsating, like it's beating near at hand, and I think that that's
my heart bracing itself for the sort of desperate riots before this
here death.

⁙

Shit, he said something about Masłoska—somebody says to
somebody, and right then I perceive, insofar as I'm in a state to
see through the gap, that it's a girl, Angelica Kosz, no less.—
And I would have bet that he doesn't read *Your Style,* that those
sorts of magazines upset him. When I met him, you know, I
thought that he's one of those basically masculine, dark, primi-
tive types. But it turned out that he's sensitive, first of all there's
that despairing just now, and it also turns out that he reads *Your
Style,* I really wasn't expecting that, appearances are so decep-
tive. If I'd known, our acquaintance also would have taken a
different course. After all, I know this Masłoska, all of that could
have looked different, she occasionally reads at The Loft, after
all, we could have gone there together, listened, felt it together.

Her poetry is just the kind that I like, about destruction, about woman's corruption by man, after all, we could have gone there together. This entire tragedy, the spilling of Nails's blood that happened, was unnecessary, simply needless.

Well, fuck—I hear the second voice. This time more with a masculine element, but through the gap I see Natasha Blokus in soft focus, and that's the correct answer.—That's fucked up, that he'd resort to such desperateness, leave him to it, Angela.

But you don't understand that whomever I'd be now, Miss Audience Choice and a revelation of the youth-literary communities, in such hard times he can't be left to a fate of suffering, of coldness on the part of his surroundings.

Well, what the fuck, I'm not going to change his diaper now, he fucked himself over with the police, he fucked himself over in town, now I have more important things, too. Did you see that upholsterer in the jeans, he took down my cell phone number.

The gap in me through which I see all this, and probably hear it, is narrow. The rest around the gap is black, boundless, and stretches to God knows where, and in addition, it hurts. I make efforts to crack that gap open more, and though I hurt all over, it works out, so that besides Angela Kosz and Natasha Blokus, in the background I see various white things, as if I'd been placed in the very middle of a duvet cover. Everything's white, and the smell is like of Lysol, so I have various visions on the subject of how and whereby I've been situated here, and above all else, where I am, because that's the key issue. I don't care about the rest anymore, whether I committed suicide or not, though I didn't. I just want to know what I'm lying on, because all I know is that I'm lying down and not even trying to change that fact, because I know that as soon as there's some diversion, an attempt to move on my part, it's bam, and they'll take me back to that room where Masłoska drives a compass into me and draws ever larger circles around me, and the audience applauds loudly, because it knows that I deserved it.

Be fucking quiet, he's waking up—Natasha says, grabs, and brutally, forcefully raises my eyelids, which I'm not even in a state to control, I'm so universally heavy, I'm perhaps pregnant with myself, I feel so heavy and boundless. Call that cunt-faced orderly, let him whip up some of his hocus-pocus so that he can come around a bit.

So then I blink pretty incompetently and see a hand-cranked image.

Hold up his eyelids—Natasha tells Angela, and hands my eyelids over to her to hold up—I'm going to get that white-tea lady, because perhaps she's gone on vacation to sip drinks.

Then, according to my grasp of it, Natasha leaves and Angela is bending over me, so that I see my own reflection getting closer to me in her eyes, I look pretty bad, what's more, I don't look at all, because I'm thoroughly covered, wired up, and sealed, for collection after payment of deposit.

Andrzej?—she asks.—Is there anything left of you?

And then defeat, because when I want to say something, regardless of the fact that instead of my mouth opening, it's still pretty closed. It's so closed that it won't consent to opening, and what's more, perhaps it doesn't exist anymore at all, it's become such a very vestigial organ. And when I want to raise my hand, it's like it's not there, either, or maybe it, too, is permanently affixed to the ground. Because maybe all of a sudden I've become a potted plant in general, I'm blooming in white earth on the sill, and Angela says to me that in order to grow better and lay down more roots, she's going to re-plant me for the spring.

Okay, don't say anything—she says, and performs a gesture of straightening the pillow—I'll tell you how it is. Because you certainly don't know. It's not yesterday anymore, it's tomorrow. That is, the next day. You attempted to commit suicide. But they saved you. At present you're lying in the hospital, and as soon as Nata and I found out from Lefty, Sztorm drove us here right away. So here we are. Nata's just gone for the nurse. When she comes back, she'll confirm my words.

Saying this, she takes combat equipment out of her purse, an ad for hell, she straightens out her eyes, so they'd be blacker. After which she reflects for a minute, counts something, maybe when she'll get her period, and ultimately decides to kiss me on the cheek.

You didn't have to do that for me—she says, painting various lines on her face with a crayon she took from her purse—

I'm not worth that much suffering, pain, loss. I know that you had to feel something when I rode away on the bike back then, leaving you alone with the trampled flower of our emotion smoldering in the ashes. Now I know: I wasn't playing fair, I hurt you, but when I was with Sztorm back then I didn't care how he is, because he wasn't like you.

I want to say something, that that's nice on her part that she was thinking of me back then, but instead of that escaping my lips, it's a bubble, which bursts spectacularly and sprays me, and maybe glass shrapnel even hits Angela in the face. I arrive at the conclusion that in the final reckoning, I nevertheless have a mouth, it hasn't come unstuck from the rest, for which I thank everyone sincerely.

Quiet, because Natasha's coming—Angela says, and a second later, her paws are back on my eyelids, complete readiness for rendering of service, like that the whole time she's been holding them and a neutral subject. And you know what? Because like that war with the Russkies was alleviated yesterday. We know from Sztorm. There's supposed to be a ship given as a present, such a symbol of friendship, on which Polish citizens are going to be able to ride in a duty-free zone. And free tickets and an open bar for city hall. For pupils and students a discount of 37 percent.

Okay, Nails—Natasha adds, sitting on my arm. That slut'll be here in a minute to get you going a little here, Eleni will belt out various fragments for you about the sun to get you going a bit here, because you're not saying anything. Or maybe another fucking awesome Greek singer. Pussy Gratis with her husband from casting, Penis Gratis.

And that's as much as I see through that gap, which Angela supports for me first, then Natasha, a veritable forceps delivery performed on my eyes without anesthetic. Then I see some more swindling and jiggery-pokery in the trade of white before my very eyes, everything is of such a very white race that I suspect that Izabela herself packed me in parchment sandwich paper and that I'm taking myself to school for lunchtime, that all around there's a great whisper echoing through the halls. That from time to time a fluorescent bulb comes on and reverberates around the gallery of faces in stone blouses, the chatty bust of Angela, the vase with Natasha's face, an interactive museum, the authentic smell of authentic Lysol B, the authentic rustle of the sheets. Let's put the crib here, Magda—a limestone crib for casting our kid, and here an artificial television. White people with white blood and flesh that's white as well, because it's poultry, limestone. And zero red, a white eagle on a white background, war among a white race under a white-on-white flag.

Eh, Nails—I hear a completely confidential whisper and am shoved farther into the depth of the bed, which doesn't even surprise me anymore. Because frankly, I'm attached to it, it's my supplemental appendage within the compensative framework of all the rest of the organs that have maybe fallen off me. Don't die yet, live for a little longer. It's me, Magda.

Don't lie—I say, or maybe it only seems to me that I say, the boundaries are fluid, the boundaries are powdered, they pour over the charts and who knows whether I'm still on a red field or already on a white one, but I don't care about that. Because that lollipop has the taste of complete bitterness for me on both sides. Don't lie, Magda, that you like came. You're dicking me around, "I'm here, Nails, I came, but April Fool's, and I'm not here at all." The end. You could have come.

Everything still could have been fine. But you didn't come.

Well, Nails, you fool—Magda says then, and I open my eyes by myself, without the use of my hands. And I'm terrified, because it's like really her, but maybe it's just a mockup of her, her dummy bought for me by the Bartender in a darts set. A baseball bat from the Bartender, doesn't he get that my arms and legs are out of order, that they've tied me up here with various tubes and it's only thanks to that alone that I'm holding my shit together. I wonder how I'm going to live like this in the longer run. Because drag your ass everywhere with all this equipment, some tanks, some radar, the cables trip you up, now move a meter's radius from the wall, dive a meter's depth in the air, and still don't tangle the plugs, because then there's a short and a personal fertilizing of the soil.

Nails, it's me, Magda—Magda says, and waves her hand at me from the bus that's driving away for vacation. It's me,

Magda, I just dropped in to chat. I bought you Marlboros, menthols, I thought you'd be glad. And a magazine about motorcycles, *Motorcycle World,* so that you wouldn't totally go bonkers here.

That's cool, I think. We're riding the bus. There's a whole lot of dust, but it's cool, the engine rumbles, everything quakes, white fields, a chalk plantation, an interactive museum, they've made so much dust you can't see the exhibits. Maybe that's speed rising into the air, anyway, because it's just the time for the blooming of the speed, the pollen of summer aplenty in the air, a nationwide allergy campaign, placement for the unemployed.

Now, listen—I hear from Magda's direction—don't be stupid, Nails. You can't be like that, after all, they want to grow themselves a rhododendron out of you for the hall.

Then she draws *Motorcycle World* out of her handbag and tries to make it so I'd be able to read to myself. But when she positions one of my arms, the other falls loose and the magazine wilts. Then Magda, driven by that off-balance behavior of mine, takes down from the shelf the radar I'm hooked up to, and I'm sort of surprised that when she takes it, it doesn't hurt me. And she plops it down on my stomach, so that I almost spat myself with pain, but my capacities for resistance are limited.

Nobody'll mind—Magda whispers to me, all heartening, and she puts *Motorcycle World* on the radar, which is beeping the whole time and is maybe my artificial heart, which from now on I'll always have to carry with me in a shopping bag, so let her watch herself with it carefully, so as not to break it. Now, right in front of my face, I see various letters marching across the pages to their anthill. And I regret that they're moving so quickly, because maybe it's the text of a song about me and my pain, which now I could sing to everybody.

But this isn't yet the end of this modernization, since Magda has most clearly decided to improve my living and sanitary conditions. She takes out an already opened pack of smokes and, with an emphatic gesture, sticks one in my mouth, and it falls out right away, but she shoves it back in deeper, almost right into my throat.

There's no smoking here—some voice is heard weakly from far off, presumably an automatically self-activating anti-nicotine campaign, which will say a second later what it thinks on the matter of cigarettes and their effects.

Is there some problem?—Magda says aloud a second later—I didn't offer you one.

Then Magda looks at me, seeing that something's not quite right with this smoking.

What do they want from you, that you'd suddenly start speaking in stereo and T-Bass?—she says, she grabs and wrenches out of me all the plugs to the cables that are trailing out of my nose and back. Now you'll feel a lot better.

Then I manage to see at an accelerated pace, as she throws those tubes to the floor, lights up my cigarette, and then I don't see much anymore. Because all of a sudden something heavy falls down onto my rib cage, maybe a stone, maybe it's my own eyelid, maybe it's a fan that's broken off from the ceiling, and maybe it's simply some cloudburst from the next floor, a snow of beds and patients. But I'm not thinking about that anymore, because I'm suddenly losing the possibility of thinking as well, which ultimately symbolizes my regression in the direction of vegetation.

⁂

Don't die . . . —such a broadcast is made over the radio. "Don't die, together we will fight our common death"—a social charity of Radio Z and Polish rock musicians.—Don't die—the radio repeats, and after that, it's like the announcer loses his train of thought because his papers have gotten mixed up.

Don't die—he says—it's all my fault.

Then the doorknob turns again and a gap appears, through which I am insolently peeping at what's outside. Maybe it's even me being born, I look out on the world from my mom, yet I don't like what's going on here. That's not an ordinary ceiling, but a moving ceiling, the ceiling's rewinding before my eyes, the fluorescent lights vanish and come back, because maybe now we're in an interactive fluorescent-light factory. And all of a sudden there are different faces as well, there's noise. It's all my fault—someone tearfully explains—I'll just be with you from now on, just don't die, after all that's not what this is all about, it's about having a good time . . . And that was all just fooling around . . . that really I wasn't with anybody, neither with Lefty . . . nor with that whole sound guy . . . understand that I was just joking, to make you angry, you idiot . . . and now everything'll be fine . . .

Don't die, Nails, that's what you're saying, Magda, you're saying it over the telephone, you're saying it over a megaphone. This is your next whim, buy me smokes, buy me stockings, don't die. If you can, don't die. Don't die if you want things to be cool between us. Be a pal, don't die, because just now I have a solarium appointment, I don't have time to make threats now, maybe later. Call me later tonight and swear that you were joking and didn't die, I'm literally jetting in a minute, but first promise that all that isn't true.

I want to think something, but don't. No thought, I have a forbidden thought, that if I have a desire to think something on some subject, the radio with the torn-out antenna broadcasts an extra-interesting nature program about the wind, that the wind's blowing. That it's blowing. It's a live-feed broadcast from town, initially there was some live reporter, ladies and gentlemen, you can't hear me, but we're witness to an unusual phenomenon, the wind is blowing all over town. It appeared from the West and has already uprooted all the white-and-red flags. Despite the fact that you can't hear me or that you totally can't hear me, I stress that eight people have already lost their hair, and the number of people who've gone missing is continuously unknown. The wind is twisting just to the left, it's tearing the balconies from the high-rises. Rumors and overinterpretations have appeared that this wind was constructed by the Germans, who want to put together a target range here and, in the remnants of the houses, build alpine walls for their special forces. The wind is blowing on an unexpected scale, it doesn't even lend itself to comparison with the Wind of 1997, whose dispatch to Poland the government blames on Moscow.

Here the feed breaks off, maybe the editor has fallen over, no biggie, he'll get a medal, posthumously he'll get the Order of the Smile and a compass from the Polish government-in-exile for particular nonconformism in the service of truth. The wind knocks the radio off the cabinet, and now a multi-hour survey of all the extant kinds of wind will be aired. Very interesting, each blows in a different direction and uproots something else, which you can't see or hear.

I'll get out of here, so help me God. Maybe I'll buy myself that kind of wind, first amateur, but then later all-professional, if somebody doesn't do right by me, I'll send the wind to his place, and good-bye, installation cancelled, the radio-and-television equipment's blown away, you can see the woman's panties, kids with a blown-out ear, and I'm sitting and steering with a joystick, I'm sipping brew, Magda's taking off her clothes, but I say, What the, take that little butt out of here, don't you see that I'm seriously occupied right now, making money, recovering a dude's debt?

Those are my dreams, everything maintained in a white-and-red key, somebody could make a movie out of it and sell it as a universal video movie, *My First Communion*. One could do business from that, put in enough right off to season it with some incidental music, walk around the parishes, do some sales, no one would even catch on that they're not his kids, since everything would be evenly white, with those like extreme close-ups.

I shouldn't have died, I tell myself, I don't even know now what I'm standing on. And if only a single honest person could be found, so that he'd fucking tell me the truth. If I'm alive. If I'm alive, then cool. If I'm dead, then indeed that'll hurt, it'll be sad, but I'll get through it somehow. But this way, generally not knowing what's going on here, I won't go for that anymore. That my dreams, my trips, that I'm well aware have totally boiled over, have spilled over all around, now we already have the movable border and the movable feast able to appear in a random place and time like a rash. I don't get anything anymore, is this the truth or not, whatever I pull out with my hand and feel, is it made from a sheet, I've already examined it precisely. How they've dicked me around here, posted a sheet over me, clear soil, but fertile, and now the sheet is growing out beautifully, the orderly comes and prunes it regularly, but it's already gotten all overgrown, it's crawled out the window and is making for town.

When I realize this, right then this character drops by. Serious. From among the sheets, from among the parchments there emerges none other than Masłoska. Maybe she's the one who took me out of the cupboard, opened the envelope, placed it on her table, and is sitting and looking. And when I start moving, she'll yell and slam me with some book. That's as much as I still put together, that it's her. Yet I have to say that she looks even worse than me, O mother. That maybe I look bad, that's logic, the cause-and-effect relationships in nature, but why does she? A swollen Chinatown, she's gotten a job in West Berlin and makes herself up as a Japanese girl, lately she cries a little to herself in her free moments about my accident, to look more exotic. Oh, how sad you've made me, my lovely, like you're the one who inflicted all this on me, but I forgive you, understanding over divisions, I've departed, but that doesn't mean that you have to cry about it as well, get drunk on Flegamina and make an attempt on your cables. Sit yourself here, read a little book, I don't mind at all, I'll move along, I'll ask you what you're reading, though in my heart of hearts I don't give a shit.

Well, it's just a study guide from school, if you want to know. Because I'm studying for the makeup—she says to me right then, which completely shocks me, that I'm already progressively forgetting the language I used to speak in.

I can even read to you aloud, if you'd like—she says, she's so good, all of a sudden she has such a good heart, she's feeding little titmice, she wipes away the vulgar inscriptions in the elevator with her drool, an invisible hand stamped full force on my face. And to my surprise, she reads me different books in digest, occasionally those stories are even interesting, all of Poland reads to children, and do you read to your child? I'm particularly moved by one such fairy tale, a certain visitor by the name of Zeno gets it hard in his trap with acid, what kind of hard core is this, I think to myself, for sure this is the pregame, and it only gets all the harder later, but they stopped writing it because it was politically unprofitable. I'm trying to give Masłoska a sign with my thumb for whether the given hero has to perish or survive, but out of spite, she'll always have read it otherwise than how I wanted, what a hardheaded cunt, I would even be willing to pay her off so that Zeno would give it back to that whore in her trap, yet not with any acid, but with a crowbar, and so far as to kill her, then they'd be even, and not that one sex rides on the other and one fucking hand washes the other fucking hand.

Okay, and the best is that there are also various questions to go with these stories. And the best are the answers to those questions, which Masłoska also reads me. They're questions on things that weren't at all in the given story, because the author forgot about them and now the reader has to fill in the empty numbered fields from top to bottom, producing a code word. A rebus of sorts. You have to guess at various things, the meaning of the title and information about the author, a profile of the main hero, and learn what happened in order by heart.

Then there are poems, awesome, more, keep reading, Masłoska, what these poets wrote to God as protest letters, that everything was beautiful in the pictures in the brochure, wounds heal and there are no accidents, but in reality what, awful sanitary conditions, dirty hotels, kitschy pictures on the walls, zero taste, and incompetent guides. How I was born from a wound on the front of my face, and it hasn't grown over since then, and I'll tell you this much, it's only gotten deeper, now I'm just speaking in metaphor. And if Disease Control cut in here, they're going to shut down your whole business, Lord, I've soiled my cuffs, my wife lost the cuff link, I demand a refund, and I'll see you in court.

Czesław Miłosz sends a dispatch from Berkeley, Edward Stachura with his inseparable guitar, a photo essay. Nothing's happening, but that's very important, go and underline all the illustrations in red, then you'll pass for sure. Or give me that book, if I survive, I'll cut those pictures out, I'll carry them in my wallet, if I feel like breaking you sometime, I'll just take them out: Hi, Dorota, the one who's strutting in the cape, that's my one cousin—I'll say. He's just getting ready to go to a banquet for artists, flirting and alcohol, if you'd like to cut in there, I can introduce you. What will we talk about, about movable margins or finer longings? You know, I've had a pain in my chest since birth, I've felt an unrest. Finally one day I looked into my own throat, and there's a false bottom in there.

Seriously, it seems to you that I'm one of those, you know, two hands, two legs, George shifts gears, it seems to you that you could remake me into a computer game. Three strikes on the cross, from a kick, from a scrap and lighting the jeans on fire, you look all over town for extravaganzas, because your level of energy is coming to an end, and for the next level you have to screw two more maidens and kill four stray dogs. It seems to you that you'd have taken care of that with three tokens and *congratulations, we have a winner,* the coins' violent precipitations, you can buy yourself everything you see, including the hanger, the counter, and the shop clerk. I'm telling you that if Nails were to open a window, then I'd open another, if he'd wiggle an ear, I'd wiggle it better, I've been tapping out his files on the typewriter and know everything, his depth is equal to the length of his esophagus, he knows literally two words: "no" and "yes" in all cases, and in various fucking configurations.

What, Masłoska, isn't it so? Now you're so smart, you're sitting there and looking yourself over, perhaps to bring you the sun here and hang it under the ceiling, and put a drink with a little cherry into your hand? You're looking yourself over, like, as soon as there's something, you're yelling right away. Mother, Mother, bring the flyswatter, it's moving.

And maybe it's some other way? Maybe what's lying here in the bed is just my representative for Poland, maybe it's only my demo tape? Maybe I feel something, too, and since you can't even comprehend that for yourself, pop out to the kiosk for 3-D glasses and then come back, because under my back, a room extends for kilometers into the heart of the earth, tangles of cables and transistors, don't look, because you'll drown, don't touch, because you'll lose your hand. Seriously, where you live, girl, you don't get anything, if you want to pass that whole business, then you'd better go buy yourself a study guide for reality plus a free tear-out crib sheet, and then we can talk. You storm into me here, I can even quiz you, sample questions with a photocopy of your ID. Pay attention, because they're trick questions: sociopolitical background? Is the Polish-Russki war just a documented historical fact or a set of occasional prejudices? How does the collective hallucination evolve with respect to wars with the imagined enemy— sketch out an appropriate diagram of the function. Is what you're holding merely a common pen? (Explain the concept aloud: phallic symbol.) What kind of significance obtains in its inscription *Zdzisław Sztorm*? (Provide an oral explanation for the term: capitalism, advertisement, joint-stock company.) The heroes' positions on the background of their life course, list the features of their character and appearance, what is "the animalization of literary characters"? To what purpose is the main hero's outlined vision of death realized? (List the premises of New Age philosophy, define the term: cylindrical-clasp composition.) Assignment for an A+: present the theory of literary subtext in the form of a diagram. And do you also have a subtext? Justify your answer. At a local disco you meet Satan—what do you say? React spontaneously to the assigned situation.

And now you're stumped, Masłoska. Now it's already an advanced course, and instead of answering, you're staring at the radar, maybe they've torn out your tongue at last. Put it in a matchbox and bury it here, right now, in the floor next to my bed, it's quite nasty, but for me, you bet, now at most you can show my personal data to the Russkies by saying it in sign language. I really sympathize with you, establish an organization, let other tongueless freaks also fight against me in Morse code, if you want I'll give you Angela's number, she'd join it, she'll jump into her roller skates and will be here in five minutes.

Masłoska, what's with you? Why do you have such an expression, huh? Well, perhaps you don't have to be so decisively angry at me right away, you know. You don't have to make your faces like as if it were dead serious, not to say life and death divided between the two sides of a saucer and a wrung-out tea bag. Hey. Maybe we can just say it's all cool, huh? I'm going to get bored, you're going to yawn, I'll put on a shirt, and you'll fasten your barrettes, a mutual UN, and not war right away and one slicing his veins faster than the other, huh? And if I'm going to die, I'll let you know whether you're dying, too, miss?—I'll think facetiously, and you'll read it out to yourself from the radar, which is on the shelf, or by the motions of my hands, you'll see how it'll be cool. If I've upset you, it was just a joke, and not that it's curtains for you.

But all I see next is that she, looking insolently into my eyes, stretches her hand toward the plug. Oh no, Masłoska, leave that alone, you'll burn yourself, this isn't a joke, electricity isn't for playing with, electricity plus a kid equals no kid and a kid-shaped hole, so stop, I know that it's just that vacation photo, a slide, me and you at the museum of cable, we're all smiley, so happy together, you're pulling on some tube, those are fantastic vacations, in a second I won't stand it, in a second I'm going to marry you, no bullshit. But you can't see that in the picture anymore, because there's a flash and all of a sudden it goes dark.

INDEED, WE'RE GIRLS talking about death, swinging a leg, eating nuts, though there's no talk of those who are absent. They're scarcely bruises and scratches that we did to ourselves, riding on a bike, but they look like floodwaters on our legs, like purple seas, and we're talking fiercely about death. And we imagine our funeral, at which we're present, we stand there with flowers, eavesdrop on the conversations, and cry more than everybody, we keep our moms at hand, we throw earth on the empty casket, because that way death doesn't really concern us, we're different, we'll die some other time or won't die at all. We're dead serious, we smoke cigarettes, taking drags in such a way that an echo resounds in the whole house, and we flick the ash into an empty watercolor box.

Meanwhile, we're plotting, on the walls we scratch out a great escape plan to the interior of the earth. And we start making preparations, we wipe off our fingerprints, clean the hair off our combs, pack our clothes. Everything such that on the world's hand there will grow a sixth, dead finger, so that it'll get it wrong, get lost in the accounts, so that it'll seem that we were never here. So that it'll hang itself on a hanger in the wardrobe, pull all its coins, matches, and scraps of paper out of its pockets and not remove them again until after everything's already over. In the meantime, to carry other things, the bodies of old girls dried out between the pages of books, the faces of anemic children.

The lid has been pried open, and the contents started on and exposed to the common murderous sun. And we're trying to tighten our eyelids, but the skin's become transparent and we see everything clearly, abandoned, clothing devoid of contents, a few days' stubble covering the room, pants bulged out by the wind, the empty packaging from us, from us, who've been eaten out of it.

We speak coquettishly: please, but instead of tunnels in the floor, a few sickly, powerless scratches made with a pin in the hands. Moths alighted on us and laid eggs on our sleeve, and now we're sick, the dressings are coming off with the skin, the panty hose are coming off with the skin, the skin is coming off with the coat. It's ever worse, I spit out a little black blister that Wanda caught in flight and now we have sudden impaired eyesight, because everything we see is caked in oil, hanged on the door at our feet, the whole world swaying dolefully in Christmas ornaments on the wind.

Do something, I can't anymore, everything has thorns, the air has thorns, the rain slaps you in the face. The hair braided itself into the bicycle spokes, it's coming out together with the head, do something, take me out of here.

And through the night a city is built on us, a repugnant city, a great Dumpster, garbage collectors stand and, leaning up against buckets, read old, disintegrating newspapers. Bridges, train and telephone lines, cars and streets extending into infinity, after which the garbage trucks circle around, tearing away people's cigarette butts, scraps of paper, and tissues. People swarmed over me, their mesh bags have worn out, potatoes, apples rolled along the sidewalk, bottles shattered, the sun sets beyond a sliver of glass and the greenhouses.

There was a buzz, drums and pipe, whispers like papers crushed in palms. When we moved our hands, everything disintegrated, only a single long trace from someone's sled remained on the face. I thought that that's it, I'm already dead, but instead of my body, I found crumbs in the folds of the bedding.

I have a great many souvenirs here: postcards with a view of the station and fingernails gnawed until they bleed, and Mom says: I don't know what you think you're doing, eating your fingernails, the reserves are coming to an end, only fingers and hands are left. You'll see, before long your own hands will grow in your stomach, they'll scratch and squeeze you from your middle, you yourself will grow in your stomach. One girl was eating her own hair and a hair monster grew in her stomach. One boy ate a pit and a whole tree grew inside him, the boughs came out through his ears and through his nose. One boy ate cherries, drank orangeade, and died. And then: That mesh bag's not for playing with. How many times have I told you: don't put your head in the mesh bag! One girl put her head in a mesh bag, couldn't get it out, and choked. A ban. A BAN. A ban on drinking alcohol and bouncing a ball against a gable. A ban on fun and games.

We smile knowingly to ourselves: Warning warning warning warning warning! we whisper jeeringly, everything threatens everything, death threatens death, sit here, sit on the mat and never leave.

And we, eating nuts, are very serious, each day we stick a fork into ourselves and die, and each morning is a Little Easter, an all-professional resurrection. We wipe our hands and toss Mom's sleek mink, a mink with sad plastic eyes, to the cats to devour, saying: Have fun together, yeah, have a really nice time. The living and the dead have crossed the line of demarcation and have merged with us into a single murmuring crowd, passing in columns and rows around our beds, we look at all of them meditatively, we nod our heads and settle ourselves on the pillows.

But perhaps now we've really gotten sick, everything's washed out, the photographs on which we bring the whole world to our mouths have become drenched in black tea. It's ceaselessly the same unending day of not seeing straight. The curtain drops about every hour, and the orange workers hurriedly change the set, turn out the light, change the weather, squirt ink into the sky. We manage to close our eyes, and they're already arranging an orchestra that smashes plates and grinds its teeth.

In the hazy light, everything is more and more the same, women, men, kids, animals, poured out into a uniform mass. And in this darkness, in the black, thick tea, we stop discerning each other, we lose our forms and increasingly recall birds: and Grandma sticks her finger between our ribs or pats us on our bottoms, checks if she can make us some broth, or sweep us up and sell us at the market. She's already making the initial preparations and in the dead of night singes our eyebrows and lashes.

A teaspoon placed in the glass, the black tea starts to swirl, to swirl around us, at first ever so softly and slowly, and then all the more violently, all the more loudly, teeth clanging against the spoon. The lights pour down on us like little orange sugar crystals, the little moon is a fingernail gnawed until it bleeds, branches are sprouting out from the wrists, everything's connected, dust, ash, the glass breakage, people fuse with animals. We're both looking more and more toward the center, the lines have been cut, inert receivers are swaying on their cables. The wind is blowing, the whole world is wind, a rain of shattering glass and a sea of spilled tea.

When no one's looking, we fiercely unravel these threads. The whole time we anticipate this moment, trembling and unsure, as if a priest were making the caroling rounds around the apartment building and you could already hear the gilded altar boys jingling their bells. We're waiting until the bell rings, all the buttons will pop off and we'll plunge, inert, and stray into the city, through the clouds, through the trees, we'll crash our heads into the asphalt gushing through the streets. We're sinking into a foaming river like winter effigies, with bricks tied to our necks, with pockets full of stones, with blazing hair.

We tug shyly when no one's looking, we make slight, meaningless assaults on these disgusting umbilical cords. And when someone looks, we hide the instruments of our crime behind our backs, scissors and knives that we used a moment ago to peel oranges.

I leave the house. A day hunched over with misfortune, the edges are so tucked up that actually since morning, since morning it's been night. Mom says, Where are you going, you're not going out, there are packs of stray dogs outside, don't go out. And thank you very much, even if they eat me, those are decent dogs and in a minute they'll return me, crumpled up, to the address sewn into the collar of my coat. I have the flat, inflexible face of the city under my feet. The city, great mine fields, rolled out under me like an unpopulated, asphalt country.

I walk very uncertainly, there's no one here, they all know about something, about something I don't know about, they've hidden at the gates. The dogs have cringed in the backyards, the cats have absconded to the cellars. A current flows through town today, each slab of the sidewalk under high tension. Today in town there's no air, instead of air they've let out gas or insecticide. A ban on leaving your house, a white skull on a black background. The people stand petrified behind their lace curtains—holding the mouths of crying children, they look with terror as I'm naively walking, as I confidently flap my coat.

Today the sky has to burst, collapse with a rain of missiles, stones, dead fish and birds, today the sky has to burst. The sidewalk is full of trapdoors, take one step in the wrong direction and suddenly you're in hell, you're frying in red grease, devils are eating you with knives and forks, wiping the corners of their mouths with paper napkins. I say: Please, you can take me, I don't want myself anymore.

Obviously nothing happens, obviously none of these things, they wouldn't be able to give me such a raw deal, not in the very middle of this reception, not in the very middle of this movie, we have to occupy our viewers for at least another hour. I meet a girlfriend and am very sorry that I can't say anything. She helps me a little, we glue all the cigarettes together and now I don't have to light each one separately, I walk along the street, dragging a fuse behind me.

*   *   *

And when we find an announcement on a telephone pole, *Very pretty little white dress for 1 Communion + little handbag for sale cheap 677 19 09*, we tear it down and want to call immediately, though we won't even squeeze it through the head and myrtle branches won't grow on our foreheads. At most we can tear off a piece of the rustling, wax-stained lace and carry it in the little change pocket of our wallet. There the lights are already out, there it's out of order, occupied, closed, we can only look through the grating as a little fur-grown evil dances the Russian trepak with everyone, it flashes the fuck-you to God, it has a collection of plastic guns, puts its hands into its pants. Behind the grating lives sweet and good evil, getting tangled up in his legs, painting mustaches on passersby. You can't really steal it away from here, the little evil flees from us on a creaking bicycle, flashing us the fuck-you, flashing his broken teeth, the little evil hides away in an itty-bitty well, into which our great, ever greater hands do not fit. We have to avail ourselves of big evil, of the true evil of adults, drink alcohol, touch men, smoke cigarettes.

And then we suddenly meditate, on the sidewalk we saw two boys cuddled together, they were tiny and Siamese, like little potatoes rolling out of a fire. They were grown together at the gaps between their teeth, grown together at their matchstick shoulders, at their squab bellies, they were holding a great ball, they had hats, they had tiny red hands, little pink flame tongues that trailed behind them like flags, flags of a pink state, the kingdom of colored pencils, and that larger one sang: I love you, friend! They wafted a trail behind them, and we breathed that pink air and knew that that doesn't happen every day. Two little deities strolling down the sidewalk, gap-toothed newlyweds, we should erect a shrine in that place, and all the prayers raised here, applications submitted, wishes expressed would be fulfilled. The little laughing God would fulfill them, playing with his woolen beard, he'd coat his cracked lips with Nivea cream, he'd mend all the scratches with Scotch tape and school glue.

And it's coming violently like a fervent light, like shattering glass, coming back from the park we smell how the Dumpster stinks and we suddenly take our lighters in hand, light up that Dumpster, and look at the flames, which, like furious orange flowers, are starting to bloom across the wall, and we run away, laughing aloud.

And when you go out, lick your finger and rub the stains from the banister, wipe the dust off the mailbox. And look at the wall. You know, just since it's been painted, those unruly brats have come and written: *Satan*. Though another party is leading in the polls.

TO BE CONTINUED . . .

I also underscore that television turned out to be my best friend, in addition a more hygienic and much more cost-free friend than any who've heretofore barged in with their unperfected butts made from organic material and in an impractical 3-D without any off switch, with only an on switch. And such a television is all Euro-sterile, culture, you turn it on, you turn it off, you have no idea that everything so unprecedentedly hygienic fits there in the middle, those houses, all those like people in various colors and at various times of day, all of them at once, from the left side a march, from the right side a procession, and from a third an old lady washes the walls of a house clean of rain with the latest anti-weather housecleaning detergent, though I actually sus-pect that it's a bunch of bull that strangers in the studio are clapping and enjoying themselves while she's scrubbing. That they've already gone shady, because that was actually done by way of a computer.

Today's September 5, 2002, a Thursday. But what's it to me that it's that date exactly, since already tomorrow it'll be some bigger one. Lately it's completely fucking up my time, that whole confusion with dates, which is the cause for the mess prevalent in the world. I have this patent for a patent office, which I won't betray, that all of a sudden we should introduce from the top down a single, decent, law-abiding date instead of the four million shitty little dates, in 254 hues not fucking necessary to anybody. To choose a single efficacious date in free, so-called self-governing elections. July 14. September 17, or, even if with difficulty, the eleventh. But regarding that, I say: I suspect that Izabela might have had, besides Zepter, some lover in town. For she's clearly not here, and she's also stopped changing as well as moving the little win-dow on the calendar, because all the time it's placed on August 16, though out the window the weather's clearly changed for the colder, sometimes even with gusts with the rains. The rains flow out the window, they're washing away the house, even the television's like as if it's been washed away and all the goods in the commercials have rotted, that's what I vaguely suspect, because the image curls up on the edges. The sun has clearly set in some distant past and gotten stuck underneath, maybe even forever, maybe even the solarium has set on Butchery Street, that's it. There are rains, an atmosphere of general disgust and new political currents of Decadence, though that Premier Leszek Miller is all assurances, that of course, though not at all. Because what to think when rivers form in the garden that are periodic at the least, not like pe-riodic streets, like to walk along them, like there are some houses, some rooms, but as soon as the sun comes out, they stop flowing and the houses stop existing, they just dry up. In the end even the weather has even stopped getting to me, and they could casually disconnect it from us, because why the fuck pay for that, I'm not going out, and whether "Out came the sun and dried up all the rain" or some other song is playing outside, that doesn't concern me as the recipient. Perhaps it concerns Izabela whether she ruins her hair in the wind, or to take a covering. For me the world is entirely forbidden and out of order, we're not letting Nails out, the comely screener Aśka shoos me away from the door like a systematic insect.

Why and because. Dr. Zit's forbidden it and Dr. Flit's forbidden shit, Dr. Flit ordered me to lie down, Dr. Shit ordered me not to breathe, and what did Dr. Monster order, that's the only fucking thing I know, that Dr. Monster in his blazing robe ordered me not to live, so I'm lying down, I'm conscientiously not living and don't say a word, because I've been reading a pamphlet and a rubber stamp, whereas meanwhile the magazines and newspapers, *Motorcycle World* as well as *Eighth-Grade Calendar,* which Magda sometimes brings as a pseudo-intellectual scrap of the second order, are already set on September, the television programs are sim-ply vying to see which channel will offer the most, and regardless of the fact that I don't believe that Izabela dicked me over deliberately and was fibbing, that date clearly doesn't work for me in the final calculations. And now I'm going to fucking inquire daily every day about what date it is, if you please, question, check, beg, demonstrate various arguments, at best in two languages, and competence in operating a word processor. I'll submit an application and CV for that shitty date, and some chick maybe even barely out of elementary school will say: Put it there, and we'll call you, but don't call us, because you're not dressed in an adequately cultured manner. I piss on that, I can live without measurements. I've already explained that to Magda, to which she replied that I can. Albeit that from all the signs in heaven and earth, I deduce most clearly that it's September, and by that I recognize, maybe I see it through the sixth window, how September is sneaking behind my back, and maybe even November as well. Also for the time being it's better not to bend for the soap, my dear gentle-men, it's a shame that they don't say that on television: Dear viewers, don't bend for the soap. You have to keep everything safe for yourself, because otherwise you'll wake up screwed someday and stuck out into the bushes together with other screwed things, couches, for the poor.

Albeit to the point, because I have bigger claims to the television than to things established from the top down by the premier and the institute as well. In fact, over many days it's turned out that it's my one sensible friend.